Postcards from Dystonia

Robert Sigley

First published in 2023 by Chunter Books

ISBN 978-1-3999-3995-9

Cover image and design by Andrew Chapman

For Tracey with love
and thanks.

Contents

Part 1

Chapter 1: The Accident

Hello. I know strangers don't normally talk on trains, unless they're Trevor Howard and Celia Johnson in the *Brief Encounter* movie, but I caught you staring whilst you were waiting to sit down. It's all right, most people gawk a bit when they first see us. It's a normal reaction, so there's no need to beat yourself up about it. Yes, my speech is a bit slurred, but don't worry, I'm not drunk. I'm not mad either.

Thank you for smiling and not running away. It's reassuring that even though the train isn't crowded, you didn't change seats. That's what people normally do around us when they find they're too close for comfort. They either go out of their way to ignore us or think we're some sort of puzzle for them to solve. You're nodding, so maybe you have some experience of this? I notice from your seat reservation that we're going to be opposite each other for quite a long time, all the way to Edinburgh in fact.

I thought you might like to know my story, rather than spending the whole journey desperately avoiding eye contact or trying to work out what's wrong with me.

My name is Adam, Adam Wright, and I want to introduce you to Myrtle, my left arm. We've been told we're interesting by some of London's finest hospitals, so we must be *fascinating.* Actually, I suppose it's Myrtle that they're interested in, rather than me. It's always her they want on camera and her they want to talk about. I don't mind, Myrtle has had a huge influence on my life, both good and bad.

Your wife and friends can leave you; your family can disown you, but when your arm turns against you, things are really bad. There's no old blues song to cover that. That ain't the blues, it's black. Real black! I can't really pull that off, can I? Not even at age 53. Maybe it's the British accent.

Now, where to start? Myrtle was born, or rather I first became properly aware of her, in 2010, just after Christmas. She was totally unexpected, I wanted Subbuteo. Before the accident, I was a plain and boring chap with a wonderful wife, Rachel, and aspirations to play the guitar. We always thought we were lucky, and even after everything we have been through with Myrtle, we still do. It's important that I say that now, so the rest of my story doesn't sound like a long whinge.

When I first had my accident (I'll tell you more about that later), I thought I would be in plaster for a month, maybe two, then everything would be back to normal. Boy, was I wrong! After a second operation, my left arm started to develop a personality of its own. It would start to shake uncontrollably. I assumed it was a nervous twitch that would pass. I used my right hand to camouflage the movement or hold it still, especially when talking to other people. When they stared or asked if I was OK, I changed the subject because I was embarrassed.

I suppose Myrtle knew I was embarrassed on some level. But then it's hard to keep secrets from your arms when you think of how many things you do with them. After my accident Myrtle became annoyed at the breakdown of our mutual respect and trust and had her revenge. She turned my shakes into tremors – but then she always was vindictive. Even before the accident, when I thought she was like any other arm, she would let me down at crucial moments by dropping something, or just being clumsy. I remember being on a date at Yorkie's Bistro in Congleton with my first proper girlfriend, Janice Mottershead. Myrtle - she didn't have a name at that point - elbowed my knife upwards, firing my peas across the room and one into the drink of the elderly woman on the next table. The woman – one of those who comes with a tartan shawl and ready-attached brooch – looked at the pea floating in her glass and declared, 'Didn't know they did olives here; bit small, aren't they?' Janice thought all this was hysterical. But I nearly died of embarrassment. I was already halfway to being ashamed of my body and this went on for decades.

After my accident, Myrtle's arrival was gradual, she sort of sneaked her way into my life. I didn't know she was there until it was too late. She first visited during the latter stages of my physiotherapy. She appeared in small bouts. I noticed tremors and jerks to start with, but I put these down to muscle fatigue. The tremors became uncontrollable and unpredictable: violent shivers attacking my whole body, lasting for several minutes on end. I would be left sweating and exhausted. I think my ignorance annoyed her, so her visits got longer and more pronounced, including slaps and physical attacks, as if to say, 'Look at me, look at me, LOOK AT ME!'

Don't worry, she only ever attacks me. She blames me for everything, from the accident to not being able to trim her nails properly. If there's anything that has gone wrong, Myrtle will trace its origin back to me and I will get blamed for it. She occasionally throws things or has a tantrum on a table in a café. Sauce bottles, chips and even a chocolate orange in the hands of Myrtle can be seriously scary weapons. She is the original attention seeker, except of course that all the attention falls back on me. Yes, it's probably a good idea to clear the train table, just in case.

For her to have such power, I want to say that Myrtle arrived from somewhere mystical and unusual; but I'm sure I found her when I fell over in Avercombe train station, just outside London – which is neither of those things. In fact, it sounds rather Oscar Wilde finding her in a train station. '*Yes, Myrtle, I know, I'm sure one day there will be a blue plaque.*' Did you see that? She sat up when she heard me talking about her, she had to get involved.

Why do I call her Myrtle? It takes away some of her power and reduces her influence. It's my revenge after all the things she has put me through and all the people that she scared away. There has never been a hero, serial killer or anyone significant called Myrtle. So obviously being called Myrtle and having the ability to have any impact upon the world, good or bad, is severely limited. I don't even think there has been a pantomime villain called Myrtle. Did you know that Myrtle was originally a unisex name? It was most popular in the year 1894, when it was twenty-seventh name choice for the whole of the USA. However, until Myrtle stops rhyming with turtle, it will remain in the nondescript shadows for some time to come. I digress, and you're looking quizzical.

It's all right, we can talk about Myrtle now. She's asleep. She looks so calm, doesn't she? Almost charming, like butter wouldn't melt in her grip. I've given her some Co-codamol. It makes her sleepy and stops her showing off or causing trouble. She always goes back to the same foetal position, lying across my chest. It's where she feels most comfortable. No, I don't know why she must lie there in that position either. It's an interesting question. I suppose it's because that was where she lived in the days before the operations. After that everything changed so drastically, and I had the shoulder replacement joint fitted and she was in an abduction sling. Maybe she thinks if she goes back there and waits, then everything will revert to the good old days. Perhaps Myrtle is an old romantic.

What was that? What is an abduction sling? Oh, it's a horrible, uncomfortable thing; it makes you carry your arm around on a cushion like it's a prize. It's very intrusive, like having a Ford Mondeo parcel shelf tied to your body.

I suppose Myrtle wants people to see her because she waves. Not all the time, and only usually at new people, but when she waves, she waves a lot. Myrtle likes the attention and acts like a member of the Royal Family meeting her public. Unfortunately, Myrtle's ideas on royalty are somewhat misplaced; I don't think the King would wave as fast as Myrtle, even if he took amphetamines. Myrtle doesn't seem bothered; after all, waving is her trademark and she has delusions of grandeur.

Of the two of us, Myrtle is who people see first. She pushes herself to the front of the queue. And yes, I am jealous. When I explain that I'm not waving and I cannot control my arm, people seem deflated, like they've committed a faux pas. So, I end up feeling I've upset them by explaining the truth. Afterwards, Myrtle giggles up and downwards, as if she has led us into her brilliant trap.

Those who don't say hello are often trying to figure me out from a distance and decide if I'm dangerous or not. I do wish they'd ask me about Myrtle rather than trying to diagnose what is wrong with me. One colleague at work thought he could tell what was wrong with me because his friend's husband was a doctor, as if this imbued him with some medical knowledge. Another said the cause of my arm movement *must* be some anaesthetic left over in my brain from the operation. 'You have a trapped nerve!' was another favourite I used to get when Myrtle would tremor. The do-it-yourself doctors also decided there was a piece of bone stuck in my arm, which every now and again touched something and caused my arm to shake. Their insight was staggering!

And the real doctors? Good question. They said I was *"really interesting"*. Doctors keep filming me in hospital and wanting to write medical papers about me. To start with, there were all sorts of theories and ideas about what caused the tremors. I stood in the Fracture Clinic trying desperately to persuade Dr Skate that I was not asking Myrtle to shake like a whisk on high speed. He developed that quizzical look on his face that they all do, '*Oh, this is unusual*', and then he asked, 'Have you ever worked with chemical fertilisers?' I felt like saying 'No, but do you think it would help if I did?'

The conclusion they eventually reached was that I have Dystonia. No, you haven't been there on holiday. It's a terrible place. Dystonia is a strange limbo land where I have lived for quite a while now. It isn't on Tripadvisor as it is a brain condition. My neurologist says my brain probably re-wired itself after the accident, when I had my second replacement shoulder fitted (in the same shoulder; I'm not completely bionic or plastic – yet). Dystonia is a bit like shell shock or post-traumatic stress disorder; my brain cannot come to terms with what has happened to me. It manifests itself mostly through Myrtle's movements, although sometimes my head, neck and legs join in as well, in a horrible version of the hokey cokey.

What happened? Thank you for reminding me to tell you. It was an extremely icy January day in 2009 and I needed to get into London for work. Despite the cold weather and the inevitable collapse of the UK's transport system, I desperately tried to get a train. I went to all the stations nearby, but nothing was running. Finally, I rang my wife Rachel and she said that according to their website trains were running from Avercombe. I arrived at the station to be greeted by a doom-laden, duffle-coated diviner with a placard proclaiming, 'IT'S THE END OF YOUR WORLD. I AM ALL RIGHT BECAUSE ME AND GOD ARE FRIENDS! BUT YOU ARE FOR IT!' The 'it', of course, not being a train, as there weren't any.

I decided the next option was to get a bus into town. I was carrying a heavy rucksack full of clothes and a laptop, and my balance isn't great at the best of times, so laden down on ice and snow I was like a middle-aged Bambi. I should have listened to my gut, which was telling me that as much as I like to honour my commitments, this was ridiculous, and I should stay at home. I generally ignore my gut because it nearly always just wants me to have a sandwich. But all the omens and portents that morning were signs that things were going to be bad: spilling tea down my suit and having to change; nearly breaking my neck on our snow-covered garden path; and the distinct lack of any traffic on the roads. Why didn't I abandon the trip? Well, because I had made a promise to somebody that I would be there. I come from a culture where keeping promises is important and being a man of my word means a lot to me. I can't control much in my life (less so now), but I can control how much I do for others.

Of course, in hindsight, I wish I hadn't left the house that day, but the meeting had taken several weeks to arrange and had been agreed with very important people. As I sit and reflect now, things are much clearer, especially in the mirror of the morning after. What was so important about that particular trip doesn't even matter now. All I can truly say is that I was stuck at the train station and needed to get a bus into town. So, I walked down to the bus stop. The pavement was slippery, and I fell. As simple and as life-changing as that. I'm sorry, I just need a minute. I forgot how painful this all still is.

I lay on the icy pavement in my dark suit and white shirt like a beached penguin. I had no feeling in my left arm. It was very cold, and the wetness of the ice was seeping into my suit jacket and my shirt, like the truth following a really awful night out. My fall attracted the attention of a few people, mainly women called Pauline.

'Are you OK, love?' said the first.

'Not really. I think my arm's broken,' I replied.

'Don't move, help will be here soon. I've phoned for an ambulance.'

'But he'll have to move or he'll freeze to death,' said another Pauline.

People are kind, but also bizarre in times of crisis. Somebody always wants to be in charge. There was a strange, yet well-meaning argument developing between the two women, but I had no intention of moving until the ambulance arrived. Three police officers came over to help and they slipped, landing on top of me. It was like three exclamation marks piling against my poor body, just to underline the seriousness of the occasion.

I passed out after that; it seemed like the politest thing to do. It is still quite fashionable in parts of the world when you're feeling you're going to die. Oh no, I used the word 'quite'. My sister Agnes always does that when she's trying to sound intellectual. Oh my God, I'm starting to sound like her! I hope this is not another symptom. You will tell me if, during our journey, I develop weird dress sense, put on three stone and start talking about soap operas, won't you?

I awoke in hospital, with Rachel looking down from the end of my bed. The sunlight behind her made her look like an angel. My clothes were folded up neatly and sitting on top of my shoes like a 'mini me'. My white

T-shirt had been cut away from my body and the end of it now protruded from the bin.

'It didn't make it, I'm afraid,' said Rachel as she noticed my line of gaze and gently flicked the rest of the T-shirt into the bin. 'You don't do things by halves, do you?' she added and smiled. Her go-to place was always optimism. If I'd lost my leg, she would have suggested my socks would last twice as long because I could now wear them one at a time. 'The doctor showed your X-ray to me. You now have no complete bone left in your shoulder. It's like looking at the stars at night. How are you feeling?'

I looked blank. She picked up a red scarf from the back of a plastic chair. 'Whose cashmere scarf is this? It's not your secret admirer, is it? The nurse said it was under your head when you arrived in hospital. Somebody called Pauline rang me after you fell over. Do you remember what happened? You're probably out of your box. The doctor says you're in a lot of pain.'

Then I remember hurriedly jumping up in bed and asking about things in panic mode: 'My rucksack? My laptop? My course! I've got to tell them I won't be there.'

And like wives the world over, Rachel gently but firmly put me back in my box with, 'I've got your rucksack and laptop. I rang work too. I spoke to Peter.'

'You spoke to Peter? But he's the head of department,' I replied pathetically.

'Yes, I know,' Rachel countered 'But he still answered the phone. He said, 'Get well soon and don't worry. He'll tell everybody who needs to know what's happened to you.'

The hospital staff were more worried about my heart than my arm - in 2006 I'd had a heart attack. You look worried too. Yes, I have a lot wrong with me, but don't feel that you must hurry through my story. I will still be here when it ends.

Chapter 2. Strange New World

Yes, there has always been some sort of incidental music going on in my head. It's continually playing, accompanying everything I do. I think it comes from watching Western TV shows and *Scooby Doo* when I was a child. It usually tells me whether to do something or not. That's what told me I could talk to you. I heard a happy tune when I saw your face for the first time and that told me that you would be OK with it. Now, where were we? They kept me in hospital for observation. I overheard a nurse say to Rachel, 'The fracture is rather nasty, but we're mainly worried about any aftershock on his heart. It's purely precautionary, so no need to worry. But I thought you should know.'

'Thank you,' said Rachel. 'Should I tell him why he's being kept in?'

'Yes, but I would make it about the fall. It might stress him out otherwise.' Of course, when Rachel approached me, she was all smiles. She was and still is a terrible liar. I chose to say nothing; my new reality tongue-tied me.

After Rachel left, I was taken for another X-ray. Myrtle wanted her first family picture, or at least a strong yet sensitive study of her in the garden. I jest of course, but at least I was conscious for this X-ray.

'Strewth, that looks really painful,' Guy, the young radiologist, said. Yes, he was from Australia.

'Yes,' I replied, 'my wife said it looked bad. There's no bone left, just bits.'

'She was right, the bits of bone look like the Milky Way or hundreds of little baby teeth. It's spectacular!'

'Baby teeth?' I pondered briefly whether cannabis featured in this man's life or if he was moonlighting as the tooth fairy. I decided that no comment was probably for the best. I just told him I felt dizzy.

'That'll be the morphine injection. They tell me you've had a fall and broken your shoulder. I need you to lie totally still for about a minute whilst I take another X-ray.' And with that he pushed my trolley into the X-ray area adding, 'OK, smile.'

I looked bemused, so he explained himself quickly, 'Sorry, I used to have a summertime job taking photos of kids on the beach. It's hard to shake off.' When I was finally ready, he said, 'Not to worry though, you'll have a nice little compensation claim there.'

'Really? Who am I going to sue, God?' I replied indignantly. 'I fell over on ice outside the train station. It wasn't anyone's fault. It could have happened to anyone. It was just one of those things.'

'But that's it,' returned Guy, 'it didn't happen to anyone, it happened to you! You could be off work for ages yet.'

Suddenly I felt defensive. It was the first time somebody had talked about lasting change from the accident and I was unprepared for it. Later that day the subject raised its ugly head again when I found myself on a hospital ward. My arm was now in a sling and the rest of me was wrapped in a bed gown like a poncho.

I tried to orientate myself by looking round the room. There was a television by the side of the bed on a giant white metal hinge. Next to this was a chest of drawers on which sat a jug half full of tepid water and a plastic glass. The room had six beds in it, all occupied by men in the latter stages of life. All of them seemed to have the same scar crossed upon their chests and cardiogram wires monitoring their hearts. Then I fell asleep.

I did a double-take when I woke up, thinking they were zombies. Then, a tall pale looking zombie shuffled into view and said, 'Hello, I'm Keith.'

I remember smiling in relief. Keith was a ridiculous name for a zombie, so obviously this was a human.

'You're incredibly young to be a hot cross bun.'

'Sorry?'

'We've all had a triple heart bypass in here. That's why we have the same chest marks. They call this the 'hot cross buns' ward.

'I fell, broke my shoulder. I suppose I'm here because I've a stent in my heart.'

'Sounds like a song, doesn't it? An old Sinatra number.' Then he sang, '*Even with a stent in my heart, I will always love you.*'

I didn't know what to say.

'Never mind,' said Keith. 'You'll have a nice compensation claim there then?'

'You're the second person who's said that to me today.'

'You could be quids in. You see Ron over there?' I looked at the corner bed where an orange bald bloke sat reading a magazine on fishing. 'He got 15k when a bus ran over his foot, that's what his tan's all about. Anyway, I'm off for a fag. Nice to meet you.'

I was astonished that someone who'd had a triple heart bypass operation was still smoking. I remember tutting indignantly and muttering something about taxpayers' money being wasted on somebody who was clearly not helping himself. The TV was now on and tuned to ITV4: the American detective show *Columbo.* I didn't really take in the episode, but I did notice the frequency of the advert breaks, especially those which told you how to get compensation. The adverts all had the same premise: a woman called Morag falling over in reception because her employer had recently polished the floor and not put out "a hazard warning sign". They boasted, 'We got her four thousand pounds. We are injury lawyer specialists with "no win no fee".'

Rachel arrived at five o'clock. 'How are you?' she asked, kissing my forehead.

'OK, I suppose. I thought Australians were supposed to be positive people?'

'They are, aren't they?'

'Well, I lucked out with the radiologist guy. He was called Guy too. He's probably the only doom merchant in the whole country.'

'What are you talking about?' she asked.

'He told me I should sue someone, maybe the council, over my fall. A hot cross bun called Keith told me that too, so did the telly and a bus ran over Ron's foot.'

'Oh dear, poor Ron,' smiled Rachel.

'I'm not going to sue anybody. There's a real "compensation culture" in here and I want nothing to do with it.'

'That's OK, we don't have to sue anybody. Just concentrate on getting well.'

The hospital didn't really care whether I sued anyone. They spent the next day making sure my heart wasn't going to conk out again from the stress of everything and that my stent was OK. I found myself covered in sticky electrocardiogram patches and connected to a monitor. So now I was not only immobile, but I felt I was on a leash. To top it all, every thirty minutes or so someone in a blue or white uniform would ask, 'How's your heart?'

I would reply with 'Fine, but my arm hurts.'

The nurse would smile patronisingly back at me, and after looking at the cardiogram say, 'Well, your heart is doing really well.'

Chapter 3. No Room at the Inn

By the way, when people say, 'Hi, how are you doing? I don't do the 'I'm OK, or I'm not so bad,' and everyday platitudes like that anymore. Now, when something's wrong I say so. I probably should have said this earlier. When I say *'I am not OK'* I am really *not* and I probably need to go to hospital. I always answer truthfully. Don't look so worried, I carry a letter in my left-hand inside pocket which lists my bona fides and what has happened to me. It really cuts down the 'having to explain myself time'. It's on hospital headed paper, which means that people take my condition more seriously.

Just before lunch on my second day at the hospital, a rather stern-faced senior nurse came to my bedside.
'How are you?' she asked.

'OK, I think. My arm is really painful,' I replied.

'Yes well, you need the Fracture Clinic for that. The next one isn't until Thursday and today is Monday. This ward is for heart patients, and we'll need your bed later this afternoon for an emergency admission.'

'Do I go to another ward?'

'No, unfortunately the Fracture Ward is full too, so we're discharging you for now. I'll call your wife so she can come and collect you.'

A smiley pharmacist called Dawn came into the room shortly after the nurse left. She gave me two boxes of Ibruprofen, another sling and a short lecture about keeping my arm still with no heavy lifting.

When Rachel arrived, she did her best to remain optimistic. 'I've arranged a cab. It's waiting at reception. You'll soon be home with your music and guitars. There will be no zombies or hot cross buns to worry about.'

'It's fine,' I replied. 'Somebody else needs the bed and they have more serious heart problems than me. I accept that.'

However, what I didn't appreciate or even truly understand was that there was now no bone connecting what remained of my left shoulder to my arm. My arm was effectively only held together with some tendons and damaged muscle. I was about to find out what that meant. After wandering aimlessly through the hospital corridors to find the car park, I finally found myself on the back seat of the taxi. My left arm was curled into the shape of my body and balanced on two folded-up coats for support. Even in the relatively flat car park, I shuddered every time the taxi went over a slight bump, sucking in my breath and adding, 'Jesus, that's sore.'

'Sorry, I can't go any slower,' said the driver.

'We'll be on tarmac soon and that will be flatter,' said Rachel.

But sadly, Rachel was wrong. The road may have looked smoother, but it was still bouncy and the up and down undulations jarred my shoulder terribly.

'You can let some of it out,' said Rachel noticing the tears in my eyes.

'OK, you asked for it,' I replied. You think tarmac is smooth and the suspension on modern cars is very comfortable, don't you? Well, it's not with a broken arm with bits of bone floating loose. I want to die!'

'Shall I stop?' asked the rather concerned driver.

'Absolutely not,' I said. 'Keep going no matter what I say. I want this over with as quickly as possible.'

'Good man,' said Rachel. 'It won't be long before we're home.'

Standing still in traffic, the diesel engine made the cab shudder and my arm ache even more. I must have looked bad because throughout the journey both the cab driver and Rachel kept asking whether I was OK. I cursed, screamed, moaned and probably cried, all under my breath of course - after all, I am still British. At the time this meant I would stupidly proclaim I was fine whenever anybody asked.

'Right, lady and gent,' said the cab driver when we reached the traffic lights. 'We have two options, because of the road works: I can go the longer way down the High Street, which will take us forty-five minutes; or we can try to negotiate Big Susan. That will take us fifteen.'

'What the hell is Big Susan?' asked Rachel cautiously.

'It's a pothole, Madam. Well, some of us taxi drivers call it a crevasse. The Big Susan part is a sleeping policeman which makes the pothole part even deeper. It's passable, but with care.'

'Big Susan it is then,' I interrupted. 'I can't do forty-five minutes of this.'

I got to know every bump, gradient and pit in the 'Big Susan' pothole intimately. After what seemed like a five-hour drive (Rachel said later it was actually about ten minutes, but of course she was lying), we were home.

'I'm sorry if I was rude or abrupt,' I said to the taxi driver as Rachel helped me out of the cab.

'Stop worrying,' he said. 'I gave that up years ago; there are better things to do with your time.'

'All the taxi drivers from Trust cars have the same bulbous nose,' I said to Rachel as she opened the front door. 'Perhaps they swap it over before they come around, for continuity's sake.'

Chapter 4: Home Sweet Home

Back home, I lay in bed trying to make up for lost sleep. This was the first time the extent of the injury hit me. Rachel had left the telephone intercom by my pillow so that she could carry on working. Of course, when I awoke the first thing I did was knock the phone on the floor. I let out an exasperated sigh and tried to reach it; but putting any weight on my newly broken arm was impossible and my entire left side became a screaming burglar alarm of pain. I immediately recoiled on to my right side, but the momentum caused me to roll right out of bed and thud against the blanket chest. I was dazed. Rachel ran down the stairs the moment she heard the clatter.

'What are you doing, you silly man?' she said, bursting into the room.

'I tried to pick up the phone,' I moaned pathetically. 'It fell on the floor.'

'Couldn't you have waited?' she said as she helped me back into bed.

'Well, no, I needed to pee.'

'I have a plastic jug for that. It's not quite a book at bedtime, but it will certainly be more effective. Here it is.' She presented me with the old measuring jug and helped me move to the edge of the bed.

'This jug was a wedding present,' I said as I relieved myself.

'Well, it was from Clive and Nadine. And I've never liked them.'

Mission accomplished; Rachel tried her best to make me comfortable. 'Let's hope you can sleep a little better now you are home,' she said, helping me back into bed. 'At least there won't be any weirdos telling you to sue anybody.'

'I'm frightened of rolling over and making my arm worse,' I replied.

'Have some Ibruprofen,' said Rachel, opening a blister pack and giving me two tablets and a bottle of water. 'That should knock you out.' Then she began wedging cushions and pillows all around me. 'There, that should hold you in place. In your old striped rugby top, you look like a bumble bee on an exceptionally large sunflower.'

'It's not great if you're Taphophobic,' I said from inside my newly padded prison. 'That means afraid of being buried alive.'

'I know. You told me. You forget we've been together since the dawn of time.'

'Well, apart from that, it's OK.'

When the painkillers kicked in, I was out like a light.

The following morning, I stood naked in front of the bathroom mirror (save for my sling) whilst Rachel put shaving foam on my face.

'There you go, my little wedding cake,' said Rachel, handing me a razor.

'You're not going to shave me?' I said, disappointedly.

'No, you can do that part; besides, I'm worried about cutting you. You've seen what sort of a mess I make of my legs. I'm not doing that to you.'

I picked up the razor and nervously pulled it against my cheek, creating a small slalom path through the foam.

'I knew you could do it,' said Rachel.

'Thanks,' I said, but as I did so, a great globule of shaving foam with strands of salt and pepper beard dripped onto my sling.

'Oh Adam,' laughed Rachel, 'you're a messy pup.'

'This is hard with only one arm.'

'Hold on a minute, I have an idea,' and with that she ran downstairs. I stood by the sink hearing cupboard doors opening and a lot of rustling of carrier bags. She returned a minute later with a bin bag with a head hole cut out of it, so it was now a poncho cover-all for my left shoulder. 'Bend down, so I can fit this over your head, we can't get your sling wet.'

Once shaving was done, we got into the shower together to wash the rest of me.

'I always wanted to know how to be bad,' I said coyly, looking over my bin-bagged shoulder at my now naked wife.

'In your dreams, mate!'

'Isn't showering together was supposed to be sexy?'

'All right then, take me, big boy.'

I promptly burst into tears.

Rachel hugged me and with tears in her own eyes she said, 'Now you listen to me, mister! One arm or no arms, you're still the best man I know, and I love you, and no broken shoulder is ever going to change that. Understand?'

I heard that at work rumours of my fall had travelled around the office quickly. Portly Peter Moores even wore his grey suit to show that things were serious.

He announced it formally during the morning team meeting, when people usually gathered awkwardly in a horseshoe and struggled to make their work sound interesting. After Peter's "Adam update", there was visible shock on the faces of some of my colleagues.

'I was only with him on Friday,' trumpeted dark-suited young Roderick into a tissue. 'I'm not crying. I have a cold. Honestly.' He even widened his eyes to prove it.

'I guess you just never know,' said ponytailed Jerome, touching Roderick's elbow.

He didn't buy milk,' squawked dowdy Diane from accounts. 'Milk Club was his baby. Now he won't be able to. Poor bugger.'

'I'll get some at lunchtime,' said Neil Black.

'No, you won't,' added Diane. 'That's Adam's job, and you're leaping into his role when he's not even cold. I'll get it. We in the Milk Club stick together.'

'This is a lot of fuss, isn't it?' scoffed Darren Jones. 'He's only broken his shoulder.'

'He will be missed,' said Diane. 'He was a trooper and the life and soul of this place. Always making time for everyone with a kind word and a smile. It's always the wrong ones who get taken before their time.'

'Diane, Adam's not dead,' said Peter. 'He's just had an accident and he's in hospital. I'm sure he'll be back soon.'

'We should get him a card,' said Jerome.

'Yes,' agreed Peter, 'that's a good idea. It will show we're thinking of him.'

'Yes, one with a cow on it to say that Milk Club will carry on,' said Diane, wiping tears and mascara tramlines from her eyes.

Chapter 5: Project Adam - Rachel's story

Waiting for the Fracture Clinic was the longest three days of my life. With only one working arm for dressing, shaving, even making tea – all those things I previously took for granted were now a horrendous ordeal. Worst of all were the two-handed things like unscrewing bottles, tubes of toothpaste, or washing and drying my hands. I also quickly found out that with only one hand I couldn't cut up my food, make a sandwich or fasten the zip fly on my trousers properly.

Rachel was brilliant, taking our 'in sickness and in health' vows in her stride. She washed me and helped me go to the toilet and did it all without complaint. She was amazing and would always keep coming up with new things to make me feel better. She could deal with what she called 'Project Adam', all except for one thing: when I started to cry. I cried a lot as my ability to cope and dependence upon Rachel grew exponentially. It was a combination of anger and extreme pain; my emotions were all over the place. Our house became a little bit of a sanctuary where we developed a routine and way to cope.

We had just about figured that out when we had to deal with a return to the hospital.

Since I could not face another taxi ride, we walked. Setting off about two hours early, we walked arm in arm through the park, as Rachel thought it would be more tranquil. The walk normally took about thirty minutes, but Rachel wanted me to take it steady and look at nature, squirrels and trees along the way, to calm me down. Even when I was falling to bits, we were always punctual. We were used to hospitals since my heart attack. Rachel was always controlled in difficult circumstances. In part, this was because when her dad was in the army, she had lived all over Europe. The exposure to that of many people on a regular basis gave her the innate ability to get on with all sorts. She'd also been through bad days herself. When she was at boarding school in Germany, terrorists blew the school up and her teacher promptly had a nervous breakdown. Rachel led her class to safety, which included pulling a girl out from under a bed and getting her hand bitten for her troubles. Rachel was only fourteen at the time. Her dad had a big, broad, tearfully proud grin on his face when Rachel was given a medal by the local mayor a month later at a school assembly. Yes, I am in good hands. Husband with heart attack and then a broken shoulder? For Rachel this is probably a piece of cake. At least, that is what I told myself.

The Fracture Clinic was full when we arrived. People sat in rows of blue plastic chairs. Where they could the chairs followed the pattern of the walls and room layout. The walls were painted in a washed-out cream colour which somehow became depressed with itself and sort of merged into a dirty grey as it headed towards the floor. There were lots of noticeboards on the wall. They mostly seemed to be there to tell people off. It was like a really aggressive set of library instructions where people shouted at each other in capital letters. 'DON'T MISS APPOINTMENTS', 'NOW WASH YOUR HANDS', 'KEEP YOUR CHILDREN ON A LEAD', 'ALWAYS WASH YOUR MOTHER ON TUESDAY'. All right, I'm lying about the last couple, but you get the idea.

The orders and warnings were interspersed with posters about fighting to keep the hospital open. The hospital was considered for closure to pay for the incompetence (or perhaps bad luck) of another hospital miles away, a motion put forward by a smug-looking politician who had probably never set foot near the place. Somebody had drawn horns and a devil's tail on his photograph. I had not known a time, for many years, when people cared enough to make a stand, and it was nice to be in the middle of it. The hospital had become a symbol of something in the community, and more power to it. I was glad the hospital had remained open and relieved that Rachel and I didn't have to travel an extra four stops on the train to get to someone who could take care of my shoulder.

As I looked around, it suddenly dawned upon me why it was so busy. This was the place where three outpatient clinics converged. There was the Upper Limb Fracture Clinic, the Lower Limb Fracture Clinic and the Pain Clinic. Each clinic had a separate door where nurses came out and called for patients. This meant at least that the queue moved a lot quicker than anybody thought it would, but not as quickly as people wanted it to. Rachel's face got even tighter the longer we waited. She gave off outward smiles, but underneath she was seething like a volcano with a sore thumb. Come the time for us to enter the doctor's consultation room, she would be ready to try to kill somebody if we just got sent home again.

As we sat in the waiting room, I looked around at the people. There was a casual numbness about those present. Hospitals have a special ability to shrink people down in size. Most people had the same haggard expression on their faces and a look of resignation in their eyes. The atmosphere was incredibly sad, as once great giants were reduced to being mere mortals by old age and infirmity. They all seemed to be wrapped up in great big coats and jackets, which alongside their pallid complexions made them look even more vulnerable. Then I heard a weird purr, purr noise. It took me a minute to figure out what it was. It was my mobile phone. Nobody ever rang me except Rachel, not even Telesales, so it took me several seconds to discover where the noise was coming from. Nervously pressing the call button, I uttered a tentative, 'Hello?'

'Could I speak with Adam Wright, please?'

It was my work colleague, Jerome; I recognised his posh overtone and his 'speak with' rather than 'speak to' turn of phrase. His call was odd because we were "only in the same team at work" and not really friends.

'Yes, speaking.'

'Adam?' he said again, like it was the start of a soliloquy.

'Yes,' I replied.

'It's Jerome; I called as soon as I heard about your accident. How ***are*** you?' He sounded like he was suddenly either my new best friend, my boss or both.

Oh hello, er, Jerome,' I replied, still surprised. 'I'm stuck in God's waiting room, waiting to see a doctor at the hospital. I'm at the Fracture Clinic.'

'You poor thing, you must be in so much pain.'

'Yes, my arm is pretty sore.'

'Yes, I'm sure.'

This was rapidly turning into a rather awkward conversation because I had no idea what to say to Jerome, and by the sound of it Jerome didn't know what to say to me either. I always thought we were same grade rivals, competing for the affections of our Head of Team, Peter Moores. Now I struggled to find a way out of our current situation. Thankfully, from somewhere the inner strength came to me to say, 'How about I give you a call later or send an email to let you know how we're getting on, if that's OK? In fact, yes, I think we're about to be called in.' I added the phrase, 'Yes, I'm coming,' for effect.

'Yes, that's fine,' agreed Jerome as he put the phone down.

But I'd told him a lie and I'd even shone my mobile phone in the direction of an imaginary nurse who was supposedly calling us in. For some reason I didn't want to speak to Jerome, and the sudden interest in my welfare from a relative stranger was unnerving and tough to take.

'That was Jerome,' I said to Rachel after ending the call. 'He asked how I was. I suppose I should have been kinder, but the lie of going in to see the doctor seemed the kindest, quickest and best way forward.'

'Well, it will soon be true,' reassured Rachel.

'But I don't know how he knew what happened. Peter must have told him.'

'Well, you spoke to work as well. The doctor told me you rang them when you were in the ambulance.'

I had no recollection of this. Then a thicket of half-remembered words permeated my brain. Yes, I ***had*** spoken to my, and Jerome's, boss – Gentleman Jim. I had told him I wasn't going to make it to the training course. Jim, in turn, had said to me, 'Good God, that's brave! Ringing me when you've just broken your arm!' Oh well, at least work was in the picture as to what was happening.

'You haven't mentioned Jerome before,' said Rachel. 'Jim I know. He's nice.'

'Well, Jim is moving to a new team this week in Birmingham. I think they must be thinking about a replacement. Jerome is much younger than me. He always has this controlled manner about him. I sense he irons his boxer shorts,' I replied. 'He has one of those daft ponytail buns. It becomes a soggy sausage roll when it rains.'

'What's he like?'

'I can't say I'm a fan. We were on the same team in a quiz once. I had provided loads of answers to questions nobody else knew. Not exactly *Mastermind*, they were only film trivia questions and the final one was "Who wrote the script for the movie *Butch Cassidy and the Sundance Kid*?" I answered with the name William Goldman. Our team won and everybody patted me on the back except him.'

'What did Jerome say?'

'He said "You know lots of small things". I replied with yes, but "I know some larger ones too," I was quite upset by his comment.'

'No, he doesn't sound very nice,' agreed Rachel, 'but you're quick to judge people sometimes.'

I have no intention of turning Jerome into the villain of this story! On the contrary, he did lots of things which helped me. However, at that precise moment in time, negative thoughts were the easiest ones to come into my mind.

Chapter 6. All Apologies

Yes, this train is taking quite a while to get going. We seem to have stopped just outside Watford Gap. Typically, there are no announcements, and so we have no clue as to what's going on. It would be helpful if they said something, even if it's only to tell us how long we might be stuck here.

I know a lot about being stuck in time at the behest of someone or something else. The same feelings translate easily back to the days just after my accident. We sat in that very full waiting room for over half an hour. As time wore on, people sagged silently in their chairs. Some chewed on Polo mints; others, the braver ones, faced the wait without anything at all. They looked like a coterie of old dolls and teddy bears who had been left too long in a musty toy cupboard. They probably smelled the same too, sitting in mute, motionless meditation, waiting for the magic side door to open with its rude but purposeful squeak.

Then, just as Rachel was about to trade me in for a packet of Fruit Pastilles, a nurse dressed in a dark blue uniform came out of one of the side rooms and stood in the middle of the room. Her hair was helmeted in place with hair grips; and if they still had matrons, this lady would undoubtedly have been one. She had all the accoutrements: resolute cleavage, upright stance and an ability to outstare a house brick. She called out the words 'Adam Wright, Adam Wright, ADAM WRIGHT!' over and over again, like it was a mantra. Eventually, my crystalline world shattered and I realised she was calling me. Rachel had already noticed and was helping me to my feet. We lurched forward towards the would-be matron, as though frightened that somebody else might take our turn without asking.

'Come with me, sorry to have kept you waiting,' she barked as we entered Doctor Skate's Fracture Clinic. It may have had a grand-sounding name, but it was not particularly impressive. It was like walking into a wardrobe: minus the white snow of Narnia, and grimmer grey and cream walls. A doctor and two other people were sitting in the corner. I took up a seat next to Doctor Skate's desk, Rachel to my right. Skate, through a rather sensible Scandinavian beard and with the utmost caring solemnity, introduced the two viewers who sat on the outskirts of the room.

'Do you mind my two colleagues being here? They are here to observe.'

'No, we don't mind,' replied Rachel after seeing me shake my head.

Both observers smiled and introduced themselves. The lady in a blue cardigan was Dutch and called Doctor Elena Van de Lear. The man in a suit was a visiting Danish Professor Magnus Olsen. Skate switched on his computer screen to look at my X-ray and pronounced, 'There's nothing left.'

'I'm sorry?' said Rachel.

'Usually we have something to join the bones back together with, but there is nothing left to use in this case.'

I felt numb; at first, I thought Skate was blaming me for having fallen over and broken my arm too badly. I gasped for breath a few times.

'This is a really bad break,' Skate continued. 'What happened?

'I fell over,' I blubbed. The occasion, the visitors, everything got to me.

Rachel continued the story. 'He was going to a training course.' She looked at me and I gave her a wave to continue. 'The footpath near the train station was very icy and slippery. He fell over, and then three policemen fell on top of him.'

'Why were you sent home from the hospital ward? You should have been admitted last week. This is a really bad break.'

'We have no idea,' snarled Rachel. 'Somebody said we'd have to wait until your Fracture Clinic re-opened as we'd missed that week's clinic. Here we are a whole week later! My poor husband has been a crying, gibbering wreck ever since.'

'I'm so sorry, that should not have happened,' said Skate. The visitors looked at the floor and said nothing. Skate telephoned his colleague, the coiffured and calculating Mr Columba, who came in and the two of them had a strange whispering debate. Then Skate telephoned somebody else, using the words 'I see' rather a lot.

'I too am so sorry for what happened. Do you wish to complain to the Trust?' asked Columba, turning to Rachel and me. Clearly Columba felt he needed to interject whilst Skate was busy on the phone.

'No, we don't want to complain to the Trust,' said Rachel. 'Is that all you do round here, apologise and tell people how to complain?' Then another doctor walked in who turned out to be the one whom Skate had spoken to on the phone. Before he could even open his mouth, Rachel leapt in with, 'Is he going to apologise as well? I don't want your apologies, I want you to fix my husband. Do you understand?'

'The next available operation for a replacement shoulder joint is on Monday. I am genuinely sorry for what has happened, but you are top of the appointment list.' Rachel glared at him, so he added the word 'honest', as if it were a shield to thwart any further embarrassing questions or comments.

But even after their hand-wringing apologies and acts of contrition, they still sent me home! Yes, those people who sat there in sanctimonious indignation and other places near Winchester still sent me home! They even told us to 'be careful'. We smiled at the ridiculousness of it all as we were given yet another mountain of Ibuprofen on our way out. What else could we do?

The next day, as I lay in bed, Rachel brought in an envelope which had been posted through our letterbox. 'This came for you this morning,' she beamed.

I struggled to tear open the envelope, so she helped.

'A get well soon card from work. That's nice,' said Rachel. 'Lots of people have signed it too.'

'Yes, it's nice of people to remember me. I think Jerome is behind it,' I replied. 'It certainly looks like his handwriting in the main message.'

'It's full of "*best wishes*", although one seems to say *"breast wishes from Keith"*; it must be a spelling mistake.'

'Probably not, he's a bit of pervert is Keith. He's the maintenance guy. Dowdy Diane signed it. She must have chosen the cow on the front to remind me of Milk Club. She's a bit like a "work version" of my sister Agnes, well-meaning but odd.'

'Oh God, that's worrying. There are quite a few "Miss yous". They can't all be from Jerome.'

I read the card several times that day, mentally crossing off who had signed it. 'My friend Neil is not amongst the contributors,' I said later to Rachel.

'Perhaps he's away on holiday. It's a nice thing that people are doing this.' Then Rachel leaned into my gaze. 'You shouldn't over-analyse it.'

Chapter 7. You Are on Hold for the Moment.

The gap between the appointment at the Fracture Clinic and the operation was only three days, but it felt more like three weeks. To all intents and purposes, I had regressed to infancy. I lay about the house like a beached whale in my blue dressing gown (apparently, this look is all the rage in the Southern Atlantic). Rachel worked from home, once again making sure I had the telephone intercom by my side in case of emergencies. Periodically during the day, because she knew I didn't want to impose on her, Rachel would pop her head around the front room door to check up on me. The first morning set the tone.

'How are you doing? Do you need anything?'

I did not take in her question at first.

'I can plump your sofa cushions up?' she ventured after my blank look.

'I think I need stronger painkillers; these don't touch the pain.'

'Well, what do you suggest?'

'They gave me Tramadol and Co-codamol in hospital. Things ending in "ol" are probably good. They're stronger.'

'Maybe I should get you some *Castrol* or castor oil. They gave you Ibrupofen because it's non-addictive, but your body gets used to it and it's not as effective.'

'There's the Welsh slayer of Greek monsters, Dihydrocodeine.'

'Good to know you're still trying to make me smile. I'll call the doctor's surgery.'

The room was very quiet as Rachel rang; I could hear the telephone conversation quite clearly: 'Hello, doctors' surgery,' said the rather shrill receptionist, called Kevin. He was work experience and straight from school.

'Yes, hello, my husband Adam Wright has broken his shoulder and has been sent home from the hospital to wait for surgery. But he's in chronic pain.'

Rachel looked around at me and smiled. She touched my hair in a pat of reassurance, but as she did this my face crumpled like a cardboard box having a boot stamp on it and I promptly burst into tears.

'He's sat in front me crying.' Then Rachel's own voice started to crack, and she began to cry too, but not before uttering through broken breath, 'I'm sorry, but I'll have to phone you back.'

In the early days, it was like that for a while; we would sort of set each other off crying, on a downward spiral of sadness. It was as though someone had got hold of our little world, given it a good shake, and we didn't know who, why or what to do about it.

'You daft sod! You made me cry,' said Rachel, hugging me and then blowing her nose. We kissed each other through the tears, half laughing, half crying, making deep eye contact; it was a pointed, poignant, almost sensual moment. Then real life pulled back the curtain – our home phone rang. It was Dr Sharma, my usual doctor; the receptionist had given him our number, and realising we were in difficulty, he'd rung back.

'I'm sorry. I'm not good at dealing with crying men,' said Rachel.

The ever-calm, ever-resolute Sharma seemed to take it all in his stride. 'That's OK, don't worry, it happens all the time. I'll have a prescription waiting for you in five minutes. You can pick it up at the pharmacy.'

Chapter 8. All in the Family

I deliberately asked Rachel not to tell anybody on my side of the family about my fall until after the operation. I explained, 'My sister and brother are difficult to talk to at the best of times, so I don't want to waste your time exchanging pleasantries about what it's like to have a broken arm, or worse still, trying to stop them coming down to see me.'

'I can't imagine not telling my mum or sisters if it were me,' agreed Rachel. 'But if you are sure'.

'Well, your sisters are vaguely normal. Besides, if we tell them, we'll only have my *oldest friend* Clive getting wind of it and wanting to visit and then telling me about the time he broke his foot and *"how it took not one, not two but three operations and it's still not right. It aches in the cold weather and squeaks in hot weather..."* And I can live without that.'

'Fair enough. I don't even know how you know Clive.'

'I met him in metalwork at school. We bonded together to stop ourselves from being bullied. Now I can't get rid of him. He's like the human version of Herpes.'

'Well, we're in this together, so as you wish.'

'Extra people create complications. When the time comes to tell them, we'll just inform one member of the family, Paula. She's always brilliantly reliable and will pass on the update. She's dependable too: she was once a nurse, so she understands what we're talking about.' I paused for effect, before adding forcefully, 'If anybody questions why, tell them it's my decision.'

Rachel smiled. 'So, we're not telling your sister Agnes first then?'

'Absolutely not, no way in hell! Not after last time,' I replied firmly.

"They say blood is thicker than water,' said Rachel.

'That's true, Agnes is best described as a bit gloopy.'

'She means well, she has a good heart.'

'Yes, I know, and I love her, but she gets even the simplest things completely and utterly wrong. Then we have to spend ages putting them right. In the meantime, everybody else ends up worrying unnecessarily, and the point of having a single information provider is completely gone.'

I don't mean to sound so harsh. But some years before, I tried to use my sister Agnes as the means to inform the rest of the family when I had a heart murmur. It didn't end well and was one of those 'never again' moments. When I had my first heart attack, Rachel had used my niece Paula as a conduit to pass news on to the rest of the family. Whilst this had proved to be very successful, Agnes (Paula's mother) had taken umbrage over not being consulted before everyone else. Agnes said it was her role as the eldest sister to be the family information broadcaster, insisting on being the first to know of bad news in future. A couple of years later, I had another heart murmur at work. I was taken to hospital and diagnosed with a borderline heart attack. After a few days I rang my sister Agnes from the ward to tell her the news.

'I need you to help me, and you will have to be strong,' I began. 'You said you wanted to know first when anything else bad or good happened to me.'

'Yes,' replied Agnes.

'Well, I'm in hospital because I've had another heart murmur.'

'Oh, my God. Are you all right?'

'I'm very tired, but I'm all right, and I'm in the best place. I'm being kept in for tests for a few days, and they're going to adjust my medication for the future. I need you to let everybody else in the family know that I'm all right. Do you think you can do that? It's quite a big responsibility.'

'Yes, I'll be all right. Don't worry.'

But I did not realise how much she loved me, and the thought of suddenly being without her brother affected her very deeply. When she rang our younger brother Bryan, he must have thought she was auditioning for *EastEnders*.

She managed to get out the words 'Adam is in hospital, he's had another heart attack' before bursting into tears. Her voice then, apparently, became completely unintelligible garbled nonsense, most of it high-pitched and totally impossible to understand, although I understand the next door's pet Labrador did get worried about me. The effect of this was awful, as it scared the hell out of everyone else. Poor Rachel spent the entire weekend having to convince everybody that I was not about to die.

This was especially hard work in the case of my 'oldest friend' Clive's wife, Nadine, who was even more removed from reality than Agnes. Nadine wanted to be 'Rachel's rock'. She provided lots of unwanted advice, including her top five funeral directors, and having seen off two husbands, her tips on how to be a merry widow.

'With a change of hair style or colour, you could be quite nice looking...' Rachel politely declined.

Thankfully, our younger brother Bryan was much more sanguine and philosophical about the whole thing and made a big point of going around to everyone else and telling then what had really happened. Needless to say, Paula was drafted back into action to deal with any further updates; and no matter how much Agnes protested, she would never have the 'family information broadcaster' (the Fibber) role again. From then on everything was simply played down, especially whenever news needed to be delivered to Agnes, so as not to create any further difficulties.

'Families and friends, how on earth do we deal with them? Why do we bother? You're nodding, so you must know what I mean.'

Chapter 9: How To Say Goodbye.

Rachel gave up the 'obey' part of the wedding vows very early in our relationship, yet strangely I inherited it - an arrangement which continues to this day. More seriously, marriage for the two of us has been about separate entities fusing into one and losing your embarrassment, sense of pride and admitting you need somebody. You get a degree of intimacy and trust in each other from recovering from a serious accident, not that I would advocate everybody has one. On occasion you also get downright cranky, and miserable too.

One morning Rachel walked into our bedroom where, propped up by pillows, I was reading a magazine. 'I have something to tell you,' she announced.

'Oh yes, sounds ominous,' I replied. 'You're pregnant?'

'Hardly. Well, it's not ominous really. You know that information that comes with your tablets? Those delightful little "get out of jail free cards" that the drug companies put in there: Don't take this medication if you're diabetic; about to operate heavy machinery; or plan to go ballroom dancing with a cactus.'

'Yes.'

'Well, we got a new one this morning: you can't eat grapefruit anymore because it reacts with your heart medication.

'That's fairly random, isn't it?'

'I know. I was going to try to act out the ridiculously dramatic warning that came with it to introduce a little levity. We haven't laughed much in a while.'

'If I'm honest, grapefruit is no great loss. In fact, I could kiss you. Grapefruit is the sweat from the Devil's balls.' And after her blank look, 'Maybe that's a bit strong, but let's be honest, it's not very nice, is it?'

I said goodbye to Rachel before I went into hospital for my first shoulder operation. I thought about it for several days beforehand, and then decided that saying goodbye to each other couldn't hurt. In the words of the late great Tommy Cooper, it happened 'one Thursday'. I was sat in the front room and Rachel came in with a cup of tea for me. 'Can you do something for me, please?' I asked.

'You look serious, should I sit myself down?'

'Maybe. I was just thinking about the accident and my heart attacks, and it dawned upon me just how quickly our life together could change or even end. It's like in the Live 8 message when they said, "Every time, I click my fingers someone dies"!' I clicked my fingers for emphasis.

'Well, stop doing it then!' said Rachel smiling.

'No, I don't mean it like that. The end of your life is a big thing to contemplate. When people do think about it, they usually do so from the vantage point that they will still be able to see it, somehow, or at least hear about it later. I wonder how many more opportunities for survival I will have. I'm not a cat with nine lives; indeed, the closest I ever came to that was Daniel Croft calling me a pussy at school because I wouldn't pick up an earthworm in our science lesson.'

'Adam, get to the point, what are you trying to say?

'I think I'm trying to say that death may come at any given moment and we won't necessarily get the opportunity to say goodbye on our terms.'

'OK,' Rachel nodded.

'Could you fetch two pillowcases down from the spare room please?'

OK,' she said, a little surprised.

After a few minutes, Rachel came back into the room and presented the pillowcases to me. She looked bewildered when I put one of the pillowcases on my head like a hat, leaving my face exposed. I then asked her to do the same.

'Really? You want me to put this on my head? Adam, where is this coming from?'

'Well, including my fall,' I began, 'two horrible things have happened to me, both of which were unexpected. OK, before my heart attack I was a smoker, but I was only 42. Nobody has heart attacks and dies at the age of 42.'

'Well, Elvis Presley did, although he was the size of a house when he died.'

'What are you saying?' I asked, examining my own gut in horror.

'Robert Kennedy also died when he was 42, but he was shot.'

'Rachel, please put the pillowcase on,' I growled, so she got the message that I was serious. After she put it on, we sat there like two solemn-looking Smurfs gazing into each other's eyes. Then I tried to explain myself, slightly stuttering over my words.

'I want you to know that if anything happens during the operation tomorrow, that I have had more fun and wonderful times with you than with any other person. I want you to know that if I'm not here, I completely trust you to carry out my wishes. I want you to know that I love you. No matter what anybody else thinks or may say after I'm gone, you are my wisest counsellor and my best friend. I know you'll do the right thing.'

'You are the same to me.' Rachel saw me crying and hugged me. She remained stoic before adding, 'I don't think I'm going to cry.'

'You are always so strong,' I said. 'You're always so practical. You are amazing. You always think of how to help people.'

'Not really, it's because I'm sat here wearing a pillowcase. Oddly, that helps.'

I knew it would add to the solemnity of the occasion.'

Part 2

Chapter 10: Operation One.

Good God, how much luggage has that guy brought? I'm surprised it fitted in the overhead rack. It reminds me of my trip to hospital for the first shoulder operation. I remember as I picked up my rucksack in the hall thinking, 'This feels heavier than when I packed it.' When I looked inside, I found T-shirts turned into ponchos with one side cut open, pens, writing pads and guitar magazines as reading matter. 'Did you remember the life size model of the *Titanic*?' I joked quite loudly.

'I want you to aspire to something, so that's what the guitar books, magazines and writing pads are all about,' said Rachel, now standing in the front room doorway.

'Well, there's no chance of giving up with you around, is there?'

'Damn right. It's the early thoughts that will make all the difference,' said Rachel. She didn't just stand by her man, she helped him stand too.

I had never looked forward to being in hospital so much. I even took another taxi to get there! One dose of dihydrocodeine later, and there we were in the hospital waiting room. I thought things were supposed to be more joined-up now in terms of computerised record keeping, but sadly not. I still had to talk them through my accident and remind them about my allergy to penicillin. Before I had the operation, a young, bearded doctor came in to talk us through the procedure.

'My name is Small,' he began.

'What, like Ted or Ian?' I asked, half joking.

'No, my name is Doctor Paul Small. I manage the theatre. I'm going to take you through what will happen today.' He started pointing at some diagrams of a human body. 'We'll make an entrance through the top of the shoulder here, pull out the older bits of broken bone and join what's left to a new shoulder joint.'

I could feel myself turning white and feeling sick, so 'Redoubtable Rachel' took over, asking, 'Will he have a scar?'

'There will be a mark, yes, but it will not be excessively big. Our skin is quite stretchy and pliable. It will return to its former shape in no time, a bit like after women have babies.' He again tried to show me the pictures, but I turned away.

'He's never been good with blood and guts,' said Rachel. 'Just explain it to me, please. He can't even make it through the *Gremlins* movie without being sick.'

After the doctor left, Rachel forced me to understand what the operation was going to achieve, saying, 'Their plan is to insert a new shoulder joint and pin it to what is left of the bone coming up from your elbow. Your range of movement afterwards will be limited, but with time you should be able to use your arm again and do most of the things you could do before.'

'Including playing the guitar?' I asked.

'Yes, including playing the guitar.' Rachel was rather in the dark in saying this, but she felt an optimistic husband was better than a scared and pessimistic one.

The doctors were trying to mask it, but I sensed that my heart problems really concerned them. I had to agree not to take any legal action against them if I died (which of course, I couldn't have done even if I wanted to), and Rachel had to do the same. Since we wouldn't get the surgery without signing their paper, we had no choice.

I sat in the waiting room for ages pretending to read a guitar magazine or watch television, but my mind was wandering because I was scared.

'Oh,' I said looking at my bedcover, 'I have one of those blankets that used to be a carpet; it's orange and has a weird weave and lots of symmetrical square holes in it. Still, it's nice that the carpet was encouraged to diversify and become something else, even if it is rather later in its career. I suppose being a carpet is a young man's game and a tougher job. All those heavy feet, you know.'

'Yes, dear,' said Rachel. 'It was her way of saying 'shut up.'

'Sorry, I'm rambling. It's hard to concentrate I've read this same paragraph about Stratocaster guitars about fifty times.'

Rachel kept busy by my side on her work computer. The time of the operation was 11 a.m. but that came and went. It was now nearly three in the afternoon, and I had fasted since 8 o'clock the previous night.

'I'm starving,' I announced to Rachel, 'And my mouth is as dry as a bone. I'm thirsty, I need a drink of water at least.'

'I'll ask one of the nurses at reception what's going on,' she replied.

But before she could leave the room, a hospital orderly called Jason came in and started to wheel me away without so much as a by your leave.

'Well, I know I'm a cheap night out, but really!' I said in a futile attempt to look brave. 'What's your name?'

'Jason, I'm the orderly.'

'I'm Adam, this is Rachel my wife. I suppose if you didn't brush your hair and wore dirty clothes, you would be disorderly. Anyway, it's nice to meet you.'

'You too, mate,' beamed Jason. 'It's nice to have someone jolly on the ward.'

I did feel rather bulldozed into meeting Jason, but nonetheless I still shook hands with him. Then it was like one of those old films where the wall moves and the condemned man is taken away to be hanged, with lots of activity and people milling around. I was half expecting a priest or vicar to appear out of the cupboard, but thankfully no one did. As Jason pushed my bed towards the doorway, I could see Rachel getting further away and my fear articulated itself into the words, 'Hold on!'

Jason halted the trolley immediately. Then I beckoned Rachel over.

'I just need one of these.' I kissed and hugged a tearful yet smiling Rachel.

'Right, I'm ready,' I whistled in the dark and off we went. I lay back, saw lights, absorbed and felt bangs, and half-heard conversations as I glided aboard my hospital trolley magic carpet through corridors and then got into a lift. I saw faces, lots of upside-down faces, and some smiled, some didn't. Some looked ill and spaced out – but enough about the doctors and nurses.

Then finally we got to the operating theatre and there they were, the dream team: Skate, Columba and Dr Small. Jason announced my arrival. 'This is Adam Wright; he likes to shake hands.' He was right. I tried to make friends with everyone in the room. It was my strategy. I took a lesson from the last kidnap victim's mother in *The Silence of the Lambs*, thinking that if everybody knew my name, it would be harder for them to hurt me because they would see me as a person. I later confided to Rachel, 'You clutch at straws when people are about to cut holes in you. Besides which, Jodie Foster, who played Clarice Starling in the movie, and I were born in the same year! There the similarity ends, but I hope you get the point.'

There were lots of lights as I lay upon the operating table. Arthur, the anaesthetist, placed the oxygen mask over my mouth and told me to breathe deeply. I followed his instruction to count backwards from twenty, getting to seventeen and that's all I remembered as I leapt rather than drifted off to sleep.

I awoke nearly three hours later in a recovery room with Rachel in an armchair by my side. She still had her work laptop on.

'Hello, my darling,' she beamed. 'They say it was successful.'

I looked at my left arm, which was now sat upon a cushion like a prize.

'Hello, wonderful wife,' I returned. 'God, I could do with a drink.'

'I'll ask the nurse if that's OK.'

'I'm sure it will be, after all they've done the operation, haven't they?' I asked in a *can't we bend the rules* sort of way.

'Yes, but we'd better check in case you're sick.'

'This room looks nice; how come I'm here alone?'

'This is the recovery room; you'll be placed on the ward later today.'

'You can let Paula know what has happened now I've had the operation.'

'Feeling guilty?'

'No, but I really can't think how we can put it off any longer without people getting pissed off.'

'OK,' said Rachel.

'Only Paula for now. I am sure that Agnes will phone as soon as she can.'

'Well, you should be awake at 8 a.m. tomorrow when they allow the first calls of the day,' Rachel laughed.

Chapter 11: Bedside Manor

After giving Rachel instructions about my family, I must have dozed off because I next woke up on a hospital ward. As predicted, my sister Agnes rang at spot on 8 a.m., opening with the immortal words, 'I just thought I'd ring to see how you are.'

'I'm fine thanks, Agnes, how are you?' I replied in my chirpiest, breeziest voice.

'I AM ALL RIGHT!' boomed Agnes in her northern brogue. She always spoke to people on the telephone as if they were a long way away because they were. She spoke in short sentences too, which made conversations even more stilted. Nevertheless, I tried to be colourful even though her questions were in black and white. I prefaced the update about my condition with the word **They** as if I was referring to some higher power which could not be questioned. This apparently is how you speak in hospitals. '**They** seem happy with my operation. **They** say it went well. **They** told me I must wear a huge great sling, but that's OK. Besides which I'm in the best place if anything goes wrong. **They** will look after me.'

'That's good, I might try to come down and see you.'

'Oh good,' I replied, sounding unimpressed. From the tone of my voice, it was very apparent that my answer of 'good' had too many letter 'Os' in it, certainly other people in the room registered this because they looked up. I love my sister dearly, but at that moment her coming down seemed a little too much to deal with.

Then there was a long pause in the call as neither of us knew what to say, before Agnes finally added, 'Oh well, I'll ring again tomorrow at the same time.'

'Oh great,' I was amazed that those words came out of my mouth. What I really wanted to say was, 'Why? I'm OK now. Can't you leave me in peace?' Of course, that was something that never happens within families: we rarely say what we mean, or indeed mean what we say.

After the phone call was over, I looked around my new-found lodgings and quickly decided I would rather have been back at home and still in pain. The reason for this change of heart was that I now shared a room with two guys who were obsessed with East End criminals from the 1960s.

To my left, there was an old balding guy who lived inside a tatty blue dressing gown and was permanently hunched from the weight of the gold medallions tied around his neck. He must have been forgetful because he wore a gold signet ring with his name, 'Syd', pressed into it around his bulbous index finger. Syd had a frequent visitor, Jed, who would spend the entire afternoon with him. They laughed. Oh, how they laughed. As they had monosyllabic names it gave them more time to laugh and say other things when they talked.

As I told Rachel the next day at her next visit, 'I have no objection to people having fun, but the breathy, crackling soundtrack of their lives really grates my nerve ends. They speak really fast too. It's like listening to a lisping seal and a Great Dane with laryngitis coughing out a cockney version of the William Tell overture. Every now and again one of them says something bizarre like, *"And Harry said, I'll set the dawgs on yer".*'

'It's good for you to vent your frustration,' said Rachel, 'but I'm glad we're alone.'

'And then, after two hours of hackneyed hilarity, when it came time to say goodbye, they hugged each other awkwardly in the way that men do when they're desperately trying to show the world they're not gay. When Jed left, I muttered "Thank God" nearly too loudly.'

'You be careful,' said Rachel. 'It's OK to think this sort of thing, but you don't want them thinking you're a snob, or worse still wanting to hit you.'

'Don't worry, I'll be careful; they're bigger than me.'

After we said goodbye, Syd returned. He then came over to me and said, 'Your missus is pretty. You're very lucky.'

'Thank you,' I replied nervously. 'I know I'm very lucky.'

'She seems nice too. What did you think of ma' mate yesterday?'

At first, I thought he said Marmite and wondered what the hell he was talking about. I was going to say, 'I loathe the stuff', but in the end I simply responded with a rather innocuous 'Seemed nice,' thinking that was safe enough.

'Ma' mate has just done time for bank robbery,' said Syd proudly.

I don't know what you're supposed to say to that, so I replied with, 'Well, he doesn't look like a bank robber.'

'I know, it's quite amazin',' said Syd. 'He did nineteen years! The Scrubs, Wandsworth, Belmarsh, he's been in 'em all.'

I gathered I was supposed to be impressed by this. I thought to add that I was really surprised that he'd been in prison because he had no stripes on his jumper or black burglar mask and didn't carry a swag bag but thought better of it. I remembered my warning from Rachel and the fact that I now had only one working arm to his two, and if his mate had been in prison, he could probably handle himself.

'He was in the army before he was a crim,' added Syd. 'He's been around the world. He can say "Take your clothes off" and "He's paying" in six languages.'

'I bet his mum is proud,' I replied.

Syd didn't do sarcasm; he looked puzzled, like a Staffordshire bull terrier trying to remember his seventeen times table. After a few moments he added a rather bewildered 'Yerse'. Then he asked, 'Was that your sister who phoned this morning?'

'Yes, her name's Agnes. She likes to keep in touch. We haven't lived together for a long time now. So, we haven't got much in common anymore. But she's lovely.'

'You never get too big for family, bruv. Remember that. When all the others are gorn, families is what's left.'

'Yes. Thank you, that's good advice,' I replied. But inside, I must admit I was feeling affronted that this low-life illiterate was giving me 'an educated man's advice'. I wanted to say *'Who the hell are you? The people you know are jailbirds,'* and although Rachel's advice held, I am ashamed to say I did mull over my revenge.

The guest in the other bed to my right was a young, wide-eyed black guy called Randolph Scott, who also somewhat surprisingly seemed to idolise gangsters, in particular the Krays and the American Mafia.

'They did so much for the East End community!' eulogised Randolph.

'Really, like what?' I replied, somewhat taken aback.

'Well, nobody would know any of them places if it weren't for the Twins.'

'Well, people who live there probably would,' I countered, but only half-heartedly, sensing resistance was rather pointless. This man had dedicated his life to gangster worship, so any form of rejection might render his religion and existence pointless. Whilst Syd did come out with the odd challenging insight, finding wisdom in Randolph's words was much harder.

'You certainly get them all in here,' said Nurse Soames, overhearing the conversation as she walked past.

I had an early stage of the abduction-sling on my left arm at that time, something the doctors had cobbled together post-operation. It had a Blue Peter/home-made feel about it, with the elbow of my newly reset arm resting upon a pillow. This was tied to my neck in a strange harness made of what looked like a tightly wrapped, orange-checked tablecloth. Given how complicated it all looked, Nurse Soames was amazed that I was somehow able to wear a T-shirt now.

'How did you get into that?' she asked, as if I had done something bad or performed a mystical deed.

'My wife designed it,' I said proudly. 'You see, she's cut the T-shirt up one side so that I can put it on like a poncho.' I demonstrated this and Nurse Soames, normally the most expressionless patient carer of all time, looked at the T-shirt and then smilingly declared, 'What a good idea.'

This was high praise indeed. 'I will pass on your compliments,' I said. Perhaps she thought I was being rude or sarcastic because her face scowled slightly at my words. I was not used to this environment, I felt scared and vulnerable. It wasn't the hospital part; I had done that before. It was the people; I didn't really know how to relate or talk to them. I was outside my comfort zone, and I thought it was starting to show. I felt that I could not really say anything to contradict their beliefs just in case I was accused of being a snob.

As I contemplated my dilemma, a nurse appeared at the end of my bed.

'Do you know where Syd is? I have a blood test for him,' asked the nurse.

I glimpsed the shadow of Syd hiding behind a screen, rapidly shaking his head. I said nothing, but as payback for his advice about Agnes I discreetly moved my eyes in Syd's direction. Taking the hint, the nurse crept behind the screen as well.

'Mr Belfield, I need to take some blood, and I know you don't like needles.'

'All right, nurse, it's a fair cop; at least Adam didn't grass me up.'

'Touché,' I mused, feeling smug at having reduced a big man to a quivering wreck.

When the conversations of Syd, Randolph or even Jed got too much, I exaggerated my pain so that Nurse Soames would increase my morphine dosage. So, the atmosphere went from being stupefying to a rather comfortable numbness which in its own way was quite heavenly. I thought they'd given me too much once, because I saw an angel walking around the hospital. It turned out to be a nurse who always came around at night, dressed in white, and was very beautiful.

'How is anybody supposed to sleep in hospital?' I asked Rachel during our next visit. 'If it's not a nurse taking your temperature, then it's an orderly offering you a cup of tea, or another patient snoring or setting their alarm off. The days drag quite a lot too. There's nothing to do.'

'What about the stuff I packed for you? Didn't it help?'

'Well, I'm so tired it's hard to concentrate, I keep getting disturbed. I'm still trying to work out how this is going to affect me in the long term. It's hard to get going.'

'Even harder if you don't try!' said Rachel firmly, sounding quite annoyed.

'OK, you're right, I'm sorry, I'll start tomorrow, I promise.'

'That's better. I'll check. You can do it. I know you can. You've just got to have faith.'

Chapter 12: Everybody Dance Now

The hospital had a secret weapon to deal with any apathy amongst middle-aged men: her name was Nurse Ruth, and she was the physiotherapist. I was sitting on my own when she arrived (the others having gone to a cardio-therapy talk). She breezed in, white uniform, lots of pens, big white-toothed smile, blonde hair in a bob.

'Hello, I'm Ruth, you must be Adam,' she smiled.

'Yes, I suppose I must be,' I replied, as if no one else wanted the job.

'I know it's only two days after your operation, but we need to think about movement and exercise.' With this she gently lifted my hand out of the sling and placed it on the bedside table. 'Now, keeping your elbow in the sling for support, I want you to turn over your left palm.'

I tried, but my hand felt lumpen and alien. 'It's hard.'

'Yes, it will be, you haven't used it for weeks.'

After a few judders, my hand eventually flopped over once; it got to the tipping point and gravity did the rest.

'Well done,' beamed Nurse Ruth. 'The first time is always the hardest. You need to keep trying. These early days will make all the difference to your range of movement later on. You need to have a goal you want to reach.'

'Thanks, I already have a goal, can I show you something?'

'OK. I like positive people.'

'Could you please pass me the guitar magazine from the cupboard?'

'This one?' asked Ruth.

'Could you turn to page 44 please?'

Ruth opened the magazine saying, 'Page 44? Ok, let me see what you have fixed on. There's a picture of a Fender Stratocaster guitar. It's beautiful.'

'It's sunburst like the one Buddy Holly used. My wife says I can buy it and play it when I get my arm back.'

'Good. That's a brilliant incentive.' She high-fived my working right arm, adding seriously, 'If you want to play that guitar, we'd better have ten hand turns each day.'

Nurse Ruth was one of those people whom God gives the right job every now and again. She was like a nurse in a World War Two movie who all the male soldier patients fall in love with. With a flutter of her doe eyelashes, she had me doing all sorts of little exercises in no time. These included opening and clenching my fist, putting my hand flat on the table, and bending my fingers back. After six long days, I was discharged and allowed home and yes, with yet another hundredweight of Ibuprofen. I also had Diclofenac, not a Welsh rugby Prop Forward, but a big-time opiate for severe pain. However, I was only given a short-term amount.

'I can't give you very much of that because it's very moreish,' smiled the pharmacist with a wink.

The Winking Pharmacist' would be a great name for a pub or a methadone clinic, wouldn't it? Maybe not.

Chapter 13: Home Again but No Jiggity Jig

Back at home, I was dutifully doing my exercises on the kitchen table three times a day. It all helped, or so I thought. I have never been a person who defines himself by his job, but I was determined to get better and back to work. I sent work an email, because speaking on the phone with my arm in a sling was complicated and difficult. I was also wary of why Jerome had taken such a big interest in me. My email to them was fairly innocuous and read something like:

'Hi everyone,

Hope all is well. I am doing OK. I've had an operation on my left arm. I have an entirely new shoulder joint. I'm fastened into a fancy thing called an abduction-sling which holds my arm still. I'm not allowed to move much now because of the stitches. I enclose a sickness certificate which signs me off work for the next two months.

I am now at home, which is a relief after being stuck in a room with Don Corleone's grandchildren! I'm still in a lot of pain, but in the next few weeks I will find out from the surgeon about how everything went. I will keep you posted on developments. Thank you all for the card and good wishes. It was very kind, and I really appreciated it.

Best wishes Adam.'

Being at home was certainly better than being in hospital, mainly because there were no would-be gangsters or bank robbers around. I also appreciated the not being watched, monitored, poked, prodded and evaluated every five minutes. Well, not by the nurses at least, though I still had my fair share of being watched by Rachel. However, this soon dissipated when she went back to work. Then I was left feeling lonely and empty as I sat alone in the house. During the worst times, I spent a lot of the day crying. I kept this undercover because I didn't want to be a burden or get in the way of Rachel and her job. I felt that I'd done too much of that already. So, when Rachel asked how I was, I always said, 'I'm fine.' It was the same subterfuge used by Errol Flynn, the 'very old' and 'very dead' film star. He died a broken-down alcoholic at 50. However, up to that point, whenever anybody asked how he was he always replied with 'Never better, old chap.' OK, not one of my better role models. By the way, Mr Flynn supposedly slept with over 12,000 women, so there was another similarity, not!

I wanted Rachel to be able to go out and do whatever she wanted or needed to. I was determined that she should not feel tied down, like she was my nurse or carer. It was at this point that the idea of having my sister Agnes come down to help struck me as a sensible move. However, after the very first thought of it, I slapped myself because it sounded too ridiculous. 'You bloody fool, she will drive you mad in half an hour!' But the thought kept coming back to me. It reached the tip of my tongue on several occasions, without quite formulating itself into words – hanging there like a circus acrobat trying to board a trapeze, then losing their nerve.

Before she went to work each day, Rachel would prepare and leave me sandwiches or food that could be easily warmed up, like soup. It was not exactly gourmet stuff, but I was glad of it. The food was left under a couple of plates or in the bread bin. There was a reason for this: my limited ability to get the lid off the Tupperware sandwich containers. My one futile attempt at this on the second day of being alone resulted in a disaster. I had to wedge the sandwich container between my knees to get the lid off. This was hard with only one working arm, and my zeal in pulling back the lid fired the contents all over the room. It took most of the afternoon to clean it up. I thought I did a good job until Rachel remarked in the middle of the News, 'Why is Sophie Raworth wearing a slice of tomato? Look, it's there on the TV screen.'

I tried to do my bit to help around the house but reaching and holding things was difficult. I also made a few attempts at washing up – leaning plates against the side of the sink to wash them. Progress was slow with my left arm still in a sling, except for the bouts of exercise.

I tried to gain some independence and start doing things for myself, like washing my face, shaving, and brushing my teeth. I desperately wanted my autonomy and dignity back. Rachel still had to wash me in the shower, as I still couldn't get around myself with a flannel or cloth. Going to the toilet presented its own problems, but thankfully I could deal with those solo. Things were worst of all at night. I was starting to become a man of a certain age who could not go for more than a couple of hours without needing to pee. The added burden of looking after me and doing her regular work had taken its toll on Rachel, and she was looking very tired. It was this more than anything which made me feel guilty and want to bring in Agnes. I would lie there in bed for hours desperately needing the toilet but unable to sit up or move without help from Rachel.

I waited whilst she slept until the pain of needing the loo or needing to be in another position became too much to bear. Still, the guilt of waking Rachel was more awful than the actual pain. Rachel and I are a partnership, which was how we describe ourselves to anyone who asked. However, after a heart attack and a broken shoulder, I was feeling less like a partner, and more like an albatross or an anvil that Rachel was stuck with. I felt things were very one-sided and I hated that my accident had happened, but I could do little to play what I felt was a full part in our marriage. My go-to place in this period, as always, was humour.

'Cut down in my prime,' I would say to Rachel's mother on the phone. 'I was always such an active child.'

'I think you're confusing yourself with someone else,' came the reply.

Rachel was OK about the uneven labour distribution. She was even sanguine about it. 'It was for better or for worse,' she said; 'those were the terms of the contract when I got you from the catalogue. Besides, you would do the same for me, wouldn't you?'

'Absolutely,' I replied, hoping to Christ that the theory was never tested. You only really find out the truth about somebody when you see them at their worst. I really tried hard to be on my best behaviour. If there was any consolation in the accident happening, it was probably the way round that it occurred. Rachel was a much better carer than a patient, and very bad at relinquishing control. When introducing her to people, I acknowledged my own lack of control and said, 'Hello, this is Rachel, my carer and parental guardian.' An arrangement which continues to this day.

Eventually, and after a bad night of little sleep (I woke Rachel three times and a fog of guilt hung in the air like Victorian London), I blurted out, 'I'm wondering if I should ask Agnes down for a few days to help care for me?'

'OK,' said Rachel a little surprised, 'are you sure? We're doing OK.'

'I think so, she wants to help, and it might be good to help you out whilst I can't do anything much around the house.'

'Let's give it a bit longer: we have our routine and we're coping.'

I nodded, but felt we were postponing the inevitable.

Chapter 14: The Agnes Early Christmas Special

'I'm afraid the guilt got to me,' I stammered to Rachel the next day as she brought in a morning cup of tea. 'I spoke with Agnes an hour ago, and she's coming down next week.'

Rachel didn't reply.

Thinking that silence was bad, I continued, 'I'm just trying to be practical: I thought it might kill two birds with one stone. It will stop her asking to come down, and more importantly it will take some of the pressure off you.'

Still no reply from Rachel.

'She's a great cook and she will help clean, honest.'

Rachel just smiled and said, 'OK, I'm not sure that this is for my benefit. You have guilt-tripped yourself into this.'

My parents had both died many years ago, and Rachel and I would visit my sister Agnes at Christmas. It was an annual event, like an unfunny version of *The Two Ronnies* or a weird *Morecambe and Wise* Christmas special. However, this time around she would come to us much earlier in the year.

Agnes was indeed a great cook, but she had nobody to fuss over now that her daughter Paula had left home. My 'oldest friend' Clive who lived a few doors down from Agnes in our hometown of Congleton often said, 'We should get her a starving person to feed up. One of them Ethiopians, he would know it's Christmas. Once he were "fattened up" they could send him back home and give her another one. It would give her some company and would help feed the world.' Leaving aside the casual racism – Clive was usually in his slippers when he made such remarks – it made sense for Agnes to come down. She was used to looking after infirm people, having worked in an old folks' home for thirty years before retiring.

London was a big trip for Agnes. Her daughter Paula put her in a forward-facing train seat as, according to Agnes, 'Going forward when you're sitting backwards is unnatural.' She also told everyone she met on the journey that she 'doesn't do escalators.'

Rachel met her at Euston station and brought her to our home. I was asleep, wrapped in a blanket in an armchair, when they arrived. It was the rattle of Rachel's key turning in the lock that woke me.

'I like your wallpaper,' said Agnes.

'Thank you,' replied Rachel.

'Did you hang it yourself?'

'No, we got somebody in.'

'Oh,' said Agnes, pausing then adding, 'Probably just as well: it's hard to get around them corners, and your walls kink at the top like a dog's hind leg.'

'Yes,' replied Rachel, wearily.

'Adam used to be a good at papering.'

From my armchair, I was staggered at Rachel's patience.

I braced myself for Agnes coming into the room. Musing under my breath, 'Dare I pretend to be asleep, or worse?' Then suddenly there she was - all five feet two of her - wearing a Parka coat and a big grin.

'Hello, Adam,' she chirped. 'No, don't get up, I'll come to you.'

Gingerly, I opened an eye and ventured the word, 'Hello.'

Agnes came over and kissed my forehead. I was sitting down - making us the same height.

'My little brother's in trouble, I don't need to be asked twice,' said Agnes. 'Now, what do you need doing?'

'Well, if you can help Adam when I'm out at work, that would be great,' said Rachel. 'You can make sure that he eats properly and does his exercises.'

'Consider it done,' smiled Agnes. 'Does he need a bath?'

'I'm right here. And no, he doesn't, thank you,' I answered very quickly.

'Only I'm still trained to lift people in and out of the bath. You only have to ask. I used to bath him when he was little. Does he still have a lovely little bum?'

'Yes, he still does,' laughed Rachel.

'I'm fine, thanks,' I said indignantly. 'You keep your hands off me.'

Agnes opened her carrier bag and produced a cardboard box. She pulled out a mug, then gave it to me declaring loudly, 'I BOUGHT YOU A COW CUP TO CHEER YOU UP. YOU LIKE THEM!' Clearly disability equalled deafness in Agnes's mind.

'Thank you,' I answered softly. 'I can hear quite well.'

'I just thought of you when I bought it. Look, it's got a little dog on it as well!'

I placed the mug on the coffee table in disguised disbelief that I could want anything like this. Rachel smiled, trying not to laugh.

Agnes would often buy cow cups to 'cheer me up'. No, I don't know why either. She had the idea that I needed to be reminded that I once worked on a farm. Rachel and I would look at each other, astounded at her taste. Agnes had singularly kept our local Oxfam shop stocked up for the past twenty years. Rachel never said anything, but I could tell from her expression that she was shell-shocked by Agnes's arrival, as if she had been deep-fried in a pan full of my sister's oddness. As we lay in bed later, she sighed heavily and said the immortal words 'Don't ask,' through gritted teeth and shaking head. 'That was even harder than taking you to hospital. You owe me big time!'

'She is not bathing me,' I muttered after Rachel turned off the light.

Chapter 15: Regression to Yesterday

The early days of Agnes's visit were great. On the first day, I staggered downstairs to the wonderful smell of frying bacon and eggs. She had laid a place at the table for me and had even been out to the shops to buy some crusty bread. Freshly cut flowers stood in a vase in the middle of the table, along with the *Daily Express* newspaper (well, you can't have everything).

'Good morning,' I said, kissing Agnes's forehead.

'It's like going back in time,' Agnes replied, bringing over a very full breakfast plate. 'When you've ate that, we'll do your exercises and get you moving about.'

'Wow, I can get used to this. I normally just have cereal to line my stomach for my morning medications, but this is fabulous.'

Throughout the day, I would hear Agnes hoovering or singing to herself as she washed up or did other things. Her work rate was phenomenal. The only problem was that she would stop every now and again and insist on talking to me for what seemed like hours. One example that comes to mind happened on the third day of her visit, when we were deciding what to have for lunch.

'Does your arm hurt?' asked Agnes after we had done my morning exercises.

'Yes, it's very painful. It's throbbing!'

'They say nothing works faster than Ibrupofen in the adverts. So, I do that.'

'What?'

'I take nothing. It's not very good, though I still get headaches.'

'OK,' I replied, a little bemused. 'I'll order something for lunch today to give you a break. My treat. What do you fancy? I handed her some of the flyers that came through our front door. 'How about fish and chips?'

'I won't eat fish!' said Agnes indignantly.

'Well, we could have a pizza then.'

'OK, but I do eat tuna.'

'Or a kebab?'

'And salmon, I do eat salmon.'

'How about steak pie and chips?'

'And cod, I do eat cod.'

'There's a new veggie place we could try.'

'Hake, I do eat hake. Haddock's not bad. And rock, rock's all right.'

'So, you do eat it then?' I said, getting frustrated and interrupting.

'Eat what?'

'Fish.'

'Well, yes, I suppose I do, yes.'

Our conversations often went on like that – a ceaseless chain of nonsense.

Agnes was lovely and so kind, she cooked and cleaned, but she was also incredibly wearing and, like a child, needed to be entertained. Paula, her daughter, had given her puzzle books for her journey, and Rachel and I followed this up with a free run of our television. As we got into our time together and got used to each other's daily patterns, I noticed that something bizarre was happening. Agnes started off her visit as a 63-year-old woman with a dodgy hip. As the days wore on, she started to move much more quickly and gracefully.

There were a couple of times when she opened the curtains in my bedroom and stood in the sunlight, and I saw a teenage Agnes standing in front of me; I had to rub my eyes. I think that from Agnes's perspective, too, our relationship had changed: I was no longer her younger and smarter brother in some super-charged London office. I seemed to have reverted to childhood and become helpless and vulnerable again. One day when I was asleep, I felt something soft touch the side of my head. I smiled and nuzzled up to it thinking it was Rachel. Then I woke up and realised it was Agnes's hand. I shooed it away and retreated under the duvet.

'It's all right, it's just me. I used to stroke your head when you were a baby.'

'Well, I'm a bit old for that now,' I replied defensively.

'You don't want a story then? I could fluff your pillows.'

I just scowled. 'No thanks, I'll just get a bit more sleep. But no more stroking!'

'OK,' said Agnes, sensing she had struck a nerve.

Agnes would just come out with things, out of the blue. Over breakfast she suddenly declared, 'Your brother Bryan's gone to see a psychopath!'

Rachel and I looked at her with raised eyebrows.

'He has a bad back,' continued Agnes.

'Oh, you mean an osteopath,' corrected Rachel.

Other times she would ask, 'Where is Walford?' She never seemed to understand that *EastEnders* was fictional.

'All the same, I wouldn't want to live in *EastEnders*,' said Agnes. 'Everybody seems so miserable. *Coronation Street* seems a lot cheerier.'

Conversation with Agnes was hard for Rachel and me. We didn't watch soap operas and had very little in common. I am ashamed to say that I spent quite a few days trying to be in other rooms away from my sister. My shaving and showers took twice as long. One day, Rachel was at home and carrying the washing basket up to the loft to peg it out. Opening the airing cupboard door, she found me hiding there.

'What are you doing up here?' I whispered tersely.

'I'm pegging out the washing,' she nodded towards the basket.

'Yes, well I hide in here sometimes when you're at work. She doesn't know this place exists. Go away, or she'll find us both.'

'Hello, hello, shall I make tea?' Agnes called from downstairs.

'This is stupid,' said Rachel. 'We're hiding in our own house!'

'I know,' I said, 'but she drives me mad. She only needs five hours' sleep, then she's up and running again like a giant Duracell bunny. You can't turn her off.'

We developed distraction activities for Agnes, such as looking through family photo albums; these were usually accompanied by Agnes's comical commentary as she looked at the old photographs: 'He's dead now. So is she.'

Sometimes I played the guitar. On one occasion, I managed a fumbled version of 'House of The Rising Sun'. It was a way of feeling human again, and I was glad when people recognised what I was playing. But as I got to the bridge, Agnes sang very loudly, 'MY FATHER WAS AN INDIAN...'

'Your father wasn't an Indian,' laughed Rachel.

'Wasn't he, what was he then?' asked Agnes, rather confused.

'A tailor,' I replied.

'No, it's your mother who was a tailor,' said Rachel.

'I don't suppose he was an Indian, he was born in Cheshire,' said Agnes.

'No, not your actual dad. The song says your father was a gambling man way down in New Orleans,' laughed Rachel.

'Oh, I thought he was an Indian,' said Agnes. 'Perhaps they didn't do ethnic minorities in them days.'

I had looked forward to Agnes's arrival, but now I looked forward much more to the time when she would leave.

Chapter 16: Bad News Bear

My next appointment at the Fracture Clinic came around very quickly, and once again Rachel and I were sitting in the cupboard room with Dr Skate and Mr Columba. Columba smiled and made small talk about the weather. Skate stared at the new X-ray of my replacement shoulder for a long time, and then at the real thing on my body and said the immortal words, 'This does not look right. It's too low.'

'The surgery went well, but your shoulder will sink over time, so I'm afraid we need to do it again,' agreed Mr Columba.

At first, I didn't realise what they meant. I thought things were going well, and I was recovering, albeit slowly. Besides which they had looked so positive when Rachel and I entered the room. Then I realized that their positivity was simply for effect and the conversation was rapidly deteriorating and I started to cry. Columba just stared at me. He was not very good at dealing with upset people, or people in general really.

'Think of the positive side of things,' said Skate.

'Yes, it will be so much better in the longer term,' added Columba, as if prompted. 'It will be so much better to do this now.'

All I could think of was more pain, more hospital beds, more gangsters to share a room with and more days of no sleep. I tried to focus on the positive aspect by asking Skate, 'Will I be able to play the guitar again?'

He looked at me smiled and said, 'Maybe you should think about the piano.'

This was his attempt at humour, but he might as well have shot me. My confidence flopped like a piece of card which had been dipped in water. I sat staring into space. It wasn't only facing up to no more guitar playing. It was everything: the operations, the accident, my life being on hold, the pain, and the indignity of not being able to do anything for myself. Everything seemed to be blocking the way ahead.

Of course, Rachel upped her positivity and tried talking me round, but I was elsewhere. I don't remember a single thing that was said during the meeting with Skate. When we got home, Rachel seemed worried. She hugged me a lot and said, 'When this is over, we're going to have such a great holiday.'

This was met with a rather stony silence from me, so Rachel tried a different tack. 'If you think about it, it's better that they redo the operation now. When it's over, you will have a much better range of movement.'

I still couldn't bring myself to join in. Our marriage was like a balance or set of scales: the more depressed I became, the more Rachel sought to lift me out of it. And she continued to try, whether I wanted to hear it or not.

'I don't know why he dismissed your idea about playing the guitar. People overcome all sorts of setbacks to do something that they love.' Then from somewhere she then showed me a picture on her phone of a soldier who now played the guitar with a false metal hand, after his real one was blown off in Afghanistan.

Still no reaction from me.

'Then there was Django Reinhardt and Tony Iommi from Black Sabbath. They both got over serious problems by thinking about things in a different way.'

'You can't be turned off, can you? You are the most maddening bloody woman I have ever met,' I laughed hysterically. I kissed and hugged her and cried, adding, 'You are amazing! How on earth do you know about that? I love you.'

'I'm your wife, and I'll always believe in you.'

'No, it's not so much that. I always know you will never stop caring and loving me. It's that you remember all the bollocks I tell you about musicians.'

'Well, I tried not to, but some of it sneaked in.'

Later, Agnes joined us for dinner and proclaimed, 'Rachel is right.'

'Well, that's always good to hear, but why this particular instance?' laughed Rachel.

'You said earlier that he shouldn't give up playing the guitar, and you named musicians who'd carried on even though they were injured or hurt. Well, Freddie Mercury, he carried on and he had Aids. That Dead Tiger drummer lost an arm.'

'Yes, that's perfectly true, Agnes,' agreed Rachel.

'I think you mean Rick Allen from Def Leppard. But you're right, some folks are amazing,' I agreed.

'Then there's that Eggy Pup.'

'Who on earth is Eggy Pup?' laughed Rachel.

'He were always breaking bones and things. He were one of them punk rockets Adam used to like. I thought he were horrible.'

'I think she means Iggy Pop,' I said.

'Thank you, Agnes,' said Rachel. 'You see, Adam, out of the mouths of babes and angels, others don't give up on dreams and neither should you.'

'Well, that's told me then,' I said. 'I just need a lust for life. What?' I ventured at their blank looks. 'It's the name of an Iggy Pop album and song. Oh well please yourselves.'

Chapter 17: The Update

This train tea is hot and the shortbread – well, once on the lips, forever on the hips. I got my gut instincts from my mother (she was rather portly).

By the way, my suspicions were right: Jerome was promoted to fill the vacancy created by our mutual boss Jim moving on. Jerome was now my line manager, effective immediately. I learned of this change in an email from Peter Moores, our Head of Unit. There was something cold about not telling me in person, but I could understand why he couldn't do that. And if they wanted someone who was able to take control right now, that certainly was not me, so the accident may have helped to decide things. Peter Moores addressed his email to me, as all bringers of bad news do, in the uniform of comforting reassurance: *'I don't want you to be concerned with or worried about anything except getting better. We all miss you here.'*

I tried to take some solace from the part about wanting me back. After a day's acceptance, accompanied by intermittent swearing about being overlooked for promotion yet again, I rang Jerome. As I later said to Rachel, 'It was better than waiting in apprehension and other places near Croydon for him to call.'

'It will show you are the bigger man,' agreed Rachel.

'I would always rather something bad happened on my terms.'

My conversation with Jerome was cordial and went as follows.

'Hi Jerome, congratulations on your promotion,' I began.

'Thank you, how are you doing?' replied Jerome.

'Not so good. I've got to have another shoulder operation.'

'Oh, you poor thing, that's awful. Just when we thought you were starting to mend. You poor thing, it's really bad luck.'

'I think I'm covered by my medical certificate until the end of next month,' I added, trying to be practical.

'Oh, don't worry about that. You can send me an updated certificate whenever you get it from your GP. Did I mention that my friend Morag's husband is a doctor?'

I nodded, thinking about how much Jerome seemed to enjoy being the benevolent boss, but I had promised to Rachel that I would not create a stir.

'I asked him,' continued Jerome, 'through Morag of course, how long shoulders take to fix. All he would say was he didn't know; complicated things are shoulders.'

'Well, that makes us kindred spirits: your friend's husband being a doctor and me having no idea how long it will take to get better.' Of course, I just thought the last part instead of saying it aloud.

'Keep your chin up. You'll be back at work before you know it.'

I smiled down the phone at Jerome's attempted humour. God, the things we do for a quiet life. We must be mad. 'Keep your chin up.'

'That's always seemed an odd expression to me. It makes me walk into things,' I said to Rachel and Agnes later on.

'At least they're keeping your job open for you,' said Agnes, adding a dose of realism which Rachel was thankful for. 'It doesn't happen that way for everybody.'

'That's true,' I replied. 'I don't know why I don't feel that way. I mustn't wallow in self-pity, but it's quite hard.'

'I think I might go home on Saturday,' said Agnes.

Rachel and I looked at each other.

'Well, you're doing OK, and you'll have your house back,' added Agnes.

'Well, you're welcome to stay longer,' said Rachel, noticing my smirk and suddenly bowed head and she gently kicked my shins under the dinner table.

'Oh yes, we love having you here,' I added.

'No, I need to see my grandchildren. And the church will want help with their meals on wheels and home visits. I've done well at keeping people from being lonely. The vicar told me that several people have said that after a visit from me, how much they perked up and how they wouldn't want another one.'

'Well, if you're sure,' said Rachel, looking sternly at my almost smile.

As Agnes left the table to do the washing up, Rachel turned to me, noticing that I was about to shriek silently with joy, she whispered softly but firmly, 'Stop it!'

Chapter 18: Operation Two

Yes, the English countryside is majestic. Even from a train window. Look at those beautiful animals in the field over there. Those are Holstein cows. They look so brilliant, like black and white chess pieces against a green board. I used to work on a farm – some of my best friends were cows - and now that I work in an office, arguably some of my best friends still are. It's quite peaceful, looking outwards at the world, isn't it? It was like this when I was at home recovering. I got used to watching the world from my bedroom window.

After Agnes had gone home, there was little for me to do but wait for my next operation. Although the extent of my last conversation with Skate and Columba had not really registered, I still knew that further surgery was required. We dutifully turned up for operation number two, when it was scheduled for a week's time, making it more or less two months to the day after the first operation. I felt it should have some sort of grand title, as it was the sequel to the first operation; I considered referring to it as 'Setting My Arm 2: The Revenge', or 'I left my arm in Avercombe Train Station', but thankfully I kept this to myself.

In Rachel's mind, things would be much improved by my having the second operation; she said, 'It will be the prequel to the rest of your life.'

I wasn't so sure. To me it sounded like yet another convenient platitude to justify further surgery. Besides which, as Jerome often said, 'The prequel is so last year.'

I had to go along with it all of course. What other choice did I have? We got there early, as before, and assembled in the same waiting room. I had the same anaesthetist as last time, Arthur. He remembered me and came in to say hello, so at least I felt I was amongst friends. There was a new surgeon in town too, named Professor Jada. He was a very precise, 'two flicks of the comb, shirts ironed by a steamroller' sort of bloke. Jada came to meet us both before the operation, along with the genuinely nice, but much put upon Nurse Fishwick. Jada seemed a lot more professional than either Skate or Columba. 'This patient has not been prepared properly for his operation! See to it immediately,' said Jada curtly, to Nurse Fishwick who looked about to cry. We both felt sorry for her as she ran to reception to get more forms.

'I thought the forms you signed last time covered us this time as well, and legally they do, but Professor Jada wants you to sign new ones because he's performing the operation,' explained Nurse Fishwick on her return.

'He seems very exacting,' I said.

'That's a euphemism for rude,' Rachel added.

Nurse Fishwick, professional to the last, just smiled, no doubt crying inside.

Jada seemed made of thorns unless you were a patient; then he was lovely. Rachel found out later that Jada was on loan from another Primary Care Trust, and it was quite a coup for Avercombe Hospital to have him. Ultra-dependable Rachel had undertaken some online research into his background; I was prepared to put up with anyone, but she was far fussier than me, and on my side, so I didn't mind.

Jada performed the second operation himself and visited me on every one of the six days I spent in hospital. I therefore assumed he called the shots on my aftercare. It was Jada who insisted I wear the dreaded abduction-sling after the operation. So, I dutifully carried my left arm in one position, lashed to a pillow in front of me, for twelve weeks. Nothing was allowed to move. It was horrible.

'I feel like a giant teapot,' I said to Rachel after a few days. 'Everything is held so tightly in position that it feels unnatural. It's in front of you all the time. Sticking out and banging into things! Everywhere you go! You can't sleep in it because it aches from being held upright in bed. It makes washing, shaving, and going to the loo virtually impossible. It's a hateful thing! It's well named too because it steals your dignity.'

But the worst thing was that for some reason everybody else found me wearing the abduction sling funny and I began to hate them for it. When I was alone at home in the afternoon, the doorbell went. I raised myself out of my chair after two attempts and shuffled down the hall. When I turned the handle, I had to take about three steps back to enable the door to open.

It was our neighbour Carol, who looked at my abduction-sling and said, 'That should not be funny, but it is.'

I wanted to shout at her, 'Yes, it's absolutely hysterical! How would you like to be in my shoes?'

Of course, I didn't, Instead I tried to make light of it. 'I feel as big as a boat in full sail. Try that in your own hallway after meeting some Jehovah's Witnesses! You need to do a three-point turn just to get to the kitchen.'

'I'm sorry, I don't mean to laugh. A parcel came for you.'

'Oh, thank you,' I said as Carol put the parcel on the kitchen table. 'I thought the doorbell rang earlier when I was upstairs, but it takes me a while to get down here.'

The abduction-sling meant that I suddenly found it impossible to do anything because I felt enormous and unbalanced! I became instantly depressed from the moment I got up and saw myself in the mirror. I felt constrained, cornered and other words beginning with the letter 'C'. Crappy? Yes, that was probably it, Myrtle, thank you. The check and balance of my sister Agnes was no longer there. I had kept a lot of emotions suppressed whilst other people were around, but now my depression/anger valve was ready to blow, and I couldn't find a way to stop it.

By the end of the first month, I was exhausted and incredibly angry. Once I got up in the middle of the night and sat on the sofa crying. Of course, Rachel followed me downstairs. She opened the door; it was 3.30 in the morning.

'Please leave me alone,' I said softly.

Naturally she ignored me and sat down next to me, so I banged my abduction-slinged arm down on the sofa in a vague attempt at self-harm.

'NO, GO AWAY!' I shouted. 'I want to be miserable. I don't need a pep talk. I don't need an action plan. I don't want to count blessings or think about how lucky we are. I just want to be alone and feel sorry for myself. I don't want to wallow in self-pity I want to drown in it. Can you let me do that? PLEASE!'

Rachel looked shocked, but she left me to it. By now I was a month into this stupid abduction-sling thing, with two more still to do and I hated it. I needed sleep. I needed space. I also needed a shave. I caught sight of this bearded, tired stranger in the bathroom mirror and didn't even realise it was me at first. I thought we were being burgled.

Every week we went to the Fracture Clinic at the hospital and dutifully saw Professor Jada and smiled at his notes on progress. By the end of the fifth week, we were back with Skate and Columba.

'Professor Jada has returned to his own hospital,' smirked Skate.

'Yes, all good things come to an end,' chuckled Columba.

Rachel later discovered that Jada didn't get on with the others in the Fracture Clinic. Each of the surgeons had their own opinions on how to do things, and they seldom agreed. Jada was prepared to share ***his*** opinions and be quite vociferous. I took this to mean he was critical of Skate and Columba, but I have absolutely no proof of this.

'We will replace your sling with a simpler version,' announced Columba.

'The arm will respond much better to exercise and treatment if it's not being penned in by a restriction or being held in one position all the time,' agreed Skate.

'Professor Jada said he should wear it for twelve weeks,' countered Rachel.

'He's no longer here; we're responsible for your care now,' said Columba.

'I never knew that the aftermath of surgery was so competitive and contradictory,' said Rachel later to me, adding, 'I did a double check online and found that most medical opinions are agreed that to have the arm roaming free and in a simple sling is the best treatment. So, we'll go along with this for now.'

'Well, I'm quite pleased to be rid of the abduction-sling, so there will be no tearful goodbyes or protests from me,' I replied.

In the simpler sling, I felt a lot more normal and was able to sleep easier. I even tried playing a bit of guitar again and found this was still possible, but painful. I could still make chords and finger pick, which is quite a big thing if you're me. The words of the person who told me to think about "taking up the piano" instead of the guitar came into my head. I wanted to show him what I had done. However, life rarely affords you the opportunity to go back and confront the doubters. Anyway, his glib pronouncement had only made me more determined to succeed, so it had helped. I thought maybe I could learn some tunes or think about a secondary career in the music industry, but sadly, as my recovery moved on, I now had to start thinking about going back to work.

Chapter 19: Physiotherapy Anyone?

As before, exercises after the second operation simply involved me turning over my left hand whilst sitting at a table. Five weeks later I attended my first proper physiotherapy session with Nurse Ruth. It was held in a kind of gymnasium for elderly folk – lots of trolleys, walking frames, old school benches and lines on a wooden floor. To fit into the surroundings, Ruth wore a tracksuit and beamed her white-toothed smile as I came into the room. I quickly learned to equate her niceness with how strenuous and difficult my daily exercise was likely to be.

'How are you?' she said smiling, as if the place was all ours.

'I'm not great,' I replied. 'With two operations on my shoulder and my world being turned upside down, I'm still getting used to things.'

'Well today, Adam, we begin the fight back. We're going to try and bring your whole left arm back to life. In no time we will get you playing the guitar again. What was it you were going to buy, a Startocaster?'

'A Stratocaster – you remembered.'

'I actually remembered because Buddy Holly was on the radio this morning and you said he played one.'

'Well, I take good news wherever I find it. I need some form of positive affirmation. If you think I can play the guitar again, that's good enough for me.'

'Good, I'm giving you a folder of where we are going, exercise wise.'

I looked at the pictures: a series of diagrams of a person doing arm exercises along with an explanation of each one. I winced at the reality of what this might mean in terms of arm pain.

'Don't look so worried. Stretch your left arm straight out in front you and try to raise it so that it's parallel with your shoulder,' said Ruth. 'Like this.'

'Oh my God, I don't think I would make a very good traffic policeman,' I said after my arm shook like a dead tree branch in a high wind and stopped not even parallel with my belly button. It was a shock at first to start to include my left arm in everyday movements again, and hard to get used to. 'It isn't every day you get to feel jealous of a drawing,' I sighed. 'This is really hard.'

'Don't be so hard on yourself. You haven't used your arm like that for ages. I want you to try five lifts each day, building up to ten, between now and when I see you next week.'

After the workout, my arm throbbed out a dull ache like an overacting ham miming to an opera singer. It was pretty moving though. I was left in tears by my own arm's performance.

'I agree with Ruth,' said Rachel when I returned home. 'You're stretching out an arm which has lain dormant for nearly four months. Stop trying to run before you can walk.'

A week later, as I entered the room for the second session, Ruth stared at me disapprovingly.

'What?' I asked, sensing something was wrong.

'I don't like your sling.'

'Well, it's what they gave me on my release from the hospital and it helps me get a seat on trains and keeps people from walking into me. So, I quite like it.'

'No, I don't mean it like that. It's the fact that the sling fastens your arm to your body at that angle. It's too restrictive. Everything is too rigid, and it will pull down our good work.' And with that she picked up some scissors and snipped away the join of sling between my body and my arm.

'From now on, just use the sling for travelling.'

The physiotherapy started off simply and ended up more complicated. From straight arm raises, I would try to extend my arm by my side – something I still cannot do properly to this day. Progress was painfully slow, pun intended.

It was at this point that my love affair with Co-codamol began. I would take tablets before the physiotherapy because it increased my pain tolerance and meant I could do more exercise. I would deliberately try to surpass whatever homework was set out for me to do. If Ruth had said "Do ten stretches," I would try for fifteen, and so on.

I wanted Ruth to notice improvement. I knew she would measure my range of movement in centimetres. I wanted her to be pleased with my progress. Yes, I wanted to impress a beautiful lady. Whatever the reasoning, at least it was motivating me to get better.

Chapter 20: On Me Head, Son

The printed diagrams of the exercises from Nurse Ruth looked like pages from an old military fitness book. I followed the new exercise instructional diagrams very carefully. Some of them were hard. They were printed line drawings of the same bloke, an army officer with a quiff hairdo and a flat stomach. I looked at my own body, musing, 'It has been a while since I looked like that.'

Each picture had arrows showing the man's arm movement direction – either that or some other fat person on the next page was throwing spears at him because they were also jealous of his physique.

Every day I had a goal to expand my arm reach. I treated my left arm like a growing child and had a symbolic mark of achievement in mind. To begin with this was another part of my body. In the first month my aim was to raise my left arm enough to touch my left nipple. Once I had achieved that, the target progressed to touching my shoulder, then neck, and then my nose. For a long time, I was obsessed with being able to wash my own hair with my left hand. I tried cheating by bowing my head and sticking it under my left arm, but all that did was give me terrible neck ache.

Then I discovered another exercise which really improved my reach. I stood in the shower and held onto the rail with my left hand and then bent my knees into a squat so that my shoulder was perpendicular to the rest of my body. I looked like a ballerina with a beer gut, but suddenly my reach was better. In a week's time I could touch my forehead and then the top of my head. After the first time I achieved the fabled left-handed hair wash of my dreams I sat in the shower and cried. It was momentous, and I gave the little soldier in the exercise drawings a 'thumbs up' the next time I saw him. I didn't tell Rachel of my new-found prowess straight away. Instead, I put some cups away in the cupboard with the high shelf with my left arm.

When she saw me, Rachel did a double-take. 'Get you, Mr Two Arms!'

'Yes, I have been practicing,' I replied blushing. That little soldier in the drawings doesn't say much but he has a great effect on me. To paraphrase Rambo, "To win at exercise you must become exercise". No, I don't know what that means either.'

Rachel and I hugged each other afterwards because it felt like a big moment.

To increase my movement and give me an added push, Nurse Ruth introduced me to the hydrotherapy team, and I started to do one session a week. Hydrotherapy is basically doing your exercises in a mid-size swimming pool of hot water at the hospital. I said later to Rachel, 'It was possibly one of the most wonderful things I have ever done. With all that warm water around me, my arm felt comfortable and supported.'

Most of all, it made me feel normal, as if movement was natural again. Strangely, the only thing I could compare it with was my sister Agnes and her inability to walk quickly on concrete or tarmac; but if you put her on grass in the park, she suddenly develops some sort of strange four-wheel drive, turbo charge. That's how

I was in water, suddenly alive again! I felt my arm was back from the dead!

There were a team of nurses who oversaw me in hydrotherapy, which helped a lot. They were all good. There were Ruth, Christine, Glenda, and Martha. Martha was rather demanding, but thankfully I didn't get her very often. After a few weeks of hydrotherapy, I became adept at doing my exercises solo and was allowed in the pool on my own. I soon found out that when you were in the pool you were kind of honour-bound to become friends with whoever was in there with you, and you ended up encouraging each other to exercise. This could be anyone from an old age pensioner with a new hip, to a person who had been in wheelchair all their life. One week I was in the pool with a 6ft 5 black guy who had been in a motorbike accident. He had a pin in his leg and was learning how to walk again. We stood in the pool warily surveying each other's injuries, so I decided to break the ice.

'New hip?' I asked, looking him up and down.

He seemed a little taken aback, but he spoke all the same. 'Well, sort of, it's been pinned. I came off my motorbike. Now I have to march on the spot, doing sixty knee lifts three times a day to help it bed in. You?'

'I fell over last year on ice outside a train station and broke my shoulder. Three police officers decided to come over and help, and they fell on top of me.'

'Sounds like a silent comedy movie, *Keystone Cops* or whatever they're called.'

'I've a new plastic shoulder now. I'm doing physiotherapy to help it bed in. They've got me here doing underwater punches to try to stretch out the muscle.'

'My name is Leroy,' he smiled, stretching out a huge hand.

'My name is Adam,' I replied, smiling back and offering my own.

After our 'hands across the water' moment, we took hold of the British bulldog spirit and very nearly drowned it as we were soon egging each other on to try to exercise harder. It's amazing what common ground can do.

'You can do another five,' said Leroy, watching my pathetic punches.

I found myself encouraging him too. 'You can do another few marches too. Go on, push, Leroy. Push. PUSH!'

'Hang on, mate, I'm not having a baby.'

'Sorry, I don't really do sports talk.'

Leroy had a back like an ocean liner, and I caught sight of a huge tattoo emblazoned across it. The tattoo said, 'BROMLEY BOUNDERS' in 6-inch letters, except they'd missed out the letter 'D' so that it said 'BROMLEY BOUNERS', which automatically registered in my mind as BROMLEY BONERS. It then struck me that Leroy was effectively a walking spelling mistake, and probably didn't know it. Suddenly I found all this highly amusing – but tried desperately to suppress it.

'Something funny?' said Leroy, frowning at me.

I gulped, thinking this guy could squash me with his thumb.

'Not really,' I said, wracking my brain for a suitable lie. 'I'm just thinking about the two us and the ridiculous predicament of our injuries.' Yes, it didn't really sound convincing, but it was the only thing I could think of in the time available.

'Yes,' said Leroy, 'it is quite surreal.'

Then, as Leroy turned around, I once more caught sight of his massive frame and the ridiculous words written on it and promptly laughed out loud and tried to camouflage it with a splash punch or two.

Leroy had heard me, but thankfully all he said was, 'You are a happy little fella, aren't you?' as he carried on marching. 'I am glad I met you today.'

'Me too,' I smiled.

After that we always tried to support each other whenever we were together in the pool. It was one of those nice happenstances where two lives heading in entirely different paths converged because of an accident.

However, it was not all good news. At the end of one of the hydrotherapy sessions my head began to sway from side to side like I was a punch-drunk boxer gracelessly avoiding imaginary blows.

Noticing this, Nurse Martha came over to me and said, 'Adam, that funny swaying movement that your head does, how long has that been happening?'

'I don't know,' I stammered, feeling like a child caught doing something he shouldn't. 'It's quite recent.'

'If it keeps on happening, do mention it to your GP at your next appointment.'

'Yes, I will,' I replied, not realising the significance of her words at the time.

When Rachel came home from work, she saw me sat at the kitchen table staring at the garden.

'Are you OK?'

'Yes, I think so.'

'The television isn't on.'

'No, I was just enjoying the garden.'

'You're not OK. You've never enjoyed the garden in your life. Last time we talked about it, you wanted to concrete over it and paint the windows black so you couldn't see it! What's up?'

'Have you noticed my head swaying sometimes?'

'Yes, I have, but I didn't want to mention it in case it upset you.'

'Nurse Martha said I should tell Dr Sharma about it. I asked her what it was. She said she didn't know, but we should get it checked out because it could be neurological.'

'OK, we can do that. What do you think it is?'

'It feels like my head is trying to burrow its way back into my neck because it's ashamed of me.'

My words must have scared Rachel a little because both of us attended my next appointment with Dr Sharma. We had no need to worry about having to describe the movement to him: I was so nervous that my head duly obliged by moving about while we were in Sharma's office.

'What do you think it is?' asked Rachel.

'I don't know,' said Dr Sharma. 'It could be stress-related after all the shock that Adam's body has been through. We should keep an eye on it for now.'

Chapter 21: Is It Good To Talk?

I found having Jerome as my boss a little weird. I confided to Rachel. 'He's quite jobsworthy, very keen on procedures which he frequently says, "are there to protect him, the organisation and most importantly me".'

'Are you are still upset at him being promoted instead of you?' she asked.

'Yes, it does grate,' I replied. 'We used to be the same rank and pay grade and together in the same team, then he was promoted over me whilst I was off sick.'

'It's not the best basis for a working relationship, but you'll have to try.'

As my health improved, I started to speak with Jerome at least twice a week at his insistence, and that's a lot of Jerome to deal with. With Rachel's words echoing in my mind, conversations with Jerome were stilted but well-meaning.

'Hi Adam, it's Jerome. How are you?'

'I'm doing OK, thank you. I'm just going to put you on speaker phone so I can write and talk if need be.'

'That's fine, whatever makes you comfortable. It's just our usual check-in so you're not left feeling out of the loop; and to avoid dislocation. How are things?'

I momentarily pondered the question before answering, what did he mean by avoiding dislocation? I wanted to say, why, are you thinking of pulling my arm from its socket or something? But no, it was the current Human Resources (HR) mantra. I could hear the rustling of papers, and Jerome almost sounded like he was speaking from a script, but then he could have just been making notes (yes Rachel, thank you, we must be fair). Jerome was keen on 'work speak'. A lot of people like it, because it's easier than being human and having to think for themselves. My reply was conciliatory, avoiding any hint of disagreement.

'I'm OK. More physiotherapy, more exercise, more pain, more painkillers. More of the same thing really.' I didn't mention the 'my head swaying', as we'd been told it was only *'something to keep your eye on'* by Dr Sharma, and I thought that was too much information.

'That's good. Oh dear, I don't mean good. I mean good that you're exercising. Everybody sends best wishes. You were mentioned in the team meeting yesterday. They were talking about making space for you in the new seating plan.'

'I should set a date for my comeback,' I interjected, feigning eagerness.

'Yes, absolutely, if you feel up to it. What about doing a few days next week?' Jerome sounded relieved that I had given him an easy in-road to bring up my return.

'OK,' I replied, and with that simple one-word response I agreed to re-join the outside world once again. Once I put the phone down and sat in a chair, I suddenly became oddly nervous and started to cry. Hearing Rachel coming down the stairs, I dried my eyes and made out I was reading a magazine.

'How was Jerome?' Rachel asked softly.

'Oh, fine,' I said not looking up.

'Really?'

'Yes. No! It was awful. How do you know these things? Are you a witch?'

'No, I just know you.' Then she hugged me amidst her laughter and my tears.

'I've agreed to go back to work.'

'Well done. I know you're scared, but it will be fine. We can prepare for it together, so don't worry.'

Chapter 22: My Beautiful Neighbourhood

I had been at home or in hospital for nearly six months, and so before I went back to work, I tried to get back into the routine of daily things by doing some of the Saturday shopping and picking up the papers. This was another one of Rachel's ideas as by then I had not really seen or spoken to "everyday people" for several months. In Rachel's eyes it was 'good people practice'. Of course, she deliberately didn't remind me how many people would be interested to see me, or worse still, would try to engage me in conversation.

As I stepped out the front door alone, I was immediately taken back to that snowy day in January when I had set out for my training course. My legs suddenly became like jelly, as if they didn't belong to me, and I felt clumsy and awkward. As I got to the edge of the footpath, a man in black suddenly appeared and greeted me with a cheery, 'Hello Adam, good to see you up and about.'

'Hello,' I ventured. Then I pondered to myself, who was that?

On the way to the shops – about one hundred metres – I encountered three more people who seemed to know me. They all repeated, 'How are you?' and 'You look so much better.' I was confused as to how they knew me, and more to the point, who most of them were. Some of them sensed this and so they introduced themselves.

Perhaps they were all related, because they had similar sounding surnames: Maureen from number 27, Arthur from number 19, and so on.

'You live in Frank and Doris's old place,' said Sadie from number 91.

'Oh really?' I replied, not really knowing whether I was meant to apologise.

'That's OK though, they're both dead now, so they don't need it,' she said, turning and walking away. I made a mental note to check under the beds and in the wardrobes when I got home to make sure Frank and Doris weren't still there.

Considering this was London, the place of anonymity, I felt like a local celebrity. However, too much of a good thing can wear off very quickly, in my case after about fifteen seconds. Nevertheless, I ploughed on with gritted teeth and a carrier bag, continuing my quest to get a newspaper and some bacon and eggs. As I came around the corner, I saw a man tying his pit-bull terrier to the step of the grocery shop. I walked on a bit further and was nearly run over by a kid in a hoodie on a bike. Why had the world become so busy suddenly? Then another couple of people nearly walked into me.

There seemed to be a lot of people about. They were everywhere! I was now raising my right hand to protect my face, and my left arm was shaking like a windsock in a Force Ten gale, sling or not. I was becoming so agitated by everything around me. *I've got to get away*, I thought. I was now sweating and scared. I quickly ducked into the newsagents. As I looked up, I was confronted by two more people.

'Adam, it's so lovely to see you. How are you? It's been such a long time,' said the owner, Kavitha, from behind her counter, beaming her welcoming smile at me.

'Thank you, nice to see you too. I'm OK. Yes, it's been a while,' I stammered.

'We've been seeing Rachel every week, coming in for things, and we've been asking about you, but it's so nice to see you in person.'

Kavitha and her husband Raj were always kind and worked so hard. Noticing my sling, Kavitha stepped out from the counter and picked up a *Guardian* newspaper from the bottom shelf. 'Here you are,' she said, handing it to me. 'Here's your usual.'

'That is so kind thank you,' I said passing over some money.

Then Kavitha's mother said, 'Hello, my dear. Gut to see you.'

I thought for a moment that the lady was calling me fat, "Gut to see you indeed!" But of course, "gut" was just how she said 'good'. I tried to smile but I was scared so I ended up half smiling and half wincing, which was neither one thing nor the other. I did return her 'hello' with a smile and a nod. At least I hope I did.

It was the same thing when I went into the butchers. Jimmy and Clive extended their jolly 'Sarf East Landan' welcome to me from behind their glass meat counter.

'Nice to see you, sir,' said Clive, 'What can we get for you today?'

'A pound of unsmoked bacon and half a dozen eggs, please.'

'A pleasure, sir,' said 'Salt of the Earth' Jimmy.

For some reason, Jimmy's manner took me back to thinking of the gangsters back in the hospital. Clive looked at my sling, and immediately I felt I had to explain myself: 'I fell over and broke my shoulder.'

They both nodded sympathetically. 'Yes, we heard. You look a lot better than you did the other day,' said Clive, filling a bag with my bacon and eggs.

I briefly pondered who they might have heard this from, and when Clive had seen me, as I hadn't been outside the house in several weeks. Then this voice suddenly appeared in my head, it simply said, 'Leave!'

After picking up the bag I walked toward the door and Clive ran after me. I didn't know why he was following me, and immediately became hunched up, scared and closed in. My hands went up against my face as a shield.

'Your change, sir,' said Clive.

'Thank you,' I smiled in sudden relief that Clive's approach was innocent. As I got back into the street, I pondered, what the hell is happening to me? Scared of Jimmy and Clive? These were people I had spoken to a thousand times before, usually about innocuous things like football, but now their complexions seemed rubbery, sinister and scary. Outside my own house, I was now frightened of my own shadow. As I walked home, I kept my head down, figuring that if I walked quickly, then my ordeal would be over sooner. Alas, I was wrong. With a broken shoulder, just carrying a few things in a plastic bag, even if it was just bacon, eggs, and the *Guardian* newspaper, threw me off balance so that walking home took a lot longer. I had agreed with Rachel that it was good for me to go outside and talk to somebody other than the wall or her. But by the time I'd walked all the way home, I was physically shaking.

As I reached my front door, an old lady called after me, 'Adam, how are you?'

I looked up and said, 'I'm OK.'

'Good, I've been praying for you.'

'Thank you, you're very kind,' I replied.

Who the bloody hell was that? I pondered, and then I bolted! I got my key in the front door lock and got inside as fast as I could. As I finally made it back into the house, I wanted to collapse in a heap from the ordeal of having to speak to so many people. I got into the kitchen, breathing loudly and heavily, and dumped the shopping down. Then I went to sit in the front room, and with head in hands I absolutely bawled my eyes out.

Rachel came down the stairs, and as I shivered in shock in the front room, I could hear her putting the shopping away in the kitchen.

'Did you talk to anybody?' she half shouted. In the other room, I was in shock and barely able to say anything. Rachel came in and asked how I was. 'You look pale, are you OK?'

'There were people everywhere! All asking the same questions! Wherever I went. It was purgatory. Is there no end to human curiosity? Surely not that many people care about me, I'm nobody! I'm not important! How the hell do so many people even know me,' I stuttered.

'People care, and they were glad to see you,' said Rachel.

'On my way to the shops I got collared by the entire world!' I announced. 'Everybody spoke to me.'

'They were worried and just being nice. It's a good thing that people care.'

'I don't want them to be nice. I don't want them to care. I want to be left alone.'

'It's quite amazing in London that people even notice.'

'I know, I was not ready for it, that's all.'

'If I told you beforehand that everyone was going to be asking about you, then you would never have gone out.'

'That's really sneaky,' I replied. 'That's all I can say. Some women are very sneaky. Everybody said the same thing: "How are you?", "You look so much better." I kept thinking who are you and where have you seen me before? You can't all know me; I haven't been out. I've either been at home or in hospital. The butcher said he saw me the other day looking very ill, and now I look so much better. How can he have seen me? Unless he's been hiding in our bathroom?'

'I may have mentioned your fall to a couple of folks. You forget, you've been out of action now for six months, and we've lived here for fifteen years.'

'I know people mean well, but it's rather put me off leaving the house again! I'm now thinking, is my return to work going to be like this? If it is, I'm dreading it!'

'You'll be fine. Most people are nice, they only ask because they care,' said Rachel. 'People at work want you back. They even said they missed you.'

'Only five of them did. The rest were "best wishes" and "get well soons".'

'Well, I'm sure they all meant it.'

Part 3

Chapter 23: The Big Day

I once owned a pair of light grey trousers which never made it outside the house. I had them for nearly ten years, but knew full well that within fifteen seconds of putting them on I would spill something down them or stand too close to a wet surface and there would be the most incriminating wet mark on them around the crotch area. No doubt I would eventually notice this as I was about to leave the house and suddenly become horrified! Incontinence, anyone? Rachel gave the trousers to a charity shop in the end. They were used in the remake of *The Sweeney* movie.

The meaning of the parable of the grey trousers was that with work looming, I was not taking any chances. In order to prepare for my return, I ironed enough clothes for a week; well, I was worried about spillages. I experienced quite a lot of those even before the accident. A tomato, a cup of tea or even a glass of water in my clumsy hands could become as lethal as a Molotov cocktail. It took ages to iron five pairs of trousers, and by the end of it my one good arm was nearly dropping off.

On the morning of the big day, and after the worst night's sleep of all time (come back, you gangsters, all is forgiven), I wearily pulled myself out of bed; well, Rachel did. I could now shave and do almost everything else for myself, but dressing was still difficult. I watched my slow transformation in the full-length mirror in the spare bedroom à la the kids' TV cartoon character Mr Benn; and gave a commentary. 'Today, kids, I'm going to become an office worker. Yes, it does sound quite dull, probably because it is. My dutiful, beautiful wife Rachel has made me a packed lunch: cheese, I think. Oh God, I am becoming my father-in-law, he's always so obsessed with detail.'

From the doorway, Rachel said, 'That would be funny, except that it's true.'

When I began the short walk from our house to the station, my legs once more felt like jelly. They did not seem to belong to me. I must have done this trip thousands of times before, but today it seemed to matter so much more.

As I walked, I felt every curve and contour in the pavement under my feet. My footsteps were echoing and stuttering in my head. I felt as if I was walking along a very narrow and extremely high mountain pass, and I would fall off the side of the world if I put a foot wrong. The mechanics of crossing the road momentarily eluded me too. I stood, hesitantly watching cars, looking for a gap and wondering whether it was safe to cross. I was now so much slower in my movements that I was convinced I would never make it across the road in time. I must have looked desperate, because eventually a lady in blue Citroen car stopped to let me across the road.

When I got to Manford train station, it was as if I'd never been away. The platform had not changed at all. The air was bracing – that's posh for 'bloody cold'. It seemed quite busy too, with folk gathered on the platform like peculiar clumps of temporary people heather. They stood in the exact places where the train carriage doors would open. 'Good to know some things don't change,' I mused quietly to myself.

When I first worked in London, I thought this was some sort of clever extra sensory perception which people had about train doors. I was rather disappointed to discover it was no such thing, as the doors always opened in the same place every time. I took up my former platform position just behind the 'M' of the fourth 'MIND THE GAP' sign, painted in some strange semolina white paint behind the yellow line.

There had been earlier train delays, which explained why, post-rush hour, it was so busy. I recognised some of the people at the station that morning from my former regular commuter days. There was the lady I used to nickname 'Rubber-Face', who could scowl disapproval in at least three languages when trains were late. I used to get the same train as her, and it gave me a strange comfort that she was here now. Next to Rubber-Face was her friend, 'Her That Follows': a strange, rather small, companion whose primary function in life seemed to be to nod eagerly and agree with all of Rubber-Face's worldly pronouncements and observations. They were both from the same fabled part of the not-quite-American West, also known as Hounslow, and they were always together.

I was also comforted to see that Latimer's Marble Stonemason Works was still operating behind platform 2 on the opposite side of the station. Latimer's normally made kitchen work surfaces and ornamental grave decorations. I had caught the train into London from Manford station for fifeteen years now; on quieter days, I swear you could hear somebody tapping out your name on your marble tombstone, ready for when you were done with this life. That place too had not changed one iota whilst I was away. Great slabs of marble still leaned against each other in racks as far as the eye could see: grey, white and some speckled strange kind of leopard skin stuff; it was still south-east London, after all.

The familiar sights on my first day's journey back to work didn't really do much to ease my tension. I waited, shuffling around from one foot to the other, and tried to listen to music on my iPod; but even Pink Floyd couldn't calm my nerves that day. I got on the train and stood as it lurched forward. A man covered in tattoos stood and urged me to sit down. Clearly my sling created some sympathy. As we swapped places, I smiled and mouthed the traditional London traveller's mantra, 'Thank you, that's really kind of you.' This, along with 'Can you move down, please', are the only words you can say on London Transport without the risk of scorn from your fellow passengers.

I got off the train and onto the Tube. It was still busy, but this time I managed to get a seat under my own steam. Then I walked along the same old streets towards the office, not wanting the journey to end and wondering why I was getting there so quickly. Finally, there it was, my place of work, the Ministry of Paperclips, or to give its more common name, 'the office'. That's all anyone ever called it! It was a building, chiselled from the finest glass and cement, looming out of the tarmac like a giant sleeping elephant with a traffic-fumed dark complexion.

It was still here. Bollocks! I was genuinely hoping that somebody had stolen it or that it had fallen down. As I got through the double glass doors, I fumbled inside my jacket and found my work pass. It was still in the same pocket where I'd left it six months ago, the self-same piece of plastic building pass attached to the same lanyard. Where had the time gone? With pursed lips I took a sharp intake of breath and went inside. The 'white shirt and black tie' security guards at the front desk looked the same as before. As I walked in, my left arm seemed to awake from within its sling and began to wave. The security guards thought I was waving at them, and a couple of them smiled. I saw no alternative but to smile back. As I got through to the lifts I felt as if I was in a dream, or at least behind a veil or sepia lens. I mused under my breath, 'Why am I waving suddenly?' I didn't like it, and I used my free right arm to hold my left arm still.

I wasn't really trying to hurry or indeed to go slow, but the lift journey seemed very fast. I was hoping to keep a low profile and not run into anybody I knew. As I went up to the third floor, I saw there had been changes while I was away. There was a new slogan on the wall of each floor. I pondered the words 'A NEW STRATEGY FOR STATIONERY'. There was mention of 'a four C plan' on another banner. Let's see, there was 'CONSISTENCY, CONTINUITY, oh and CUSTOMER CARE'; I forget the final one, but it could have been Colin. All the same, you did rather sense that the person who wrote this magnificent set of buzzwords was probably considered the biggest 'C' of all by their colleagues by now.

I got out of the lift, rounded the corner and immediately ran into Jerome and Roderick. Jerome looked good on his promotion, in a dark blue suit; black-clad Roderick looked his usual self – recently exhumed and in dire need of food.

'Adam!' Jerome purred. 'Come in and sit down.' He called the team over and started introducing me to people I already knew. 'Look, everyone, see who's returned!'

As I shook Jerome's hand, my left arm, freed from its shackles, once again waved several times at others who had now all gathered in a group. Thankfully they just waved back, taking it as meaning I was pleased to see them. My friend Neil Black shook my hand in the business-like way men do when trying to suppress emotion, before adding, 'Sorry I didn't sign your card, I was on leave at the time.'

As I shook my head in forgiveness, Mary Swanson, Peter Moores' Personal Assistant, hugged me. Peter was out that day ('being ironed' according to Neil), but he was keen to be represented, hence Mary's appearance. The dour Scottish printer, Gavin Keep, who was not in my team, said, 'Oh, it's just you. I thought it was a queue to meet someone important.' His unintentionally funny reaction broke the ice, and this gave way to many 'How nice to see yous' and 'You're looking wells'.

But I still felt on display, like a prize show dog. The whole occasion - and having to re-meet so many folks I already knew - all got to me and I made my excuses to retire to the toilet; it seemed the one place where people would not follow me. I was wrong. I stood in there looking at myself in the mirror and wanting to die. Then Sam Maxwell, a gaunt-looking guy with a pallid complexion made worse by his dark suit and black shirt, came in and shattered my tranquillity. I made out I was washing my hands, except I couldn't do that with a sling on.

'Please could you press the soap thing for me? It's hard with only one arm.'

'Sure,' said Sam smiling. 'I'm Sam, I'm on work experience.'

'Yes, thank you, I'm Adam. You look like a lot like Roderick. You two would make excellent gothic bookends.'

Sam laughed, probably forgiving the remark because I was only just back. (From then on, I secretly nicknamed Sam and Roderick the Zombie twins).

For some reason I felt obliged once more to explain myself. 'The sink is too high and far away for my left hand. I can't press the soap dispenser and press the tap at the same time. I was struggling with this quandary for several minutes but to little avail. So, I'm glad you came in.'

'It's no trouble, it's nice to meet you,' he said, as a huge globule of white creamy soap hit my right palm.

I elbowed the tap on, and the creamy liquid slid off my hand and dissolved down the plughole. I shook my right hand and then placed it under the whirr of the hand drier. 'Thanks. Now that I'm a temporarily disabled office worker, I shall write a snotty letter to the tap manufacturers immediately.'

Sam left and I reflected on what he meant by his 'Nice to meet you' comment. Is it nice to meet me? He looks like a vampire. No, stop it! It's your first day back after a long time off. Give him a chance. He was caring, that's all. God, when Rachel's ideas get into your head, they're difficult to shift.

The difference between my outward demeanour – merrily smiling and laughing – was stark compared with the paranoia and insecurity I felt inside; but thankfully only I knew of my secret battle for now.

Once back on the office floor with the group, Head Printer Peter Vardy came over and shook my hand.

'How goes it?' I asked.

'Fine,' he said, then noticing my waving arm, he hurriedly added, 'I can't stop, I need to get these export figures worked out by close of play today.'

'I can help,' I offered.

'No, it's fine, really.' He seemed to be still looking at my waving arm and recoiling. It was a sign of things to come, although I didn't know it yet. 'Besides I'm sure Jerome has plenty for you to do,' he added, defusing any umbrage.

Dowdy Diane came over and hugged me and tearfully said, 'I kept the Milk Club going for you! It's not been the same without you.'

'Thanks,' I said, trying to ameliorate her earnestness.

My return eventually dissipated down to nothingness. Here are the top three welcome home comments and whizzes of pearldom I got that day:

'It won't be long before you're back to normal.'

'We really have missed you.'

Then later I overheard the same person ask someone else what my name was.

'We knew you'd get fed up with daytime telly eventually.'

Chapter 24: Shake, Rattle and Deny

London is a place where nobody needs to know everyone else's business. It's a welcome contrast to growing up in Congleton, where everybody gossips and judges' people. I pondered many times how I could just visit Agnes on trips up north to find out what everyone else was doing. In contrast you can be yourself in London and nobody bats an eyelid. In my first week of living there, I saw the world's hairiest transvestite on a tube train: he was a Greek gentleman dressed in a ladies' business suit, and his five o'clock shadow was breaking through on his homeward journey. Nobody gave him a second glance.

It felt odd having to support my left arm again. At first, I didn't realise how much muscle they had removed in the operation, along with all the bits of bone. With the sling removed, my left arm hung loose. It would follow me around like a drunken bore at a wedding, continually interrupting and trying to engage the rest of me in conversation. I didn't know quite what to do with this sudden added weight, and yes it was heavy!

'My trailing arm makes me feel like Igor in those old comic horror films,' I explained to Rachel.

'Except that it's not funny or scary?'

'No, it's not. It pulls down on my neck terribly and gives me backache unless I prop it up on a chair arm or go back to wearing my sling. Nurse Ruth told me only to use the sling on train journeys. When I'm at my work I must to try to use both arms. It's not easy: I tried to get my left arm involved in some typing today, but it wasn't keen.'

'That's a good idea, referring to your arm like a person, and trying to persuade it to come back and join in with the rest of you.'

'It is?'

Yes, I think so. It might help defuse things with people. Disability is a hard sell amongst most people, and a bit of comedy to demystify things might help.'

'OK, I'll think about it.'

One day I was sitting at my desk and looking through some of the emails that had come in during my absence. I noted that each one was entitled 'Adam Next Steps', so it gave the impression that work was already beginning to think about me as being different, or what their alternatives were. The list of emails made me start to relive the sequence of events up to now. Before long, my brain was swimming in bad memories and discovering that people's so-called 'insights' and 'advice' didn't help. They seemed to be hinting at my early retirement and making sure that the company wasn't liable. As I reached the email halfway point, my left arm suddenly started to tremor quite vigorously. It lasted about thirty seconds, but as I didn't know what it was, it felt like a lifetime. The office was already quite hot, it being June, and so the effort and effect of the tremor made me sweat like a hippo in a power shower.

But far worse, to my mind, was the fact that some people in the office stopped what they were doing and watched what was happening to me. There was quite a bit of 'offstage mumbling' too, which thankfully I could not hear properly, although I did hear someone say, 'That's really weird.' I was embarrassed and scared and quickly retreated to the toilet. I locked the cubicle door, pressed my back against it and cried. I stood there alone, asking myself, 'What the hell was that?'

I looked at my left arm in disbelief. It had just decided to move on its own! 'I did not tell you to do that,' I said. 'So why did you do it?' My arm sort of shrugged, then waved its palm downwards as a sign of contempt. 'OK,' I remonstrated, 'the waving I can cope with, because people think it's cute and wave back. But the tremor thing is horrible.' My arm now turned away like a sulky little child and folded itself in a HMMMPH! pose. The whole thing was weird.

I wanted to look at the instruction manual for my left arm, to see if the fault finder had any tips. Hmmm, I mused, yes, let's thumb the imaginary pages together. Here we are, imaginary page 24, 'Surprise Arm Waving and Tremor', see Manic Depression and Madness, yes here it is. Now what does it say? 'You've had it, mate. Go throw yourself off a bridge immediately.' Sadly, the human body does not come with any manual or instruction kit.

Leaving that aside, your left arm cannot simply decide to move or do things on its own, can it? No, of course it can't! Perhaps I had imagined the whole thing. Perhaps it didn't happen. Yes, that was it. If I had a blanket, I would have thrown it over my arm to put things out of sight and out of mind. I mused to myself: So, my arm moves on its own accord; what am I going to do? I'm going to ignore it and pretend it never happened, that's what. All very British and unemotional.

After a few more minutes, I had composed myself enough to return to my desk. But when I tried typing again, my arm immediately went into another tremor. There were more anxious looks, louder mumblings and other Cornish fishing villages from the surrounding populous. I mused to myself, Damn it they've all noticed! How long will it be before this gets back to Jerome? Then to our Head of Unit, Peter Moores? They will think I'm mad. I'll be fired in no time. This is all so embarrassing!

'Are you OK?' asked Roderick, silently scraping back his chair on the carpeted floor and walking over.

'Yes, I'm fine,' I replied quickly and defensively. 'The doctor said my arm could shudder and tremor a bit whilst the replacement shoulder beds in. Every now and then the new joint touches a nerve, you see, and that's what causes the movement.'

'I see, that must be really disconcerting,' said Roderick, nodding and looking scared at the same time. I was not sure whether he believed me.

What the hell am I talking about? I mused. Shoulder bedding in? I'm lying my arse off! Trying to make normality out of something that patently isn't! We all go too far when we do that and start trying to normalise the weird. More importantly, why did I feel the need to do this? Probably because my own attitude to disability was just as completely warped and naive as anyone else's. Why did it matter if my arm shook? Well, I was worried in case people thought me mad and tried to send me home. In my eyes there would be no consultation, just a decision. I could imagine their words: *'We are worried about you. We feel it would be best if you were not here.'* Compassionate but callous. But then British people *always* turn mental health conditions into equations of etiquette – mental health equals scary and unseemly; not being normal equals being incapable; crying equals privacy, and so on. Keeping things hidden and never discussing them is the done thing; well, that and telling you not to worry about something – commonly known as the 'I'm-not-too-bad' fixation. I quickly put my sling on, fixing my arm in place. 'That's better: look, everyone, she just wanted a little sleep, that's all. Oh well, at least she didn't cry.'

Roderick smiled at me awkwardly and raised his eyebrows to everyone else.

'What the hell am I saying?' I mused. 'My arm had gone into a weird spasm, and I'm lashing it down to make it stop, trying to camouflage it by acting like I'm putting a baby to bed.' I tell you, I couldn't wait for the day to end.

Luckily, work let me travel home early during the first few weeks of my return so that I could get a seat on the train. Come three o'clock, I was out of there quicker than a greased pig who heard someone mention the words "bacon sandwiches."

Chapter 25: Myrtle's Naming Day

Whenever I returned home after work, I was grateful for the silence, the lack of questions and the absence of prying eyes. However, one particular day when I got home, the house seemed enormous and foreboding. Rachel was away at a work social event. There were pots and pans left out unwashed on the kitchen work surface because Rachel had not washed up for a few days. That's not a criticism. With me being incapacitated, she was having to do everything and neither of us wanted Agnes back again so soon. So, I thought I would surprise Rachel by doing the washing-up.

As I took off my sling and placed both my hands in the water, my left arm made a grab for a wooden spoon lying nearby and then threw it across the kitchen. I stared in disbelief at my arm's behaviour. Then I tried to reason with it. 'What are you doing now? I didn't tell you to do that!' But my left arm wasn't finished, and before I could question anything else, it grabbed a whisk and sent that flying as well. I stared open-mouthed, as it raised its way out of the water and grabbed a saucepan and whacked me in the face. I fell to the floor. I must have passed out, because when I woke up and my blurry-eyed vision reoriented itself, I was in a chair with Rachel standing over me.

'Hello,' she said softly, still with her coat on. I didn't realise it, but she had found me on the kitchen floor.

'Hello, OOOOW!' I said, suddenly discovering the pain on the side of my cheek which was quite badly bruised.

'I know you're frustrated and in a lot of pain, but you shouldn't throw things and then leave them lying around the house.'

'But I didn't,' I protested.

'Yes, you did,' she nodded. 'I know, I picked them all up. There were loads of them: knives, forks, spoons, even the whisk, all over the place! Luckily, nothing breakable. Oh, and a saucepan.'

'But I didn't. My arm did. My left arm attacked me!'

'Well, your left arm should stop it,' and with that Rachel turned to my left arm and said firmly, 'Behave yourself!'

My arm recoiled in anger, slapping my face. 'Looks like she heard you.'

'She? A bit sexist, isn't it? Assuming something bad must be female?'

'Not really, almost everything that bosses me around is female. There's you, your mother, your sisters, my sister, next door's cat. I'm going to call my arm Myrtle.'

'Why Myrtle?' asked Rachel.

'Because it sounds like turtle, which makes her seem less foreboding.'

'Okay, Myrtle it is then. Is she tired after her earlier exertions? She looks calm.'

'Well, she's worn me out, I imagine she's tired too.'

'She looks cute, like a naturist version of Sooty the kid's TV puppet or a very thin, well-plucked Emu.'

Suddenly Myrtle reached out and slapped my face again, and in response both Rachel and I snapped at her like stern parents with a simultaneous, 'Stop it!'

'Are you OK with the name Myrtle?' I asked once I had wedged my arm between my trunk and the armchair as a forcible restraint.

'Of course, it's your arm! I know you're having problems with it. I've seen you.'

'You've seen me?'

'Yes, I've been watching what's happening to you. I see your arm lift up on its own, it's like a little periscope. It does it in bed sometimes when you're half asleep. It's like it's saying, 'Look at me, look at me!' I see it shake. I watch your crumpled expression and then your blind panic as you fight to control it. I'm not blind. I know you're going through a lot of difficulty.'

'What do you think it is?'

'I don't know, but you're not imagining it.'

'Thanks that means a lot.'

'I can see it happen,' continued Rachel. 'I don't think your arm is possessed by an evil spirit, or that the replacement shoulder joint used to belong to a serial killer or the world's worst juggler - that would explain all the cutlery being flung everywhere. No, it's far too well behaved. It doesn't attack either of us often enough for that, vomit pea soup or say, "Your mother knits socks in hell!"'

'What are you saying? Are you expecting it to strangle me or something?'

'No, it's just that I would expect a demonic possession to be a bit more animated. I think that for now at least your arm just doesn't want to be part of you.'

'So much for my grin and bear it coping strategy,' I said.

Rachel's comments surprised me, because I hadn't realised the extent to which my arm was showing my anxieties in front of everybody. Myrtle's voice, which I'd always thought mute for everyone else, was very loud indeed and tended to drown out the rest of me, especially as it was the first thing people saw. I was also annoyed that my 'camouflage strategy' of wearing sandy-coloured shirts and keeping my head down was clearly not working. I mused to myself, 'If it's like this at home, I wonder what it's like at work? My stress levels are always twice as bad there.'

My arm acting independently from the rest of me was difficult to accept at first. I wondered if I was going mad. I didn't feel or look any different. I checked I was still there in the mirror each morning. I mulled over Rachel's comments. Was my arm undergoing some sort of demonic possession, or was it now choosing to become a separate entity or person in its own right? Since the possession angle was too scary to even contemplate, I went with 'my arm becoming a person in her own right' strategy. It was at that moment I began to refer to my arm in the third person in public, and Myrtle was properly born. Naming my left arm Myrtle had several advantages for me. It meant that I had someone to direct my anger towards, and more importantly someone to blame. It also cut down the need for an exorcism, thank goodness!

'Myrtle quite likes her new name,' I said to Rachel over breakfast.

'I'm not surprised,' said Rachel. 'It's us acknowledging her as a real person. We just need to be careful in case she thinks about conquering the rest of you.'

'It's hard when your body parts choose not to want anything to do with you in one breath, then try to disrupt the rest of you in the next. I will have to try to win her over, buy her some hand cream, nail varnish or something. Her birthday must be the day I fell over, 10 January. That's a way off but when the time comes I'll go out and buy her a bracelet or something to remember it.'

Chapter 26: Myrtle's Brexit

For the next few days, I reflected on Rachel's words. I lay awake at night, trying not to torture myself with pictures of Myrtle as an evil spirit. Although I was sure she could carry off a small set of devil horns as well as the next arm, I did wonder what Myrtle was doing during her episodes of sitting up in bed and looking around in the middle of the night whilst I was asleep. I became scared that the previously United Kingdom of my body was undergoing some form of rebellion or unrest. Could it be that Myrtle, like some bad-tempered miniature version of Cornwall, was going for full-blown independence? 'Hangers on, will he?' as some folk say down there when they hear someone stretch the truth or go too fast.

Whatever Myrtle was doing over the next few weeks, my condition worsened. When I was walking down the street, my head and neck would suddenly begin to sway of their own volition and my arm would tremor and shake. This also started to happen when I was in conversation with other people. During these times it seemed as though, like the episode at the hydrotherapy pool, my head was trying to slowly screw my neck back into the trunk of my body. On top of this, I felt completely unconnected with what was going on around me. I couldn't look anyone in the eye when the movements were happening, because I *was* ashamed, worried that people would think that what was happening was my fault or that I was doing this on purpose. Those standards we all have, such as *'I'll never let anyone see me like this,'* began to waiver as I simply couldn't maintain them.

There was not much rationality or support for me from Myrtle, but there was quite a lot of bile and self-destruction. Myrtle was always quite canny towards outsiders. She would not appear until she could have maximum impact. You could say that her appearances coincided with those times when I was undergoing the most stress, such as when there were more people around, or at least people I wasn't used to. Rachel and I attended a family get-together with Rachel's parents, Maxine and Roger, along with her sisters Teresa and Mary. We were at a restaurant in Central London and being served by a waitress who stared with alarm at my head wobbles and because Myrtle kept waving at her while she was taking our meal orders. After looking at the specials menu, I ordered gammon, egg and chips. The waitress brought it over along with an incredibly sharp knife. Whilst Rachel was firing ketchup into appropriate places on the gammon slab on my behalf, Myrtle sensed her opportunity. She grabbed the knife and started wielding it like a psychopathic orchestra conductor, getting quite carried away with her own self-importance.

'SOMEBODY HELP ADAM,' said Roger, in one of those time-stood-still moments. His voice was loud cutting through the background noise making the restaurant fall silent. Myrtle chose not to hear Roger's warning. She was now swishing the knife blade towards me. She had those Hitchcock high-pitched violins going through her mind and was thrusting the knife repeatedly to their shrill note bursts. Sensing an impending problem or possible murder, Rachel disarmed Myrtle.

'Sorry, but that was getting rather close to your left ear,' justified Rachel.

'Well done, Rachel,' said Roger. 'I'm glad you stepped in. I hate to think what would have happened if you hadn't.'

Myrtle slapped me in frustration, then threw a drink over Rachel and me.

'NO!' scolded Rachel. Myrtle, deflated, sank back down to the table like an admonished puppy. It must have looked weird. The people at the other tables stopped and stared. The knife had tomato sauce on it, which had also ended up being fired over me during Myrtle's histrionics. I now had a tomato sauce stain in the shape of a cut or gash across my cheek. The returning waitress looked at my cheek wound and did a double-take.

Roger was unabashed, adding, 'No, he's all right, it's just tomato sauce', before joking, 'We can't take him anywhere.'

The effect on my confidence after episodes like the meal was shattering. I started to think that Roger was right, you *couldn't* take me anywhere. I needed to be in some form of rubber room where Myrtle couldn't hurt me.

I was also convinced that Myrtle had a role in the deterioration of my voice, because my flapping and shaking arm, lack of body coordination and buckling legs made me feel more like a creature than a man. In my head, creatures don't speak, and so my voice became a noise. My words were trapped in my mind, unable to come out unless they were stammered or cloaked in gibberish. I began to bray, rather than speak. 'Hello' morphed into 'Dello'. 'Nan-new-nelp- me' was not an instruction to a grandparent, but a request for assistance, 'Can you help me?'

Similarly things were starting to get bad at work and I couldn't stop them. I felt I was becoming secondary to my injury. I worried that people would think of me as a set of symptoms first, and a person second. My fellow workers were shocked by my transformation, and I became the subject of a lot of underground gossip which eventually spilled over into the team meeting. Thankfully this happened when I wasn't around; I only got to hear about it afterwards, on the work gossip chain. The intention of the meeting was well meant, an open question from Peter Moores, 'How can we help Adam Wright?'

To start with there was silence, with people looking at each other and then the floor. Nobody wanted to go first or be seen as the bad guy. Eventually Jerome started the discussion with 'Adam looks in a bad way. His speech is getting worse, and his arm tremor is unnerving.'

'He's not putting it on,' added Roderick, shaking his head. 'I heard somebody suggest that, but it's far too weird for that.'

'Yes,' agreed Jerome, 'it's certainly not something you would choose to do at work if you could help it. Did I say my friend's partner is a doctor?'

'Well, real or not, it's not nice to see,' said Diane. 'He was supposed to be presenting at another team meeting yesterday. His arm was flapping around, he was like an injured bird. And his speech. Well, it was awful! They said he sounded drunk! Someone from the other team came and got me to take him back. They were embarrassed. We shouldn't let other teams see him like that. It's not professional. It reflects badly on us.'

'Quite right, Diane,' agreed Peter Vardy. 'We shouldn't let him see visitors from outside either. He'll upset them and we might lose work.'

'I'm rather more worried about hurting Adam than upsetting visitors,' said Peter.

'Can you catch it?' asked Darren Jones abruptly.

'That's cold and unfeeling, isn't it?' said Neil Black. 'He's our friend and colleague.'

'I'm only saying what others are thinking,' said Darren Jones defensively. 'This is an office, not a day care centre for loonies. It's horrible to watch.'

'He's not mad. It's a disability, and I'm quite sure you can't catch it,' said Jerome firmly.

'I think there's scope for keeping an eye on things,' said Peter. 'I don't want us assuming we know best and deciding things for him, at least not yet. We'll speak to Human Resources and see what our options are.'

Things were left in a strange limbo land where nobody quite knew what to do. For now, there were only disparate mutterings of discontent, not yet a unified or unanimous voice; though I did wonder how long it would take to become one.

Chapter 27: Better Rude than Mad

I was oblivious to the meeting of my colleagues and so called "friends". But under my own volition, I did decide I needed a coping strategy at work to get through the day. As my voice was so unpredictable, I simply tried to speak less to people and keep out of the way. To counter the tremors, I would deliberately do less with my left arm and fasten it in my sling on the bad days. Unfortunately, the bad days became every day. Yes, this was burying the problem, but I had quickly concluded that Myrtle found manual labour tedious and unnecessary. She would *much* rather get other folks to do it for her. I reasoned that was probably what the restaurant episode earlier was about. This was not simply restricted to cutting up food – there was a whole list of things which Myrtle would rather have the 'servants' do.

She had little or no desire to carry things or turn on taps. She enjoyed washing up though because she liked warm water. She saw the sink as her own film-star swimming pool and had a touch of the 'Joan Crawford' or some other diva about her. Bette Davis once said, "Until you're called very, very difficult, you're really nobody at all." I sensed that Myrtle was a pretty big fan of hers. Myrtle used to wear a washing-up glove with the fingers chopped off as her take on a 1950s swimsuit, and she used to fold up a J-cloth as her towel. I am lying of course about the last part: she used a sponge instead, but it was kind of you to nod and smile.

At work, when I would try to get Myrtle to help, she would throw things in response, out of protest or spite! People would duck as a stapler or pencil flew past their heads. Other times she would sulk. Myrtle would usually sit on my desk, balanced on her elbow. She looked like a cross between a snake and a miniature velociraptor, and she would turn around and regally survey all about her, occasionally opening her palm as if she was yawning. It must have been weird for the others who sat nearby or walked past, because she seemed to be staring at them whilst I carried on typing or whatever. She did all this on her own, whilst I tried to carry on regardless.

In the early stages of my return-to-work, I continued to plough my way through some of the thousands of emails which had arrived whilst I had been away. It was weird looking through the correspondence. 'Was all this stuff really about me?' I asked myself. It seemed so far away and, as I read through some the emails about my accident, as if they were talking about someone else. It felt like I was taking over from a dead person and reading about their demise. In terms of getting back up to speed, I was given the new departmental Paper Strategy to read by Jerome, along with its recycling supplement. So clearly there was no end to their cruelty.

'We will soon have you back in the fold, with a new performance agreement.' said Jerome, trying his best to engage me.

'Can't vait,' I replied. My voice was becoming bad, but thankfully sarcasm was harder to spot with a speech impediment. Conscious that my speech was bad, I began communicating with a series of nods, smiles and shakes of the head, and the occasional 'yes' and 'no' like an over-encouraging version of Clint Eastwood from the *Man with*

No Name films. Only I didn't wear a poncho, carry a gun or have a horse. So, no trouble with that simile then.

Colleagues at work quickly noticed a change in me. Previously, I'd been quite vocal and enthusiastic in my work activities, priding myself on putting people at ease. Now I was monosyllabic in conversations because I didn't want people to think I was insane. Strangely, I preferred being considered rude to being thought mad. As I later told Rachel, 'I was going for enigmatic and aloof, but I could never quite manage it.'

'Can't really see you as enigmatic,' replied Rachel. 'You talk too much.'

'The tremors frighten people. Sam Waters cried when he saw me in the canteen, which caused his dark hair dye to run. I hadn't seen him for ages, and he seemed shocked by my transformation. I blamed myself of course.'

One day from my desk I saw the tanned, rotund and bearded Nathan Brock talking to Roderick and Jerome. Nathan had recently returned from holiday in Tunisia. He was the man who'd organised my trip to the training course on behalf of the board member Sir Brian Willis. It was on that visit that I fell over and broke my shoulder. I reckoned I should at least get up to say 'Hello', so when Nathan stood up to leave the room, I called out 'Hello'; but it came out as 'Nellow' as he left. No response, not even a half turn around. Nathan had clocked some weirdo trying to talk to him, but in that sour-faced British way he chose to ignore me in the hope that I would go away. But I would not go away, I had invested a lot in this by getting to my feet and speaking aloud. Others in the office stopped and watched.

'Naden, it's Edam Night [it's me, Adam Wright],' I called again, a lot louder and audibly frustrated. My voice was always a lot clearer when I was annoyed.

Nathan turned, looked at me and did a double-take. 'Adam, I'm sorry, I didn't recognise you at all. I thought it was some weirdo following me. You look so different.'

'Owse-sit-gowing? [How is it going?]' My words rushed out of my mouth and collided with each other.

'Oh mate, you look terrible, are you sure you should be here?'

'Yed-di-think-so,' I replied, not knowing quite what to say now I had his attention. I composed myself and slowly stuttered out the following sentence: 'I know why this all happened! I booked a course of swimming lessons at my local pool, and a week later I fell over on the trip to Kent.' It was an attempt at humour. I also added 'Nexercise benfats noon' [Exercise benefits no one].

I caught Nathan looking at Myrtle, and so I tried to stop her shaking with my free arm. Myrtle seemed annoyed because I had not introduced her, so she went into one of those hurricane tremors she saves for special occasions; and what could be better than embarrassing me in front of an old friend.

'I heard you broke your arm, but I didn't realise it was this bad. All this from a fall? You poor bugger.'

I nodded and there were tears in my eyes.

'I feel responsible.'

'I yam responsible!' I replied. I wanted him to recognise that *I had made the decision to try to travel* when the weather was awful, and the trains were not running. I'm a proud man, and I didn't want to let those people down who had put themselves out on my behalf. If anybody was to blame, it was me for not accepting the limitations of the day. That's what I wanted Nathan to take away from our meeting. Whether he did so or not, at that time, it was nigh on impossible to say, in all senses of the phrase.

Chapter 28: There Are Limits

When I first got on this train, I noticed quite a few *suits* on their way to work. Some were "old stagers" like me with their frayed checked shirts and jumpers. But there were quite a few "players" too, -people who want to get on at work and accordingly try to look the part. They had fancy attire, fancier laptops and snazzy mobile phones. They looked as if they would make short work of the new starters and old timers in their work jungle.

I have never been a careerist, but I did care what people thought. During my first return to the Serengeti of the office, I made many futile attempts to keep Myrtle hidden. In my head I felt that if I didn't do this, then like an old, injured antelope I would be taken down by the younger lions and gobbled up at any moment. I was also worried as to how long it would be before my condition might be 'out of my hands' and perceived by the seniors as me being incapable of work. Then I would have no say in anything at all. I would just walk through the soft curtains of madness never to return. After all, you don't hear of anyone functioning and holding down a job with a disability, do you? Well, actually, of course you do! But that was my rather uninformed view back then, and I imagined it was also everybody else's.

One day I was at my work desk when the telephone rang. I picked up the receiver, stuttering out the word 'Dellow' [Hello].

'Hello, I'd like to speak to Jerome, please,' said the male caller.

'Dot near' [he's not here] I replied, as the person's words trailed off, adding the word 'Dessage?' [Can I take a message?].

'He's obviously not there. It's a terrible line. Can I leave a message please?'

The caller was being kind in suggesting that the telephone line was to blame for his lack of understanding, and not my dreadful voice.

'Yed.' [Yes] As the word came out, I wondered how I might write this down when my right hand was occupied in holding the receiver. And Myrtle? Well, she was busy counting paperclips. Unaware, the caller began his message.

'This is Jerome's partner, Christopher. I'm supposed to be meeting him for lunch. Please tell him I'll meet him in the Big Bun sandwich shop at one o'clock. Please pass the message on to him. Thank you, goodbye.'

'Yed,' I replied. Not realising the call had ended, I tried to wedge the telephone receiver between my right ear and right shoulder whilst picking up a pen with my now free right hand. Almost immediately I got a lightning bolt of cramp in my neck from how I was holding the phone. I gently slid off my chair, landing softly on the floor. I looked up and Myrtle was sat on my chest showing off her new paperclip earrings: one on her thumb and the other on her little finger, shaking back and forth like a hyperactive Whitney Houston in miniature, except that I didn't believe she would always love me.

Roderick and Sam Maxwell came over and helped me back onto my chair.

'I'll answer your phone if you like,' said Sam.

Feeling threatened that somebody else was about to take my place, I directed my reply towards Roderick: 'Call was for Durham, mat Kistpoher's big bum at non o'clock' [the call was for Jerome, he is to meet Christopher at 1300 hrs for lunch].

'Jerome's got a big bum at one o'clock. What is he on about?' said Sam. And then he smiled at me. 'Jerome has a big bum every day!'

'No, he means Jerome is meeting his partner Christopher at one o'clock for lunch,' translated Roderick. 'Maybe "big bum" is the Big Bun sandwich shop.'

I nodded. It was a 'Lassie is trying to tell us something' moment (Lassie being the golden-haired border collie dog from the old movies).

Sadly, the by-product of episodes like this was that it scared and worried the very people I was trying to persuade that I could still do my job and deserved to be at work. Disabilities did not mix well with my work colleagues, but I would not really appreciate this or even know it until it was too late.

Seeing my difficulties, Roderick wanted to help me; later that day he worked up the courage to suggest something. 'I'm not being mean, but why don't you use your right arm to hold the phone and write the message with your left?'

'Because AAYYYYaa'm right-handed!' I blurted.

'Oh, I see! So, you can't hold the phone and write messages with the same hand. That must be awfully difficult.'

I nodded. I wanted to say more but couldn't. I wanted tell Roderick how I'd tried every option, including wedging the phone between my right shoulder and my head or neck, but the phone kept falling out as it gave me the most appalling neck and back ache. Remembering

Rachel's words, as to how people were only trying to help, I gave Roderick the benefit of the doubt, even though he'd shown that he thought disabled people couldn't think for themselves.

My keyboard abilities were also suddenly now much limited. Myrtle's aversion to manual labour meant that she wouldn't join in with typing, and so writing the simplest email took twice as long. I couldn't hold down the shift key for capital letters, as I couldn't reach that far across the keyboard with one hand. I became a slow and ponderous typist and my work on documents suffered. Now all this effort at work was causing me pain and stress, so my painkiller intake was massively increasing. People noticed, because I couldn't get the blessed things out of the blister pack without help. Suddenly my work colleagues were attempting to decide my dosage for me and giving advice. 'These are strong, should you take that many?'

In reply I wanted to say, 'Well, doctor, if you read the packaging, you'll see that it says "as and when needed" for mild to severe pain.' Of course, I said nothing, viewing my younger helpers – these 'Johnny and Jenny Two Arms' – as a potential threat to my very work existence.

As I later confided to Rachel, 'I could feel the hot breath on the back of my neck of those who want to step into my shoes, whether my feet are already in there or not.'

Underneath my stuttering voice and shaky exterior, I was thinking they would help me along and then slyly push me out of the picture. Senior management would see them as my kind benevolent work colleagues. I would get the casual brush off or the Hoover of oblivion, 'Perhaps Rod should handle this one, Adam.' With that simple sentence I would be left to one side, bypassed into the annals of work history.

Chapter 29: It's Not All Witchcraft

At first, when I came out of hospital, I did all their recommended exercises religiously; I even wore a dog collar whilst doing them, or at the very least said a prayer for luck. As I said to Rachel, 'Oh, you start off believing you will get improvement in your range of movement, and for a while you do. But, and it's a big butt (especially if you sit down a lot like I do), you soon reach the walls of your emotional bathtub and find out you've got as far as you're going to go. No matter how many times you increase or change your exercises, you will never again have the same range of movement and dexterity you had before your accident or life-changing event.'

For me there was a dawning of disappointment in front of the bathroom mirror: it was like stepping out of a dark nightclub into a brightly lit toilet where you look at yourself and say, 'What the hell am I doing?' I caught myself trying to lift and stretch Myrtle to get her to the same height as my right arm, and not even getting close. I stood there, white and sweating, like a lopsided sallow semolina. It was then I realised that I was no longer symmetrical. Dr Skate had said this would happen to me during one of the consultations, but I hadn't really clocked what it meant. Now here it was all laid out in front of me. It was horrible and I cried. I fought back, of course, and went on a health kick, doubling my exercise regimen, buying some sweat bands and a garden spade, thinking of myself as Mr Rotovator.

Maybe it was the people at work commenting on my increased painkiller dosage, but now I also started to worry about the number of tablets I took. The heart pills were non-negotiable, but the painkillers were; and so, on the advice of Dr Sharma, I duly went along to Avercombe Hospital Pain Clinic to talk about the alternatives. The Pain Clinic, thankfully, did not involve a buxom leather-clad Dutch woman pointing at Co-codamol, cracking a whip and saying, 'Stop eating too many pills, you maggot!' No, it was much more sedate and reasonable.

It was run by the balding blimp Dr Williams, who sat behind an equally huge desk setting out non-medicinal alternatives. Dr Williams gave me a notepad. 'This is your pain diary; I want you to use it like a confessional and list when your pain is at its worst; then we can think about ways to counteract it. But we aren't going to use drugs. When you feel pain, I want you to try going to a happy place, instead of immediately going for your medications.'

'Ow dew meeean?' [How do you mean?] I asked.

'Well, when you start to feel pain, think of something else much nicer, and you might feel better. It's amazing what the mind can do. Let's try it, close your eyes.'

I closed my eyes.

'Imagine you're starting to feel pain. Now, I want you to picture walking along a beach. It's a beautiful sunny day, and you have no shoes and socks on. You can hear the sounds all around: seagulls, the gentle lapping of the waves. There are lovely seaside smells too: you pass one of those outdoor market stalls which sells candyfloss, doughnuts, pasties and cakes.'

Thinking this was getting a bit too weird, I sneaked a one-eyed peek at Dr Williams. The good doctor's eyes were now closed, and he was drooling at the prospect of food. 'You see big fat golden chips that have just come out of the fryer,' he continued, 'little soldiers: bottles of salt, vinegar, mayonnaise and burger relish all standing to attention. Your wife is away at her sister's, so you can have some...'

To bring him back to earth I spoke aloud as I wrote, 'I'm not sure this is working.'

'Are you sure?' he replied. 'I'm starving. OK, well, you could try Lycra. If you buy yourself a Lycra vest from a sports shop, it will add an extra layer of support to your arm. It needs to be a snug fit, mind, like a second skin to have the full effect.'

I did try this, but only for a short time because the pain of getting the thing on and off was too much. It also did nothing for my figure – a bullock in ballet shoes came to mind. My vests – I had to have two, of course – currently reside on the failure shelf with all the other 'seemed like a good idea at the time' quick fixes which Rachel and I had been through. This included other heroic failures such as strong opiate painkillers, the abduction sling and the tens machine. The latter was a delightful little number which sent an electric current through my arm as an alternative treatment. People's reaction to wires sticking out of my shirt was that they thought they were being recorded, or that I was a potential terrorist. In those days trying to pioneer disability aids to the masses was hit and miss, mostly landing nowhere near.

Chapter 30: Becoming Mr Liability

We all have a work persona, and mine was Mr Reliability. I was not pretty, or some sort of granite-jawed hero. But I was helpful and friendly to everyone, especially at the tea point where others would share their woes. Dowdy Diane from accounts would always tell me when she was in dire straits with her husband. I would jokingly tell other people, 'I think she did their backing vocals.' Call Centre Caroline told me about the 100-plus verrucas on her feet and her attempts to get rid of them, and instead of throwing up or running away I would commiserate and console her. I was one those people that other folks confide in – whether I liked it or not.

Aside from my listening qualities, I was also diligent at work and looked out for others. I was the one who left last; the one who made sure nothing was left unlocked when everyone else had gone home. I walked around switching off people's computers if they were left on. If I'm honest, it was mainly switching off the screens. I was not obsessive! All right, I had to check if my cupboard drawer was locked at least eleven times before I left the office or my family would die, but I was not obsessive. I also started off the office Milk Club and bought milk. Sadly, our office was the crime capital of the world. You could buy a pint of milk in the morning and guarantee that it would be on eBay by the afternoon, stripped down and sold for parts as cheese. Not to mention the great milk theft of 2008. Nobody did ever find out who the culprit was. I wondered if people had missed my input whilst I was in hospital, and who had bought the milk and maintained the 'clear the desk' policy whilst I was away.

In those days, I was Mr Reliability. But after the accident happened, the 'R' and 'E' fell off and I felt I became Mr Liability. More worryingly, I noticed that after the 'falling off my chair' episodes, I was never left on my own in the office again. Jerome saw to it that there was always somebody there keeping an eye on me. However, they were never subtle; it was like some bad surveillance company which had undercover spies wearing raincoats and dark glasses, or other team members hiding behind plants. Their excuses for being there bordered on the implausible, too. For example, one of the Zombie twins, Roderick or Sam, would say that he had a sudden 'important deadline' to meet or email to send off.

'Nothing we do is ever that urgent,' I muttered under my breath.

During the second month back, I was encouraged to take part in that most tortuous of events, the Unit meeting. The new Managing Director Martin Snead stood in front of a suitably awestruck mass throng and gave one of his 'inspirational' speeches. 'It was horrendous,' I reflected to Rachel later. 'The only thing that this man could inspire was a coma. He's such an arid speaker that when he opened his mouth, sand shot out of it. The first two rows of the meeting looked like a beach in Torquay after ten minutes! He began by talking about 'our objectives' and his vision for the year ahead. I thought he was talking about needing new glasses, because he kept saying, 'I can't see further ahead than the Autumn targets.'

'Well, it sounds like you're back into the swing of things, at least, if you're able to complain about it,' said Rachel laughing.

But I left out the worst bit. There was no armrest support on my chair, so after thirty minutes of listening to this aged enlightenment my arm was nearly dropping off and I was whimpering with pain. Most unhelpfully, Myrtle started waving at everyone on the way out, and bang went my anonymity. It was a weary, windscreen wiper wave too, with my left knuckle intermittently touching my forehead. Myrtle had been doing this on trains, and whoever was on the receiving end would wave back thinking he or she was being friendly. It was only after the fourth or fifth wave that the wave recipient sensed something was wrong or questioned why this was happening. Myrtle of course was enjoying it, thinking this a member of *her* public. After the waving usually came the tremors, which were Myrtle's form of soliloquy. At the Unit meeting I desperately struggled to control Myrtle's enthusiasm; but her attention-seeking waves brought over many people who had not seen me for ages. It was like a horrible birthday party where loads of people who I used to know, and had desperately tried to avoid, came back to visit. When the event ended, they stood in groups like a series of pit stops in a conversational relay as I tried to bumble my way through the crowd.

'Adam, dear, how are you?' grated Susan Concert. I had worked with her in administration around two years ago; she was always smiley, superior and shrill. 'Heard about your fall, jolly bad luck.'

'Adam, good to see you're back, and the rest of you,' punned Frank Beard. He was one of those people who thought he was the life and soul of things. If he was, then the party was seriously ill or in dire need of a blood transfusion.

'You look terrible!' smiled Ernie Elver. Yes, it's an unusual surname and it would probably have been much better if a baby eel had turned up instead.

Just wanting out, I tried to make it through the crowd by just nodding and smiling. My voice was awful that day, and I hoped my lack of reply would shorten the encounters. But Myrtle loved it and she shook up a storm. I was exhausted, not only by Myrtle but by how suddenly interesting I supposedly was. With all the waving, I felt like some weird celebrity. To cap it all, every time I smiled at people, my head wobbled and my face grimaced like some slow deflating balloon. So not only did I look weird, but now I appeared to be shrinking too! Not that anyone said anything about it to my face. They were still British after all; belittling and criticism were still private activities amongst friends and did not involve the victim.

Unbeknownst to me, my appearance at the Unit meeting caused a minor sensation amongst my work colleagues. A couple of them were armed with pitchforks, torches and banners at the next team meeting. They gathered in their usual horseshoe, but the meeting contained no good luck for anyone. My friend Neil Black was at the dentist, not that his presence would have helped much. Now some of my previous supporters were wanting me removed from the office – right away, like a lynch mob in a horror movie driving out a monster. Their vehement attitudes just seemed stoked by fear and Darren Jones. He had decided to fully come out against my remaining in post. He was a balding belligerent braggart, who Jerome noted had been a rival for my job when it was advertised two years ago.

'Ok, I'm listening, what's the problem with Adam?' asked Peter Moores.

'He's an embarrassment,' said Darren Jones. 'I'd be too ashamed to come into work if it was me. The other sections think so too. They think we're mad to keep him.'

'So, this stems from the Unit meeting yesterday?' asked Peter.

'Yes, and other times,' said Darren. 'He falls over a lot and off his chair.'

'He's off his trolley, more like. He's popping pills like a junkie,' said Diane. 'You need to do something. He's hurting himself by being here and upsetting the rest of us.'

'Yes, well, his doctor has prescribed his medication. So, there's nothing we can do about that,' said Jerome.

'Nobody should take that many pills,' continued Diane. 'He can't eat his food properly either. He spills things on the floor. We'll have mice before long.'

'You can't understand him, he sounds drunk,' said Darren, 'and he looks terrible.'

'It's uncomfortable to see,' added Diane. 'It stops me doing my work; I can't be looking out for him all the time.'

'Diane, how many times have you had to "look out" for Adam?' asked Peter.

'Well, none,' replied Diane, 'but that doesn't mean I haven't thought or worried about it.'

'It's just too weird,' added Darren. 'We're not medical people or nursemaids. He needs to be in a mental home or something.'

'So, do I take from this that you feel that Adam should be got rid of because he's behaving oddly and doesn't look very nice?' asked Jerome.

Diane and Darren both nodded along with several others.

'Well, that could be said about any one of us,' said Peter. 'Not exactly grounds for dismissal, is it?'

'He's just worried about getting sued,' sneered Darren.

'No, I'm not. I'm worried about being fair. Can Adam still do his work?' asked Peter.

'Well yes, but he's a lot slower than he was,' said Roderick.

'Of course he is. He's only got one working arm,' said Jerome.

Peter was getting fed up with the kangaroo court. 'Well then, perhaps what we should be doing is asking what can we do to help him? Has anybody sat down and worked that out? Listen to yourselves: This is Adam Wright, for God's sake, he's been here twenty years and you lot are talking about throwing him on the scrapheap. Well, not on my watch. I don't give in to lynch mobs or vigilantes, so I suggest you stop that right now. However, I agree we can manage this better. So, Jerome and Roderick are speaking with Human Resources to get more help and advice going forward. We need to exhaust every avenue before letting people go. I'd do the same for any one of you.'

Chapter 31: Being Discovered

In between workdays, I was still attending medical appointments at the hospital. These were with Nurse Ruth, who like her colleagues had also seen the signs of Myrtle's arrival. Unfortunately, the doctors tended to dismiss her opinion because she was only a mere physiotherapist and a woman, so what could she possibly know? Turns out quite a lot. She was forever suggesting ways for me to improve my range of movement and different types of exercise. She was also incredibly good at judging whether I could do more exercise, and when I'd had enough. She always got me through to the point of conking out without ever actually letting me do so.

Then an incident happened during one of the afternoon physiotherapy sessions which was unforgettable. Myrtle decided it was the perfect time for a performance. She has always liked the idea of matinées and used them as training for the 'big theatrical starring roles', when she must perform in front of senior doctors and professors. By now it seemed to have registered with Myrtle that she was interesting. It started just after I took off my coat and sat on the bench waiting for Nurse Ruth to start the session. Suddenly, Myrtle rose and began to wave of her own accord, and then she 'karate chopped' herself against my chest, heading back to the place where she once lived in the sling. At the same time my head did its turtle impression and tried to burrow itself back into my neck. Nurse Ruth looked at Myrtle and then at me with surprise.

'How long has this been going on?' she asked curiously, still staring at my trembling and waving left arm.

'Fu-weets,' [a few weeks], I whimpered, as if I'd been discovered doing something bad.

'A few weeks?' translated Ruth.

I nodded, not looking her in the eye. I always felt guilty that the shaking was somehow my fault, but I didn't know why. I still don't.

'I thought you were shaking last week, but I didn't say anything. It seems to have got worse, more noticeable.'

I nodded again. Then I asked, 'What-is-it?'

'I'm not sure what it is. Does it hurt?'

'Yed trobs and I cry.' [Yes, it throbs and I cry].

'You cry? How long does it go on for?'

I held up two fingers.

'Two minutes?'

'Yed, till Myrtle get tired.'

'Myrtle? Who is Myrtle?'

I touched my left arm with my right and said, 'Myrtle.' I wanted to say calling my arm Myrtle seemed better than thinking of the alternative – demonic possession or madness - but I thought it impossible to explain. Then Myrtle went into a prolonged tremor for about a minute. Ruth waited for her to stop.

'OK, Adam, I'm going to take off your shoe and sock, I want you to push against my body with your foot. Do you understand?'

I nodded and duly did as I was asked. Ruth looked anxious after my bare foot touched her stomach and I pressed as hard as I could.

'I think you have Clonus,' she said, noticing my concerned stare. 'I'm going to take you to see another doctor. Clonus is not curable, but it is manageable.'

'Clonus? What the hell is Clonus?' I mused. It sounded like the name of some weird devil dwarf or a clown's bottom, but in reality it was a strange involuntary movement disorder. Back then I became a beacon for strange and weird new things, especially when nobody really knew what they were. I mused, 'Well, medics probably have to say something. Saying "I don't know" might make them appear stupid, but on the other hand, getting it wrong might make them look even more stupid.' Of course, I said nothing. It was bad enough that I didn't know what Clonus was, and now I was being told that I could have it and would possibly have to learn to live with it!

Straight after Nurse Ruth's physiotherapy session, I was taken into another part of the hospital where I had the longest ever interview with possibly the most beautiful male doctor I've ever seen. Dr Shepherd had jet black hair, china blue eyes, a resolute chin and shoulders which any expensive armchair would have killed for. We sat there for hours talking about life, Myrtle and just about everything. Well, the doctor talked and, because my speech was very bad, I wrote my answers down on an A4 pad.

'Nurse Ruth has told me a bit about you,' began Dr Shepherd. 'This is a very interesting and unusual case. Almost unique. What do you think is wrong with you?'

Dr Shepherd read and summarised my replies aloud so as he was sure he understood my answers. It made for slow but accurate progress.

' "You don't know. But you have a theory. OK, go on, I'm always ready to learn" .'

I nodded, then wrote some more and the doctor précised my notes.

' "You think your arm blames you for what has happened – your fall. OK. You think your arm goes out of

its way to try to embarrass or undermine you. You think that your arm needs to punish you for hurting it. Her motive is revenge" .'

I nodded.

'You said *"her"* are you talking about another person?'

I touched my left arm and then said slowly, 'Myrtle.'

'Myrtle? Your arm is called Myrtle?'

I nodded, then wrote some more words on the pad.

' "Well, she's obviously not a Roger or a Darren",' read Dr Shepherd flippantly. 'No, of course not. Could she be a Sharon or a Tracey?'

I got very indignant at his words and started writing furiously on the pad. Dr Shepherd continued to read aloud. Then he paused, looked up at me and said, *' "It's better than contemplating whether you're going mad, growing a brain tumour or being demonically possessed".* I see. You cannot get your head into that space without wanting to hurt yourself. *"Thinking of my arm as someone else is easier to process".* Yes, I suppose it is. But you *do know* that your arm does not have the ability to think for itself, don't you?'

I nodded.

Dr Shepherd continued. 'Your arm does not have a brain or a mind. So, you must accept that it must be you on a subconscious level who is telling, er, Myrtle what to do. It could be a form of self-loathing or self-harm.'

I nodded, then wrote the following words in the pad: *' "Not sure Myrtle would agree with you" .'*

Dr Shepherd hmm'ed at my last remark. He then asked a lot more questions, beginning with, 'When does the tremor happen most often?'

He again read my answers aloud*: ' "It's usually worse when meeting new people or being in new situations or places. It's nearly always at a time when you feel uncomfortable, uncertain, vulnerable or scared. It happens a lot at work" .'*

'When you feel scared, what do you think is going to happen?'

' "I don't really know... but I feel that whatever is going to happen will hurt me; I'm sure that I won't be able to stop it or fight back with one arm, and it will be horrible. I dread people staring at me and making fun of me because I'm different" .'

After he finished he reading thought for a moment before adding, 'Why does this upset you so much? After all, it's just words.'

'There speaks someone who was never bullied,' I mused, getting upset. Dr Shepherd read aloud as I began to rant on the pad, *' "WORDS DO HURT! There is no truth in the rhyme, 'Sticks and stones can break my bones, but words can never hurt me'. A bully wrote that! Words can be horrible! They can be absolutely vile, they can and do hurt! They are how people reject you. Try saying that little 'words can never hurt me' adage to someone who threw themselves under a train because someone said they were useless, too fat or not good enough. Their pain was entirely caused by words. I know how that feels. I was bullied as a child and made to feel different, never good enough. I was looked down upon because my family were poor. All those unkind words from the other kids were the soundtrack I grew up with. Murmurings in the background, not much in isolation, but if you add them together it becomes a sort of blanket of bullying. I hated it then and I hate it now. At least if I'd broken a bone, that might have got me some sympathy" .'*

'I'm sorry for upsetting you,' said Dr Shepherd.

Myrtle suddenly started to tremor and shake. When the tremor subsided, I wrote some more, which Dr Shepherd again read aloud. *' "After the accident, I always have to depend on somebody. I feel as though I'll never be independent again. The downside of being 'interesting' and 'unique' is that you don't fit in. I feel like a freak. There is no hiding my emotions anymore. The shaking shows my fears to everyone. Myrtle puts everything, out on display" .'*

'OK. How long do the tremors last?'

I wrote and the doctor read aloud again. *' " She tends to shake until she can't shake any more. This lasts usually about three or four minutes. The fact that she is not moving now probably means she's tired. She reaches a plateau and after her frantic activity she becomes calm" .'*

'So, it's a bit like sex. She spends herself?'

I nodded.

'Hmmm, do you tremor in your sleep?'

After contemplating this for a few seconds, I wrote, *' "I don't know. My wife Rachel said that Myrtle sits up whilst I'm half asleep and looks around. Normally Myrtle tends to lie across my chest. She has a thing for my right nipple – she guards it jealously" .'*

'Why do you always turn everything into a joke?'

' "I'm just trying to defuse the situation and gain acceptance. What happened was horrible. I think if I make people laugh, they will like me more" .'

'I suppose that must work, because I like you.'

' "I try to keep very still in bed, so I don't turn and roll over on to Myrtle. I worry about breaking my arm again. I know the chances of that are slim, but having a plastic shoulder doesn't seem as strong as what was there previously" .'

'Is the movement worse when you're at work?'

' "Yes, much worse. It's harder to control. I feel scared and vulnerable like people are looking at me and questioning my right to be here. I've had heart problems. I think that people are worried about hurting me. Two heart attacks plus a broken shoulder plus brain disorder or whatever Myrtle is equals I should not be here" .'

'How do you know?'

'I can see it in their eyes.'

'I see. Are there any things which help?'

' "Things are worse when there is no support under my elbow. It pulls downwards and aches. My arm pulls on my neck, which affects my speech. Exercise helps. I do swimming exercises without water – breaststroke arms. That calms Myrtle down. It stretches out the muscle and makes my arm stronger. It's weird doing exercises on trains and in front of the loos before meetings (well, the cubicles are too small). Exercising feels like I'm fighting back" .'

'How does this condition make you feel?'

' "Tired and fed up. The pressure to attend work and take part makes Myrtle worse. I feel like an outsider; the town weirdo; that I don't belong because I'm different. Nobody wants me to be there" .'

'Well, I'm stumped. You may be relieved to know that I don't think it's Clonus. Clonus is a neurological condition that occurs when nerve cells that control the muscles are damaged. It causes involuntary muscle contractions or spasms, usually in a rhythmic pattern. This is not happening consistently enough in your case for it to be that. We need to keep you for more tests. I would like my colleague Dr Sinclair to look at you.'

Chapter 32: Let's See What Happens If...

After my mammoth medical interrogation, I was admitted to Avercombe Hospital. It backed onto Lowell Park, which was a nice, tranquil, rural setting, full of tall trees with a river running through it. There were banks of heather outside the hospital entrance, and in the summertime there were also banks of Susan and Christine, along with some nice bloke called Carl, who was very popular. I used to walk through these lovely surroundings on my way to physiotherapy, but when you're inside the hospital as a patient, you can't take advantage of any of these things. Instead, you end up gazing forlornly out of the window and wishing you were somewhere else.

After the Dr Shepherd consultation, I was put in a private room. Rachel was at her mum's house in Swindon. We both thought the physio visit was a standard appointment and Rachel was surprised when I phoned her.

'Yam-in-nospital,' I began.

'You're in hospital! Oh God! Do you want me to come home?' asked a worried Rachel. 'No, of course you don't. It's all right, I'll speak for both of us. Interrupt only if I go wrong. You're in the best place. You know I'm supposed to be going out to the theatre with Mum and Dad tonight. But I feel like I should be with you. No, you're right, I should stay with them. I know you'll be really annoyed if I come home because we bought the tickets, so I'll stay here. You'll give the doctors my number in case they need to speak to me, won't you? OK? I'm imagining you nodding down the phone. Promise you'll give them my number and that you'll be OK!'

'Promess befime' [I promise I will be fine], was the only other thing I said.

Yes, long-married couples do develop telepathy between them. But oh, the lies we tell each other to make ourselves feel OK. I wasn't fine at all. I was quite scared. I didn't know what was going to happen, and after my mammoth medical interrogation, I really didn't think that the hospital knew either.

The next morning, the stout, short and Scottish Doctor Sinclair came into my room with a group of shiny students – two males and a female. The smiley students all wore glasses and hung upon Sinclair's every word and boy did he know it! He was showing off, gobbling up all their attention and hero worship with a spoon. I must have indicated to Sinclair that I wasn't impressed, or maybe I didn't give him the required dose of awe. Either way, I rubbed Sinclair up the wrong way. To be fair, by now I had been in four different hospitals and on the receiving end of life-changing operations, so I found it hard to get excited about the next 'expert in a white coat'. Sinclair had his revenge by treating my condition as a novelty.

'This is an interesting case,' said Sinclair in his antiseptic Scottish accent.

It quickly registered in my head that I was now a case rather than a person.

'A fifty-year-old man with a movement disorder in his left arm,' continued Dr Sinclair, as if hearing and disproving my thoughts. 'Would you stand up please, sir?'

It took me several attempts to get out of bed, but nobody helped. As I stood up Myrtle promptly awoke and stretched out like a rather wobbly windsock. Noticing the new audience, who of course were there just for her, Myrtle tremored her way into overdrive, bringing the rest of my body into her frenetic fallout. Before long I was sweating with my head tilting and body swaying.

'This is interesting,' said Male Student 1, taking Sinclair's gaze back to me and away from the pretty female student. 'Have we ruled out Clonus?'

'Quite a puzzle,' added Male Student 2. 'The movement looks... *palsied*.'

'Yes,' I agree with Gavin. It's Cerebral Palsy,' said the Female Student.

'No, no, you're all wrong. Watch what happens when he closes his eyes,' said Sinclair with a certain amount of glee. 'Would you do that please, sir?'

I did as I was bid. I thought Myrtle kept on moving, but there must have been a change in what was happening. Nobody told me what it was.

'Watch what happens if we introduce another task into the mix,' said Sinclair. 'Now would you count aloud down from twenty please, sir.'

Once again, I obliged their curiosity, although now I was starting to feel like a freak that they were playing with or gawking at in a sideshow tent. I worked out that my movement apparently stopped or slowed when I was counting, because Myrtle didn't seem to be able to multi-task. The students again took turns proffering various diagnoses on what was wrong. It was like a bad episode of *The House* TV show.

'No, no this is all psychological,' said Sinclair dismissively to their theories. 'Let's see what happens if he marches on the spot with his eyes closed?'

My face crumpled. I started to cry feeling like a performing monkey.

The Female Student Doctor, largely silent up to now, stepped out of her medical training 'tower of power', suddenly realising that I was effectively being treated like an animal for their training or amusement.

'Can we stop? This is cruel and upsetting,' she piped up, to restore the balance. 'Look what you're doing to the poor man. He's crying.'

'It's all right, I'll give him some drugs,' dismissed Sinclair, as if giving out medicine was a reward. The woman's comments and added glare gave the group a reality check and they left the room. Later a nurse came back with a prescription for the Benzodiazepine-Diazepam. I did ask the pharmacist what the drug did. She looked at me and said, 'It will make you care less about things and stop you worrying.'

On my hospital release day, I said goodbye to everyone and, feeling like a demobbed soldier, I picked up my kit bag and headed home. However, I only got as far as the lift when another doctor appeared. Myrtle took a shine to her and waved, then began shaking. The doctor looked at me with a mixture of puzzlement and concern.

'Hello,' she said, noticing the name tag still visible on my wrist.

'Hel -lo, Diave been discharged.' Myrtle then decided that she really liked this doctor and decided to go into a huge tremor to impress her.

'Of course you have,' the doctor replied. 'Could you come with me, please?' Then she led me back to the ward reception. The doctor did later apologise for thinking I had escaped rather than being released, but all the same it did show the weird attitudes of the world to disability, even amongst the supposedly well-informed.

Diazepam did soften my world and make me care less about things, but I didn't realise that the pharmacist's words would join together with such alacrity and effectively make me a liability, a 'careless' liability. I was spaced out and the world seemed very weird and echoey. I shushed a large plant as I got outside the hospital just in case it dobbed me in as an escapee. Looking back, given my new cheery stupor thanks to the Diazepam, somebody should have helped me to get home. But, because of the busy day-to-day running of the hospital, nobody did.

Chapter 33: Shifting Sands

With Rachel still away, I returned to work the next day. The Diazepam was making me feel drunk. I told Jerome and Roderick about the hospital, and both seemed genuinely pleased that I had found something that supposedly would help with my condition. Jerome and Roderick decided to see if the situation would improve before acting in response to the recent team meeting, and in particular to Peter Moores' request that they work out "how best to help Adam."

However, from my fuzzy new world, I was already questioning whether taking Diazepam was the right move. When I listened to other people speaking, I found them muffled and distant, whilst my own voice seemed to be talking in slow motion. Things were clearly not right. The effect of the Diazepam was really disconcerting. It did stop the movement to a degree, but it also sedated me and made me question my own reality. I felt 'Dazed and Confused' and other Led Zeppelin numbers. Worse still, I felt I was heading for the 'The Land of Make Believe' but without the Bucks Fizz, which translated as completely spaced out. During my Diazepam period – Pablo Picasso had a blue period, so why shouldn't I have Diazepam one? – I never quite seemed to be able to figure out what was going on. Intermittently, my face would twist into a gurn, and my tongue would loll out. Not an attractive quality unless you happen to be a bulldog. (Actually, during this time I was followed home by a greyhound called Nigel; he still writes). I now found that in the office people became blurred shapes, and for good measure they had an oozing melted quality to them like figures from Salvador Dali paintings. Their words too suddenly seemed slithery and slurred. I found conversations difficult to follow, with speeches sticking and whirring like a very old movie on even older VHS video tape [ask your parents].

The Ministry of Paperclips were proud of their progressive attitude to disability, but I was never quite sure whether they categorised me as disabled. It seemed more likely that they thought of me as weird, mad or just embarrassing. Later that day I got into a lift with the Regional Head, Dominic Bower. He was their 'shining example of success in spite of having a disability'. He was blind and he had risen to the top. The fact that he was obnoxious, rude, sexist, deluded and hideous company didn't matter. He was the person wheeled out to talk about disability whenever it was needed. He always had his guide dog with him, so his disability was easy to understand, nice and visible.

'Are you enjoying being back, Adam?' Dominic suddenly asked.

'How did you...?' I asked, rather shocked that Dominic (a) knew who I was, (b) knew my name and (c) knew I was here.

'Know it was you? The dog told me. He tells me all sorts of things.'

'OK,' I stammered.

'Make sure you ask for help. We don't want you being jam.'

I must have looked confused because the guide dog Simon said, 'J.A.M. means "Just about managing".' Then added, 'Don't worry, I think he's nuts as well.'

After a few days, Myrtle got used to, or overcame, the Diazepam and returned to her former disgraceful self. Having discovered that the drugs now 'didn't work', I had to consider other options for countering Myrtle's antics. This was where the 'caring less' part of the Diazepam really kicked in. I decided I would go public instead of keeping my conversations with Myrtle private and out of the way. I'd show the world how to deal with mental health by becoming a poster child for it.

In my mind I would break new ground by getting people to discuss topics which were previously thought off limits. Before we went into work meetings, and in full view of everybody who cared to watch, I would sit Myrtle on my lap, compose myself and ask, 'Are you going to behave today?' Myrtle would nod, then lure me in close, by raising her palm and pretending to be deaf, only to slap my face. I tried everything I could to calm Myrtle down, even going as far as rocking and burping her like a baby. Of course, people didn't know what to make of this; some walked away shaking their heads in disbelief, whilst others found it upsetting. One wag suggested my glove puppet had no clothes on; and his friend Louise, after watching Myrtle slap me, tried to defuse the situation with, 'Little cow, isn't she?' It was like music hall but with a horrific slant. Sometimes, after a meeting where Myrtle had been particularly difficult, I tried remonstrating with her, and she turned away from me like an errant child. No doubt if Myrtle had been able to speak, she would be making noises like 'No', 'Humph' and 'Shan't' and drumming her fingers into the floor. Of course, word of my 'newly even more weird' condition quickly got around the office.

I didn't realise that there was such an office grapevine. It wasn't quite Marvin Gaye – more like Marvin disappointing-and-dismal. The work grapevine already seemed to have made up its mind about me. I overheard the following conversation in the gents' toilet from two people washing their hands.

'Have you seen Adam Wright?'

'No, why?'

'He's turned into a right nutter now. His brain has gone. He talks to his arm! His arm shakes, his head wobbles and the words that come out of his mouth sound like gibberish, like he's talking backwards. It's a total transformation, it's horrible to see.'

'Do you think it's contagious?'

'I don't think so.'

'Do you know what happened to him?'

'All I know is that he fell over.'

'All this is from a fall?'

'Yes, it's amazing how your life can change in a moment. Amazing and quite sad. He should be in a hospital or at least at home.'

'Poor bugger, why is he here? People shouldn't have to watch that.'

This was the shape of things to come. The comments increased as my condition worsened. The commentary seemed universal and more audible. A week later I went to the disabled toilet after a meeting and overheard two women in the corridor discussing me and Myrtle. One of them was Dowdy Diane.

'Oh my God, did you see him in there? He was like some sort of escaped lunatic with his arm flapping around. At one point his arm sat on the top of the table and looked around like a drunken snake. It was quite scary.'

'I couldn't understand a word he was saying; his words were so badly slurred. Do you think he drinks?'

'No, but I know what you mean. His arm started conducting the meeting conversation a couple of times, using his index finger as a baton. It was weird.'

'It was horrible. I felt sorry for him.'

'I couldn't come into work if I was like that. I'd be too embarrassed. You don't bring madness into work. It upsets people.'

'He shouldn't be here. He had a heart attack a few years ago!'

'What's he still doing here then? He should be medically retired.'

'Yes, it's hard to say it, but "old Wrighty" has had his chips this time.'

Chapter 34: Fifteen Is Barbara. Who Knew?

Office gossip is like an iceberg: four-fifths of it is normally hidden from view. If you get a bad feeling from those around you, then you can bet your life there is much more to it than you know. I sensed that things were going to come to a head very soon, and I was right. The culmination of things came in a morning meeting to discuss that afternoon's board meeting about Paper Market Supplies and Sales. Technically, it was still my job to organise these meetings. However, this time around, Roderick had done most of the leg work by sending out the invitations; and that day, Jerome, Roderick and I were going to iron out the shape of it and compile the chairs brief.

Roderick and Jerome sat in their smart suits looking like my legal team. I sat there like the defendant, in jeans and a T-shirt. We all had notepads and pens - it was the height of polite officialdom.

The meeting began simply enough: it was Jerome's attempt to formally re-introduce me to my work. The idea was to ease me in gently. This sounded great in theory. Unfortunately, the reality would not quite live up to it.

'What orders and sales have we had in?' asked Jerome, looking over his designer glasses at Roderick, before giving a smiling wide-eyed aside to me: 'So much happened whilst you were away. It's been a busy time.'

I was quiet, nodding only occasionally, but Myrtle was fed up and began bouncing around like a ballet-dancing Jack Rabbit; then she started throwing things.

'We've had the UK performance figures, but we're still waiting for the big report to come in,' answered Roderick nervously, as Myrtle swished a pen past his left shoulder.

'The Overseas Report on paper exports?' nodded Jerome.

'The very same,' returned Roderick like a Victorian detective. 'They promised it last week, but nothing has arrived.' He even held up his blank notepad as proof.

'I'll have to call them again,' tutted Jerome. 'Honestly, they have such a convoluted clearance process.'

'The Gettysburg Address took a shorter time to clear,' joked Roderick.

'This place has definitely been missing you, Adam,' said Jerome. 'Your skills at persuading people to get their papers in early were always legendary.'

Jerome was trying to be kind, and I wanted to join in the conversation and say thank you and try to help. But my words got stuck, so Myrtle took her chance and pushed her way to the front of the queue. She was sick of her Diazepam diet and subsequent stupor; she wanted revenge. She rose up and stretched herself out in front of me like she was trying to give out a warning to remind me that she was *STILL* here. Then she started to tremor. No, a tremor doesn't capture it. It was a full-blown eruption that made my whole body shake uncontrollably for about five minutes. I couldn't get her to stop; I felt hapless, helpless and hopeless. And my tongue lolled out again, which gave me an added 'village idiot' quality for good measure.

'Are you OK, Adam?' Jerome asked.

I sat post-tremor, breathing like an asthmatic bulldog, covered in sweat. After about four or five attempts, I spluttered out the words, 'Yed yam OK.' The tremor gave my voice a strange vibrato quality. Things would not have been quite so bad if the meeting had remained amongst the three of us, but to add to my misery, our Head of Unit (the blue-blazered – well, it was only another meeting day – Peter Moores) entered the room.

'Who is coming to the board meeting this afternoon?' Peter asked breezily as he sat down and loosened his tie.

Myrtle, never phased by grade or authority, doubled her efforts to embarrass me by slapping me across the face and shaking even more wildly.

'The usual suspects: Duncan from London, Mortimer from Overseas and Sir Leo from the board,' said Jerome.

Wham! Myrtle slapped me again and then started to pound the table.

'Sounds like a good turnout. Are we ready, Adam?' asked Peter.

I nodded a pathetic 'Yes,' as Myrtle grabbed my notepad and threw it across the room.

'Jolly good,' said Peter as he watched the pages fly past his head.

It was like that scene in the *Carry On Up the Khyber* dinner party where the British upper class ate a formal dinner whilst a huge battle raged outside. The only difference being that the huge battle was going on inside the room, between Myrtle and myself. Everyone else chose to ignore or disregard my predicament and maintained calm in the face of adversity, the classic British stiff upper lip. As my tremor continued, I was sweating, shaking, and it was severely affecting my speech. But still Jerome just smiled and asked, 'Adam, how many copies of the board papers will we need?'

'BAAABAWWWAAAR,' I said quite loudly.

'What did he say?' said Peter.

'It sounded like "Barbara," ' said Roderick. 'Is that his wife?'

'No, his wife is called Rachel,' answered Jerome.

'BAAAAAAAAAAAABBBWWWWWWWWW ARRRRRRR,' I repeated.

'He is just making a noise now,' scoffed Roderick, half-scared, half-wondering why they were still indulging me.

'SSSSSH! He's trying to tell us something,' said Jerome. 'What is it, Adam?'

I was trying to say 'fifteen, fifteen copies of the papers'. But I ended up feeling once again like the dog Lassie in the old films, trying to tell his stupid owners that Johnny was down a well and hurt. Nobody understood me. So, I wrote it down.

'Fifteen,' said Jerome, 'Barbara means fifteen. Oh, isn't that interesting? I must tell my friend Morag that. Her husband is a doctor, you know.'

'Thanks, Adam, that's really helpful,' said a bemused Peter.

Jerome's attempt at a caring stance made it worse and made me feel patronised. This whole thing was supremely embarrassing. In fact, the only way it could have been more so was if I suddenly found out my flies were undone and my penis popped out. That aside, it was still excruciatingly awful. Myrtle had been saving up all her bile for this opportune moment. She even stuck a middle finger up at me, but I was the only one to notice that part, thankfully. Myrtle knew all my weak spots and pressure points. To her it was the perfect revenge to get back at me for what I had done to her by breaking my arm and trying to kill her with Diazepam! I was in a dreadful way, there was no disguising it, and to cap it all off my speech was nearly gone.

Unsurprisingly, they kept me out of the afternoon meeting, and later that day I was called into a room by Peter and Jerome. I tried to smile, but being sat opposite the two of them was like a scary job interview because I knew what was coming.

'We are really concerned and worried about you. We want you to go back to your GP for further advice,' began Peter. 'Jerome has compiled this rather helpful list about the symptoms of your condition. It might be useful to show it to your GP.'

I looked down at the piece of paper and hoped it said, 'Pick up dry cleaning, buy milk and bread,' but sadly it did not. Instead, it was a list of dates and times when my symptoms had been at their most acutely embarrassing. I noticed that some of the dates were when Jerome was not in the office, so obviously my instincts about my being watched were correct. If this had been *Treasure Island*, this would have been my 'Black Spot' moment when everyone pronounced judgement upon me, and I would have to walk the plank.

'Things seem especially pronounced,' explained Jerome, 'when you get excited or agitated. You sometimes talk backwards, or your words choke up inside. There also have been occasions where your words come out extremely fast in a stream of consciousness with no spaces between them. We're worried about hurting you! You will be placed on gardening leave for the time being.'

'Your job will be open for you as long as you want it,' added Peter.

'We have ordered you a taxi,' said Jerome.

Yes, it was all very British – in that they could not

deal with something and so they hid it away, moved it out of sight. On the one hand, they were probably right in that I had to go. All the same, I became remarkably upset and disgruntled at my exit. I refused their taxi. It was the one time I came close to hating them.

As I left and stood on the pavement outside the Ministry for Paperclips, I felt the piano of responsibility slide off my back and land on the concrete floor with a huge resounding crescendo chord. I didn't know it then, but I wouldn't have to worry about work for a quite a while after that.

Part 4

Chapter 35: Into the Void

The family in the train seat behind us have been on their holidays. I just heard one of them say that it's all gone too quickly and he's not looking forward to going back to work.

It might be some people's idea of heaven to be paid to be at home, and for a while after the accident I was probably amongst them, but the novelty soon wore off. At first, when I closed the door, I felt like I was shutting out the rest of the world; that gave me some satisfaction because of what had happened. But you cannot live like that for very long. You always get some form of contact with the outside world, even if it's just a letter or a pizza advert. I would never be able to fully board up the windows and stock up on tinned goods to wait for the end of the world.

Then there was Rachel's job to think of, as one of us had to earn money. I tried to put a brave face on it during the first few days, so that Rachel could go to work in peace. Of course, she would periodically check on me through the day. Whenever she rang to see how I was, I would try to sound chipper or make her laugh. One afternoon the phone rang, I saw it was her number and picked up the receiver and said quite firmly in my poshest voice, 'DON'T BE DISGUSTING!'

'Sorry,' said the poor man on the other end of the line.

'Oh God!' I replied, then quickly hung up. I laughed hysterically at my mistake, which quickly turned into tears. The caller was one of those 'Do you want to take part in a survey?' people, which does sound disgusting, so I was half right. But I still felt sorry for him, musing to myself, 'I should not have done that.'

I quickly found out there's a strange dreary isolation and loneliness to being at home. You feel forgotten. It is hardly the Disney bluebirds carrying away the calendar pages accompanied by happy music. No, it feels more like a flock of manky old pigeons and seagulls flying past and crapping on you. The silence is deafening, and you start to think you can hear your own hair growing. As the hours, then days, gently trickled by, I went through them wanting, no begging, for somebody to talk to. Yet, when they did call, I hated it. I would scream at the phone, 'WHO THE BLOODY HELL IS THAT?', 'WHAT DO YOU WANT?', or 'LEAVE ME ALONE, YOU BASTARDS!' My emotions were all over the place.

Work leaves a big hole in your life when it's gone. There's a huge social interaction to work, and that takes you outside yourself. When work is no longer there, your horizons telescope and suddenly you have nothing else to think about but yourself. Now that's fine if you have a good relationship with yourself, but if like me you *don't*, that's quite a big thing to come to terms with.

Hospital physiotherapy appointments and exercise were out too, whilst my condition was still being determined. It was quite a few days before I saw or heard from anyone. Instead, my day was filled with the sound of house noises, like water running through radiators and the numbing sound of the heating coming on. I would sit in my armchair talking to myself. 'This is it now, is it? You just sit in here all day.' Faces from the past would appear in my mind, and I would play word tennis with them, trying to fend them away. My long dead mother was one of the early ones, 'If you had stayed up north, this wouldn't have happened. You'd still be whole and not have everybody fussing over you.'

I shook my head. 'You don't know that. You died before I left.'

'Given up, have you?' said my equally dead dad. 'Never could stick to anything.'

'I did stick to things, but they weren't your things. I got a job outside farming, and I was successful. This house shows I was successful. The woman I married shows I was successful. The job I do shows I'm successful.'

'Shouldn't that be the job you did have? Before you blew it.' This was a young voice speaking, somebody from my schooldays – a cold, sneering voice.

'Paul Bindon? What the hell are you doing here? Get out of my head. This isn't 5th year metalwork. You can't bully me now. I'm not listening. You're not here.'

'But you will listen. All of your "friends" at work, all of 'em turned their backs on you, didn't they? They saw through you. They couldn't wait to be rid of bad rubbish.'

'People do like me,' I countered. 'I'm a good bloke. You're wrong. Go away. Go! GO! GO! LEAVE ME ALONE!'

Then I felt the reassuring pat of Rachel's hand on my forehead. 'It's OK, it's me. You're dreaming. It's OK now, you're safe.' She hugged me and I cried.

Aside from bad dreams, I discovered that my day now had no shape or purpose to it. When you think about it, work does quite of a lot of good for a person. It gives you a reason to get out of bed, enables you to feed and clothe yourself, and gives you a routine for eating and sleeping, and it teaches you things. When *all* that is taken away and you have no real purpose, you feel like a fish that has been dumped on the dockside but is still flapping around. That is how you will stay until somebody gives you a new stream or tank of water to swim around in again. That was largely how I saw the outside world now: a big vat of water to splash around in, which was beyond my reach. I lay marooned, flapping on the bank and rapidly drying out.

Whenever work came into my thoughts, whether it was Paul Bindon's words in the dream about nobody liking me in the office, or whether I should have been sent home, I jumped into denial. Then I would have probably jumped into any stretch of water. Each morning after Rachel left, I tilted my toothbrush at the shower curtain, ranting and raving about how unfair everything was. 'I was holding down a job despite everything, but now I've nothing because they took it away.' At the front of my mind was the idea that I would quit. 'I DON'T NEED THEM! I CAN DO IT ALONE!' But my words, those stilted, shrill shrieks, were whistles in the dark. A new reality was beginning to dawn and I was starting to ask myself, 'What happens if I don't make it? What happens if things don't change, and my future is a whole lot worse?' I had no answers, but for now it was only me asking those questions.

I was being paid sick pay by work, and Jerome would call every now and again, asking if there was anything else he could do. I would blow hot and cold and speak to him in broken stilted sentences, still quite annoyed that I had been turfed out of work. 'No parslap far three momf' [I haven't seen a payslip for three months], I said curtly.

'Sorry, what was that?'

'Paysleep,' I blurted.

'Payslip! Oh God, no, you won't have had any,' replied Jerome. 'They're all online now, and because you're at home and can't log into work, you won't see any of that. I never thought about that. I'm so sorry.' There was another pause before he added, 'I'll get payslips sent to you by HR.' Then, thankfully, the ordeal of conversation was over again for another few days.

I would occasionally surf the internet to look outward at the world. But this made me depressed, because I didn't feel part of it. Myrtle was quite a puritan about internet pornography. She had decided 'that sort of thing' wasn't appropriate, or that I was committing a mild form of adultery by attempting to look at it. It was rather like having the spirit of Mary Whitehouse temporarily take possession of your arm, because Myrtle would ache, then try to punch me during any form of a porn search. Oddly, she did allow me to look at pictures of middle-aged women in overcoats. Not sure whether that's a fetish, if so lots of people have it; probably most of them middle-aged women who need to keep warm. All in all, it was not the most convivial of atmospheres and certainly not sexy. In the end, I gave up and looked at Myrtle and exclaimed, 'OK, you win! No more porn!'

After my sorry experience with the internet and new-found celibacy, I turned full-time to daytime television. I smiled at the TV listings and my mouth watered at the memory of some of the wonderful TV detective, cowboy and comedy shows that I used to enjoy when I was a boy; they were now all being repeated on Freeview. Unfortunately, the programmes had not stood the test of time. They now seemed to ooze stupidity, stereotypes, bigotry, racism and sexism from every programme pore.

The problem was that I had grown older, maybe even wiser in the meantime, whereas the old TV programmes would always represent a specific moment in time and couldn't change. The fashions were awful too, at least that's what I told Rachel. 'All right, a few of Dennis Waterman's cheesecloth shirts were OK in *Minder*, but *just* a few of them, mind you.' On another level, thinking about the TV shows reminded me of work and really hammered home the point that I was no longer there.

There were other things that I found depressing too, like looking at my guitars and not being able to play them. I would still touch them and say, 'One day, guys.' Music was still out of the question, even if my arm would keep still enough to play a guitar; all Myrtle did before, during and after was to ache. Myrtle didn't like noise, and if I was playing the guitar, it meant that I was not focusing on her, and she thought this was somehow wrong.

Chapter 36: Testing Times Ahead

Two weeks after work sent me home, Rachel and I went to see Dr Sharma. As we entered his room, Myrtle was in full flight and Sharma stared at her.

'No more Diazepam,' I blurted.

'Sorry?' said Sharma, trying to be kind.

'He doesn't want any more Diazepam, it doesn't agree with him,' translated Rachel. She then explained what had happened. 'It made him completely vacant, work got very worried, and they sent him home. It was scary and it really upset him.'

Sharma looked disconcerted by Myrtle: she was scowling at him, fingers pressed together, raising her knuckles slowly, turning forward like an angry emu in profile. Normally Sharma looked impassive but on this occasion he looked worried, even spooked, by my condition. I mused to myself, 'If Myrtle has this effect on trained medical people, what hope is there for the rest of society? They'll think I need an exorcism or putting down.'

I stood for several minutes whilst Dr Sharma examined me and watched Myrtle's movements. As he looked at me, I said, 'Not me!'

'He says it's "not him" making his arm move,' translated Rachel.

I didn't know whether Sharma believed me, but whatever he thought, he still signed me off work for three months. And his remedy? Well, that was to send me to various hospitals for a barrage of tests. An electromyograph was one of the earliest, which was basically having an electrical current run through my arm.

'The current looks for obstacles and breaks in your nerves, and tries to locate any leftover fragments of bone,' smiled baggy-eyed Dr Bridges as he attached electrodes to my arm. 'Soldiers returning from wars overseas get a lot of electromyographs.'

Hearing that did not make it any more glamorous: it was still singularly one of the more miserable couple of hours of my life. Myrtle hated it too and was at her most uncooperative. She kept finger-walking across my chest as if trying to get away. This increased to finger-running as she saw the electromyography machine. Maybe she thought we were trying put her on death row and have her executed. On reflection, it can't really have helped that I watched the movie *Dead Man Walking* the week before, which Myrtle possibly used as her frame of reference.

As Dr Bridges went to switch on the machine, Myrtle shook and threw off her electrodes. Then she jumped off my lap and started to slap me. This was incredibly frustrating for the doctor, and I could see in his scowling eyes that he thought I was being deliberately awkward. I mused, 'What can I do to counteract Myrtle's behaviour? How do I take control? What would you have me do? Put Myrtle over my knee and spank her? Send her to bed? Don't feed her? I can't stop this. I wish I could. Sorry, I have a degree in drama, occasionally it leaks out; being an office worker never quite sated it.' But of course, I said none of this. Instead I said, 'I've an idea,' and covered Myrtle's hand with a tissue.

'You're blindfolding your hand,' said Dr Bridges. 'Now I've seen it all.'

'Yes,' I said awkwardly. 'It sounds crazy, but it might help.' Whatever the reasoning behind it, Myrtle stopped shaking and the doctor performed the test.

On the other side of things, there weren't really any more conventional suggestions from the professionals on how to manage Myrtle either. I later remarked to Rachel, 'There are no counsellors who specialise in acting as mediators between former arms and their owners, sort of "body parts reunited". Can you imagine it?'

'Indeed,' said Rachel. 'Now Myrtle, I think Adam found you punching him to be a pinch point in your relationship. I don't think he feels valued by behaviour like that. How did it make you feel? What do you mean, it was payback? No, it doesn't really work like that, does it?'

Having no work or social engagements for a while meant that I became a series of medical appointments instead of a person. I must have been terribly boring to talk to. I saw our neighbours' eyes glazing over whenever they bumped into me going out the front door. Oh, they would always ask the right things: 'How is it going, any breakthrough yet? Does anyone know what's wrong?' But they tended to nod in the wrong places whenever I replied with 'Bine pine, dank cue' [I'm fine, thank you], 'Bin dospickle' [been in hospital], 'Tots arests' [lots of tests]. I could see that without Rachel around, I may as well have been speaking Hebrew or any other type of male drink. Conversations became rather embarrassing all round. I couldn't really think of things to say, and they couldn't really understand my replies. After a few minutes in this weird conversational cul-de-sac, there would be the inevitable, 'Oh is that the time? I must go and pick the kids up,' or 'I think I left my mother on.' This would then be reinforced by the phrase, 'Where has the day gone?'

The next test was a Carpal Tunnel Syndrome examination. Isn't that more about the hand than the arm? Good point, yes of course it is. But by then I was way out of my comfort zone and past caring about whether a theory seemed outlandish or not. So, when I was referred by a nurse to have the test for Carpal Tunnel Syndrome, I didn't really mind because at least it felt like I was doing ***something*** to fight back. I turned up and sat in a chair whilst Myrtle lay prostrate with her palm upwards across a desk, looking like she should be fed grapes. Doctor Slim, a man who wore a plaid shirt and looked a little like he kept his family in a freezer, ran more electrical currents, this time through my hand. Myrtle was blasé about this, having already done the electromyography, and considered herself a stage veteran; or maybe it was because I was given a sedative beforehand, but whatever the reason, she was as good as gold.

I tried to chat with the doctor and even went as far as suggesting 'Snot me hind [it's not my hand]. Topal funnel findrome is about the tand' [Carpal Tunnel Syndrome is about the hand]. However, the doctor wasn't interested in talking and didn't return any of my conversational probes. I was obviously just the patient, and therefore stupid. After all, what could I know? Afterwards the doctor turned to me and said, 'You haven't got Carpal Tunnel Syndrome – that's to do with the hand!'

'Cold you! [Told you] Craps ayy've trackthaw funnel findrome' [Perhaps I have Blackwall Tunnel Syndrome then]. This attempted levity simply brought a blank stare; looking back, it was probably just as well the doctor didn't understand me.

But then doctors tend to forget you're a human being and not simply a puzzle to be solved. I had an MRI scan a couple of times and lay inside what seemed like a metal spaceship whilst somebody played an incredibly slow and dull drum solo for an hour. It was like being inside a bad Led Zeppelin album.

The horrible drumming noise, I found out later, was the outer tube repositioning itself to take photographs of my brain. But at the time it was horrible and claustrophobic. Rachel declared, 'You have a pretty brain. It looks like a neon-lit gateau. I saw it on the screen.' There's not a lot you can say in reply to that. The result? Well, thanks for asking, they found no abnormalities, tumours and so forth, so that was comforting to know. Though in a way, I was hoping that they would find something. Then at least I would have a cause which Rachel and I could fight against. But that was not to be, for now at least.

Chapter 37: All in The Family

We were unsure about how to tell my family that my condition had worsened. Rachel rang my niece Paula and asked her for advice. They agreed that honesty was the best policy, and Paula updated the rest of the family including her mother, Agnes. Unfortunately, rather than take Paula's word that things were OK, my oldest friend Clive wanted to see me in person. At first, I tried to keep him at bay with phone calls, but sadly this didn't work too well, as the following exchange shows.

'Hello Adam, it's Clive.'

'Nellow Crive, Tadam' [Hello Clive, it's Adam].

'How are you going on?'

'Yam OK. Yamome' [I'm OK. I'm at home].

'You're at home.'

'Nyess' [Yes].

'That's good.'

There was a pregnant pause, worthy of triplets. It wasn't unexpected: we could never find anything to talk about when I was healthy, so why should now be different?

'Been nintospickle' [I have been in hospital], I blurted out, partly from frustration but mainly from excruciating embarrassment to end the silence of the phone call which by now seemed to be placing my entire life on hold.

'Your voice is going now!' Clive reacted. Before adding with a large tot of misunderstanding, 'I'm going to ring off now because you're getting tired.'

I was left holding the phone in relief. One of us had to end the conversation. It was a mercy killing. Well, I mused, 'My being tired was as good an excuse as any.'

For some reason my family and friends always wanted to speak to me and not Rachel. Having to give health updates by phone was never ideal. It tended to rely on me answering when people asked questions, and this was hard. It was also debatable as to whether people understood me when I did reply, because my voice let me down. It did that a lot, so Clive was right to some extent.

A few days later the phone rang again, and this time Rachel answered it from the bedroom with her usual cheery 'Hello.'

'Hello Rachel, it's Clive. Were you at home yesterday?'

'No, I was at work, why do you ask?'

'Well, I rang Adam to see how he was doing; and well, he kept making animal noises at me. I'm telling you because it might be another symptom of his condition.'

Rachel bit her lip to stifle her laughter, adding, 'Should I take him to see a vet?'

'No. I really think you should have Adam looked at by a specialist.'

'OK, thank you for your advice. That's er, helpful.' And with that she put down the receiver and went to find me. I was watching TV when she announced, 'I don't know whether to hug you or strangle you. That was your friend Clive on the telephone.'

'Oh, I'm sorry,' I said.

'He's quite worried about you. I know you don't like him, but making animal noises down the phone at him makes things worse. I can't quite believe we're having this conversation.'

'Have you ever moo-ed at one of your friends?' I asked Rachel.

'No, I can't say I have,' she replied.

'I was just paying him back for some of the years of opinionated stupid advice he's given me; it was quite liberating making cow noises at him.'

'Well, Clive wants me to think about having you committed. Don't look so worried, I told him no. I know you like using your condition to flummox people, but it's not the best way to stop them from worrying about you.'

Rachel as usual was right: my 'amusing' prank had backfired. The unwanted upshot of this was that some of my family and friends came to see me. Sadly, I couldn't persuade them all to visit in one go – in one fell swoop. But then getting my family and friends to agree on anything was like herding cats, minus the cute ambivalence.

My oldest friend Clive and his charmless wife Nadine were the first to visit. Their visit was more like an inspection. They sat in our front room drinking tea, competitively devouring shortbread and judging the furnishings.

'I don't like your curtains,' declared Nadine. 'They're too dark.'

Rachel tutted quietly but said nothing. Suddenly my arm started to shake. Clive and Nadine both looked horrified: the first time they'd seen Myrtle's tumultuous tremor. Nadine even elbowed Clive in the midriff to draw attention to it.

'What do you suppose it is?' asked Nadine, nervously crossing herself.

'I don't know,' said Clive quietly to Nadine. 'His arm seems to move on its own.' Then he passed on his wisdom to me as if he was talking to a deaf person. 'YOUR ARM SEEMS TO MOVE ON ITS OWN.'

'Nyeess' [Yes], I nodded. I didn't mention that I now called my arm Myrtle. I felt that this was a step too far, which Clive and Nadine probably couldn't handle. I mused, 'They'd think I've gone t'other bit.' This was a saying my dad used to use, when he thought somebody or something was barmy.

'Perhaps there's some anaesthetic still left in his bloodstream from the operation,' said Nadine. 'That might be causing the tremor.'

'It's a tremor of some sort,' added Clive thoughtfully, 'and no mistake.'

'But it's not constant, it's like it loses power. Like it dissipates after being stirred up,' said Nadine. 'I think that's what the shaking does. As he gets tired, so his arm is still. Then the anaesthetic clots up again and the shaking re-starts. It's like a self-fulfilling prophecy!'

'My wife is a care assistant, you know,' said Clive proudly.

'Really? Oh God!' said Rachel before quickly correcting herself. 'I mean, oh good! We must mention that to the hospital. Excuse me, I have to pop to the toilet.'

I could see from Rachel's shoulders moving up and down as she left the room that she was laughing at Nadine's absurd suggestion.

'She's been a saint, hasn't she?' said Nadine. 'But maybe you need a medically trained person to help you. I'm available if you need me.'

"We're fine, thanks!' I interrupted firmly. 'Yes, she's an angel. I'm very lucky.'

Naturally, Rachel and I baulked at Nadine and Clive's assessment and offer of help, but not aloud – life's too short. After all, they were trying to help, even if their input had all the sensitivity of a bulldozer trying to peel a potato.

We had another similar visit from Nadine and Clive later in the year. No more shortbreads lost their lives, but this time there was a side order of rudeness thrown in.

'Who bought this? I don't like this,' said Nadine, picking up a wooden giraffe from the front room mantelpiece.

'It's from Cape Verde. We went there on holiday a couple of years ago,' answered Rachel. 'Adam likes giraffes, so I put it out on display again.'

'Cape Verde? Isn't that where Batman lives?' asked Nadine.

'No, doesn't he live in Gotham City?' asked a bemused Rachel.

'I thought he lived in Cape Verde. Perhaps that's where he buys his clothes.'

'Haven't they found out what's wrong with you yet?' Clive declared after murdering a fourth Jaffa cake.

I shook my head.

'I thought they would have figured it out by now,' added Nadine. 'You want to have a word, tell them to pull their finger out. It's been ten months now.'

'When they do fix it, they need to get it right,' said Clive. 'When I broke my foot, it took not one, not two but three operations, and it's still not right. It aches in the cold weather and squeaks in hot weather.'

'He ticks when he walks,' said Nadine. 'It's like walking with a clock. Do you speak with the doctors, Rachel? Perhaps you could tell them to hurry up. Mrs Glennister's quite posh – she got her husband prioritised when he broke his arm.'

'Yes, but Jack Glennister's in the golf club and a Mason,' clarified Clive.

'Did you mention our theory about the anaesthetic?' asked Nadine.

'Yes, we did,' said Rachel, 'but they think it's a brain disorder.'

'Oh well, I suppose they know what they're doing,' said Clive.

'Perhaps they could give you a blood test to be sure?' added Nadine.

'They already have; the doctor has categorically ruled out the possibility of any leftover anaesthetic in his bloodstream,' said Rachel, quietly but firmly drowning their crackpot theory in a bucket of realism.

Chapter 38: The Pit and the Person

My life was on hold, and I lay around the house for days on end. I just wore my dressing gown, not even bothering to get dressed. I said to Myrtle, 'This is what you end up doing when you can't work or play the guitar. This is deep blues.'

I decided the next best thing was to watch music, if I could not play it. I started to watch my music DVD collection: all those DVDs I got for Christmas but never got around to seeing. I got through about two before being able to say, 'I've been there and done that.' I quickly realised that rich rock stars telling their life stories and complaining constantly about the cruel hand life has dealt them is a bit whiney and twattish.

Like in the early days, before going to work Rachel left me some ready-made sandwich lunches, sorted out painkillers and a wheat bag for me to warm up in the microwave. I used to place the hot wheat bag on my neck when the pain got too much. But technology and I have never been a good combination. I must have left it in the microwave too long, because as I explained to Rachel the moment she arrived home, 'The bloody wheat bag thing burst into flames!'

'What?' said Rachel, 'How the hell did you do that?'

'I followed your instructions to the letter,' I moaned to Rachel as she cleaned up the panful of water I'd thrown into the microwave to put out the flames. We threw the microwave out, as we couldn't get rid of the smell. None of this helped my self-confidence. I was starting to believe I was useless and hopeless. I became sullen and withdrawn, and the words of the school bully Paul Bindon would once more echo in my head: 'Useless, totally bloody crap at everything. You shouldn't live near people.' Paul Bindon had been my nemesis at school, driving me to self-harm and worse – a suicide attempt. I wound up seeing a psychiatrist and Bindon was expelled from school. Though why Bindon was coming back into my thoughts now, I didn't know; but the very mention of his name made me feel worthless, scared and hopeless.

I fought back - well sort of. I tried self-convincement: sitting in my chair, beating cushions and repeating the words, 'I'll be back, you'll see. 'YOU'LL SEE! YOU WILL ALL SEE,' like some terrible movie cliché. 'I can cope.'

Then Bindon's weasely voice chimed back with, 'No you can't. You were useless at school, and you're just the same now. Pathetic and weak. Real men don't cry, and they certainly don't go around whingeing and whining because they've fallen over. They fight back. You're just a Wright cry baby. Wright cry baby!'

I never mentioned Bindon's continual appearance in my head to Rachel; I thought she might think me mad. But I was more worried that Bindon was right in suggesting I was useless, and mentioning his existence to somebody else would somehow legitimise this. My protests about coming back were all bravado and hot air. I didn't have any kind of plan of what to do. Being sent home from work had hit me hard, but the lack of a proper answer to what was wrong with me certainly hit me a lot harder. I thought the world had turned its back on me and didn't want to know.

The line between night and day became blurred, and I started to live in a weird twilight. I looked in the mirror in the morning and saw this knackered old twerp standing there. He didn't even stand upright, he seemed hunched and fearful, and I wanted him to go away. But he could not go anywhere because this knackered old twerp was me. Aside from the body beautiful becoming the body beastly, there were other things which fell foul in my life. Jerome had stopped phoning for the moment, after I had been overly sharp with him in one of our pointless catch-ups. I had made it known via Rachel that I didn't want to speak to him for the time being. Even with this perfunctory instruction, I still got emails from him; and annoyingly Jerome was still trying to be breezy. On the other hand, I was glad we didn't have to talk, because my voice was terrible.

My stupendous list of things to do – write a novel, become a guitar virtuoso, find a new job, sleep with the modern-day equivalent of Natalie Wood – was looking sad too, as I was not doing any of it. I was spiralling downwards. My mood was much blacker, and anything which required any effort seemed virtually impossible. I began to question what my life was for and whether it had ever amounted to very much. I would lie awake for ages hoping and praying for sleep. But most of all I wanted to turn the clock back to the snowy day in January and not fall over.

And yes, I contemplated ending it all. This was not some grandiose protest against what my life had become to the people at work, Paul Bindon or anybody else I could shine the beacon of blame upon. No, I was just genuinely exhausted and pig sick of it all: my arm, the lack of cure, being stuck in limbo, the wallpaper in the bedroom – well, it was silver stripes, which when you're tired can look like a cage. All this contributed to my rather half-hearted suicide attempt.

I decided that I would end it all by sitting in a wardrobe for two days. Well, all the dressing table shelves were full.

Rachel was away, visiting her sister. Sitting in a fitted wardrobe and waiting to die was not the first thing on my list, but it was one of the things that happened. In my befuddled state of mind, it seemed quite the Bohemian way out. I always wanted to die in the most comfortable way possible, and for this occasion I even placed a cushion inside the wardrobe. My idea was simply to sit in there for two days and not take any heart medication in the hope that I died. Not the most cunning plan, but I had briefly examined lots of other ways of dying.

Hanging seemed far too painful. I also mused to Myrtle that 'Nothing will take my weight'. I had become a bit of a porker since Myrtle had arrived. I thought about attaching a noose to a light fitting, but was worried about waking up amidst a pile of plaster. I was always a tidy suicidalist and wanted an ending that affected nobody else. Besides being a gruesome ending, hanging yourself, I had read, gives you a huge erection. The thought of dying and being found with a huge erection sounded terribly embarrassing, not to mention rather wasteful.

I thought about drowning myself too, but could not actually get into the bath unaided, which made that form of suicide a bit of a non-starter because somebody else would have to be there. I thought about slipping a pizza delivery person a few extra quid to help me into the bath, and then I would ask them to leave. But this wouldn't work because they might want to stay to help me back out of the bath again. Besides, they might steal something when I was dead. In the bath I would need to be naked, and before I knew it I was back to the whole embarrassing erection thing. Drowning yourself in a shower seemed impossible.

Then there was electrocution: this one quickly seemed impractical because I was worried about hurting Rachel when she returned. What if I fused the lights? 'Well,' I mused, 'Rachel might come home in the dark, fall and hurt herself. There would be nobody there to help her because I would be dead.' No, that was no good. Wrist slashing, no it would make such a mess. Besides, it would probably hurt, and I was a total coward when it came to pain.

'Drug overdose, no, what if I vomited?' I said to Myrtle. 'We have a nice, fitted wardrobe and that would make it difficult to clean. No matter how you try, you can't get rid of the smell. Not that I have vomited in many wardrobes. Besides, I hate being sick, vomiting always hurts my throat. What was that you said, Myrtle? 'Oh, you poor little manic depressive, you!' 'Thank you.'

So, the 'wardrobe of death' was the best thing I could come up with. I would sit there, wait till my heart meds wore off, then conk out or starve to death. I sat waiting, resigned to my fate. I looked around at the grain of the wood on the inside of the wardrobe and thought how beautiful it looked with its knots and subtle shades of brown and lighter brown. I wrote a rather pithy note. I thanked everyone for being there, 'including my friends and enemies'; balance was very important in suicide notes. I even wrote one paragraph as a series of the letter R's prefacing it with 'This paragraph is dedicated to the letter R, which has always been sadly underrated in my opinion.' Having a lot of rrrrrrrr's together also sounded like I was growling or angry. Yes, the letter was self-indulgent, but I hoped it was not dull. I wanted to try and make whoever found me smile. Well, it's a tough enough job being a police officer as it is, so there's no need to be miserable about taking your own life.

I read a bit of the *Bible* aloud and I began talking to Myrtle. 'I suppose you're happy now you've exacted your pound of flesh; now that everyone thinks I'm completely bloody nuts because I have no control over my own body. How much more of the limelight do you want?'

Myrtle seemed subdued because she was getting what she wanted; she even stroked my cheek and then patted me as if to say, 'Yes, you know you're doing the right thing. You had your go and messed it up; it's my turn now.'

It was quite a poignant moment, and Myrtle recognised this by lying across my breastplate as if I was nursing a child. I lay there for what seemed like hours in silence, reflecting that this was the end. 'What about Rachel?' I mused. 'She'll come home to a dead husband.' No, it wasn't very nice, but I was helping her in the longer term. In the rat race, I was a dead weight, a passenger. Rachel, well she was young and pretty and somebody would snap her up very quickly. I just hoped I would be a nice memory, one of those people included when the priest says 'Let's take a moment to remember those not here' during his lookback at the year during midnight mass. Yes, that could be me, and probably my best ever career move. Being dead – you didn't have to do ANYTHING, and you always came out ahead; sounded just like my kind of job.

But the human body lets you down during those moments of poignancy, and you end up needing the toilet. I climbed out of the wardrobe, banging my head on the door. Then I saw the clock on the wall. I'd got in the wardrobe at 12.00 and now it was 12.27. So, my big brave two-day suicide attempt had lasted all of 27 minutes. Pathetic!

Maybe Paul Bindon was right: I couldn't do anything right. No, that wasn't it, as any average psychiatrist would probably say that the interference of my bladder meant that I didn't want to do myself in after all. But then again, no average psychiatrist has ever probably been turfed out of work with a broken shoulder or banged his head on a wardrobe door after a suicide attempt. God, it hurt!

Chapter 39: The Day Work Came Home

I never mentioned my rather pathetic suicide attempt to Rachel, just in case she had me committed. All right, that's not the real reason, I was actually worried in case she laughed! It seemed pitiful that I couldn't even end my own life, and if you also added in things like my ineptitude with the microwave and other technologies, it seemed like a big deal.

'God, I'm depressed,' I tutted after Rachel had gone to work. Paul Bindon, the school bully, had disappeared from my thoughts and dreams, which was some good news. But life still went on even if I didn't feel or want much part of it.

Later that week, somewhat surprisingly, work came to visit me as I could not go to them. I want to say the guilt hung around the room like thick Victorian fog, but it was actually mixed in with a bit of relief and humour. There were three of them when they arrived: two of my bosses, former and current, Jerome King and Jim Sampson, and our Head of Unit, Peter Moores, in a brown suit (apparently grey was 'too serious' and blue 'too everyday'). They platooned into the front room and sat in a smiley awkward silence, where words came out in short spurts like somebody accidentally sitting on top of a tube of conversational toothpaste. I tried to remain business like and calm under pressure, while Rachel hovered. There was no room for sentiment or emotion here, at least that's what I told myself; although my voice was so bad that nobody could really tell what mood I was going for.

'When we first arrived, we heard children and thought we were at the wrong house,' said Jim smiling.

'We thought Adam doesn't have children,' added Jerome.

'Nest daw,' I answered awkwardly in nervous word mumbles and jumbles.

'He means next door,' translated Rachel after Peter's blank look. 'You get used to it. I suppose it's easier for me, after all, we've been together since 1542.'

'I hope you don't mind us coming; we felt it was the best thing to do,' added Peter. 'Much better than emails. We're so sorry about what has happened.'

'Is there any progress yet?' asked Jim. 'Any sign of treatment?'

I shook my head and looked at the floor. The question upset me, because somehow I felt it was my fault that they'd not found what was wrong with me, or a cure.

Rachel took over the conversation once more. 'We're going to see the neurology department in the new year in Avercombe Hospital. Our GP has referred Adam to somebody called Professor Khan.'

'It's zoological,' I blurted out.

Everyone laughed at my faux pas, which reduced the tension.

'I think you mean neurological, my darling,' corrected Rachel. 'We couldn't get an appointment before Christmas, no matter how hard we tried.'

After tea I took them upstairs while they looked at my guitars and made pleasant conversation. I even managed to pick out a tune on the Delilah the Taylor guitar.

'Is that *Brain Damage* by Pink Floyd?' asked Peter.

I nodded, albeit without realising the irony. Thankfully Jerome and Jim laughed.

'They were nice,' said Rachel after they'd gone. 'Maybe they felt guilty. After all, you being sent home from work was kind of their fault.'

'Maybe they were worried in case we sue,' I replied. 'I suppose I should be glad they didn't want to fire me. I'm very tired. This takes a lot out of me.'

'I know. You did well. At least they apologised. That's the weird thing about being English, isn't it? We're always so grateful when somebody apologises. You can drive a steamroller through my life, but if you apologise, that makes it all OK.'

There was a second meeting in the New Year when a desperately earnest representative from Human Resources (appropriately called Ernest) came to our house along with Jerome. I bought some cream cakes as a peace offering/ice breaker, but weirdly they would not accept them; maybe just in case it was considered a bribe or something. They tried to remain dispassionate and uninvolved, which came across as rather cold and distant, like communicating through Perspex.

It was at this meeting that I realised how much Jerome's prowess as a manager mattered to him. He was a control freak, and most of those around him let him get away with it because it was too much of a hassle not to. He would spend ages trying to do things or get things done properly. To Jerome the list of things he'd done about something equated to how much he cared about it.

'Flexible working policy has been changed to accommodate you working from home in the future,' began Jerome. 'So, you're having an influence on work without even being there. Since we last talked, and you mentioned your mortgage payments, I want you to know that we're looking into whether you qualify for something called Disability Payment. This will mean that you don't have to worry about the time limit on your return.'

'Tank cue,' I replied, bursting into tears. This was immensely kind. So much for my own remaining cool and professional.

Chapter 40: Out of The Mouths of Babes and Angels

Before I could see Professor Khan and continue the search for what was wrong with me, I had to get Christmas out of the way. My father-in-law Roger came over and whisked both Rachel and me over to Swindon in his large Range Rover. Rachel thought a change of scenery might do me some good. I, of course, was dreading being on display with so many others in the house, but from the moment I arrived everybody was very kind. They tried to make it like Christmases of old, with lots of singing and eating. Rachel brought along a guitar (Janey the Baby Taylor), which our brother-in-law Philip played. It was great and made me feel normal again. I almost forgot about being disabled, the outside world, work, treatment programmes, and so did everybody else.

So much so that my nephew Tim nearly pulled my arm off. Oh, he didn't mean to. He was five at the time and didn't really understand disability. We were sitting on the heavily grey-carpeted floor of Rachel's mother's house. We were playing the board game Enchanted Forest with our nephew and niece, Tim and Antonia.

'I want to play football in the garden with Uncle Adam,' declared Tim.

'After this game is over, darling,' said Rachel.

That didn't really cut it for Tim. He grabbed Myrtle by her elbow and tried to pull me up to take me outside. For a 5-year-old, he had a good grip and was quite strong. Myrtle recoiled in horror as she felt his sharp determined tug, then recoiled as if to say, 'Well really, how dare you?'

'Play football with me in the garden,' repeated Tim. Disability and difference were totally unfamiliar concepts to him. He just wanted to play football, like he'd done in the summer of last year, and was not sure why he couldn't now.

'Hold on, Timmy', laughed Rachel, before adding, 'don't break your uncle's arm.' The pain became too much for me and my eyes were watering.

'I made you cry,' said Tim. 'I'm sorry.' He seemed genuinely shocked that he had hurt me, so I gave him a hug and kissed his cheek to say I was all right.

'That's OK, he's a bit delicate,' Rachel replied.

'How is your arm?' asked Rachel later in bed.

'Sore,' I said. 'Tim has a good grip and a strong pull for a little lad.'

'But that's kind of it, he just saw you. He didn't see your disability. That's nice. Kids don't judge or notice difference in people until it's pointed out to them. It's the reaction of others which dictates how they will react.'

'Yes, but when they do notice difference, they can be horrible. One day when I walked through the park and Myrtle was shaking, some kids threw sweets at me.'

'Oh, I'm not saying that all children are wonderful, but before the wisdom of adults and parents gets in the way, and they point out a difference, kids are curious and fairly accepting of whatever is put in front of them. They don't have this yardstick thing that we call normal. We should try to make more of that.'

Chapter 41: The Dawning of Dystonia

My main life lesson from my fall so far was that the bedrock of my life is located way below where I thought it was. When the removal men have been in and packed away all your self-esteem, confidence and pride, you are left with nothing. You must look for the things that define your personality, and when you do, you are suddenly left with no option but to contemplate other ways of living or being. This is when the stuff you are made of – your bedrock – kicks in.

Most of us don't ever have to contemplate making extreme changes, or face questions about how we'll exist, live, or pay for things if the worst happens. We are happily cocooned in our own little world and seldom have to deal with it all disappearing or changing. In terms of practicalities, the meeting with Jerome had helped to ease the financial side and gave me time to recuperate. But the health issues persisted, and after the family Christmas had gone and the mind-numbing normality returned, then I resumed the new visit programme which Dr Sharma had assembled.

First I pitched up at Neurology in Avercombe Hospital and met the distinguished and legendary Professor Khan. I had to admit that whenever I had previously heard Khan's name, it was said in reverential hushed tones. So part of me was looking forward to meeting this man, even it was just out of curiosity to see if the reality lived up to the fable. I was rather expecting some sort of epic muscular hero type, always on his mobile, who had the catchphrase, 'Get an MRI, Yasmine.'

On first impression, I felt rather let down: he was a little bearded bloke in a dark blue Armani suit standing knee-high to his assistant, Susan, who was rather dowdy. But, of course, size is not what counts amongst neurologists. I liked mine nimble, small and slim. Khan was the first person to proffer an explanation as to what was happening to me and to mention something called Dystonia.

'Your brain has rewired itself after the shock of the fall,' said Khan. 'Dystonia, yes it does sound like a place, and sometimes it is. It's the place where your brain is currently stuck. It's like a song on repeat. Your brain is taking you back to the accident and just before, because it cannot cope. It cannot process the change between then and now. Your body has undergone major trauma. It's a bit like shellshock for soldiers. You're stuck and it's horrible and we need to find a way past it.'

All these things rang true with me more or less straight away. I wanted to say thank you, you're the first one to really have a handle on my situation. But all I could really utter was 'Gats reet' [That's right].

'What's the treatment for this?' asked Rachel excitedly, 'and do we have timetable for recovery? What are the key milestones in his recovery plan? How can we tell whether this is working or not? Will he make a full recovery?' Rachel was a civil servant of many years' standing, as you can probably tell from her questions.

'Wow, that's a lot of questions. I can't give you specific answers to any of them,' ventured Khan cautiously. 'But I do think speech therapy and Cognitive Behavioural Therapy (CBT) will almost certainly help.'

Rachel and I looked at each other and smiled, almost wanting to cry and say 'Khan, you're brilliant. Where have you been all our lives? Why couldn't we have been referred to you a year ago?' Of course, we didn't. We simply had a quiet moment of recognition that we might finally have met somebody who could help our situation, and we were glad that Khan was on the case.

Khan turned to his assistant Susan and said, 'Get him appointments with Duncan and Marcia.' Then he turned to me, looked into my eyes and after a few seconds said, 'It could be that we don't cure this. We may just make you come to accept it. You need to face this as a possibility. You should be prepared for that. We will almost certainly improve things, but you may *never fully* lose the Dystonia.'

'OK,' I nodded and tried to make out that I was following the logic.

'Don't worry, we're realistic,' replied Rachel. 'We're not expecting miracles. We've had a year of not knowing anything. So, Adam and I are grateful for whatever you can do. Just being here today and speaking to somebody who has half an idea of what we've been through has really helped.'

'There are other types of treatment which could help the situation and help stop the tremor,' said Khan, looking at my shaking arm. 'You could have a Botox injection in your left arm to paralyse the muscle. It will stop the movement of your arm...' he paused for effect, 'but you might not be able to do anything else. I have a clinic at the Prince Regent hospital on Tuesdays. What do you think?'

I couldn't believe what I was hearing; after all this time we were finally talking in the realms of cures and stopping the shaking. Myrtle perked up at the mention of the word Botox. She sat up and looked around like one of the Loch Ness Monster's long-lost grandchildren. Myrtle thought it would help her beat the ageing process, but then she had always seen herself as a sort of "arm world" version of Peter Pan. I didn't fully register the second part of Khan's sentence about not being able to do anything else if I had the injection, thankfully Rachel did.

'Could the Botox paralyse the rest of his arm?' asked Rachel. She had listened very carefully to everything Khan said, and although his words sounded like there was an opportunity for me to become normal again, Rachel's question was like a bucket of cold-water reality check.

'It's possible there may be other parts which are be affected, yes,' said Khan.

My joy turned to horror, because the potential limitations such as no more guitar playing now fully dawned on me. Rachel immediately looked at Khan and said, 'This is something we need to think about and discuss.'

'OK, fine. You'll see me in a month here, anyway, so let me know what you think.'

Rachel and I left Professor Khan with hope for the future. This was something we had not had in quite a while, and it felt good. We hugged each other for a long time when we got home. It was one of those moments when you feel the embrace of another person reach inside you to something deeper. Rachel and I have an unbreakable bond. She has seen me at my very worst and not been completely repulsed by it. For me she is the beacon of light that helped me through it. That is something special if you can achieve it with your partner. Though I don't recommend having an accident and nearly losing your left arm to discover it.

Chapter 42: Speech Therapy

The 'Marcia' that Professor Khan mentioned was Marcia Makepiece. She was a speech therapist at the Prince Regent Hospital. Duncan was Dr Duncan Madden, an aptly named consultant neuropsychiatrist at Owsley Hospital just across the road.

The two of them were amongst the bunch of heroes who consulted on my case. It was in speech therapy where I found my biggest breakthrough. I got an appointment to see Marcia Makepiece quickly. Before I knew it, I sat nervously in the neuroscience wing at the Prince Regent hospital with Myrtle going into orbit. It all helped announce my arrival at reception. A combination of nervousness and excitement meant it took me quite a few attempts to get my words out to the receptionist, and eventually I gave up and just showed her my appointment letter.

The receptionist smiled and told me to go and sit down. Then I saw her on the telephone telling somebody I had arrived. The waiting room was quite noisy, and *Countdown* (a sort of TV Scrabble and numbers quiz show) was playing on the TV in the background. It's strange how that programme has followed me at my appointments. I mused to Myrtle, 'They must wait for me to arrive in some places and then switch it on.'

Inside the waiting room, the people were a real mixture. There were some golden oldies shuffling and softly scraping their slippered feet across the shiny floor. There were quite a few young children too, playing near the water dispenser. Mothers were using different tactics to quieten them: one shone a torch onto the floor asking, 'Can you see the light?' Another long-suffering mum screamed at her son peeing in the toy box, 'MARLON, YOU ARE GROUNDED TILL 2028!'

Disregarding Marlon's inability to play outside until he was 27, into this strange melee came marching Marcia Makepiece. She was a short, blue-uniformed, bustling lady with her red hair neatly trimmed into a bob. She stood in the middle of the double doors and declared, 'I'm looking for a Mr Wright.'

'Well, aren't we all, dear,' said a nearby overcoated old lady in response.

I had not heard Marcia calling, but Myrtle waved, and Marcia came over to collect us.

'From the description I have, you are Mr Wright,' said Marcia when her eyes met mine. I nodded, as if ashamed, yet at the same time slightly relieved at being recognised. I don't remember saying much to Marcia to start with as we were walking towards her room. However, Myrtle decided she liked Marcia immediately and so stuck herself out in front of me and started flapping around as if trying to converse with an old colleague. Occasionally Myrtle would look back at me as if to put her tongue out and say, 'Look where I am.' But then she always did have delusions of grandeur. I was worried about being able to say anything coherent, because my speech was very bad by this point. But I need not have worried, Marcia talked enough for both of us.

'Imran told me all about you,' she began.

I looked blank.

'Professor Khan's first name is Imran,' she explained, 'like the cricketer, but he isn't sporty, though he doesn't discourage people from thinking he might be.'

As she went on and on, she sounded like the poshest woman in the world, making King Charles III sound like a stallholder on Stepney Market.

Eventually we found Marcia's room. It was just like her, slightly dishevelled but full of knowledge and ideas. Books, files and papers stacked all about the place were seemingly ready to burst with enthusiasm at any moment. Marcia beckoned me to sit down, and then sat opposite and stared me full in the face. Myrtle chose to perch on the table, joining in staring at me as well.

'Your arm likes to be in charge then,' smiled Marcia.

'Marm is Myrtle' [My arm is called Myrtle], I stumbled.

'I've heard. So, this is the famous Myrtle? This is a first for me.'

I wanted to ask, 'How do you know?' but saw in my file that one of the previous doctors had noted Myrtle's name. Myrtle like a star-struck schoolgirl wondered, 'What did they say about me?' but I was determined not to go there.

'IyyammAdddaaaamm' [I am Adam], I nodded to her perceptive comment about Myrtle liking being in charge.

One of the most horrible side effects of Dystonia was that my words came out as just a noise, and I was the only one who could understand me fully. Things became especially bad when I was around people I had never met before. Even the simplest phrases could turn into the most unintelligible rubbish, with words running into each other or even sometimes coming out backwards. Saying my name usually ended up as 'Yam Edam WREET'. Yes, it was a rather cheesy means of introduction.

But Marcia was not fazed by any of it. 'Don't talk, please,' she said. 'I'm going to pour you a nice big glass of water which I want you to try and drink as quickly as possible. In one swig if you can.'

I raised the glass to my lips and Marcia pulled out a stopwatch and began to time me. It took several attempts to drink the water, and I was gasping for breath afterwards. Then she looked at me and said, 'It's OK, have a break to get your breath. I don't want you to drown.'

Then Marcia pulled out a satsuma from her desk drawer and said, 'Now I want you to eat this piece of orange.' Whilst I put the orange in my mouth, she watched and again timed how long it took me to swallow it.

'All gone?' she asked when I had stopped chewing.

I opened my mouth and showed her it was empty. It was odd how quickly I became under the spell and direction of this woman. Then Marcia gave me a newspaper article.

'I want you to read aloud from this. It's rather boring, I'm afraid, about the demise of the high street because of the internet.'

I began reading aloud 'DDerrearreraillllwwaystat-tttions in all mayyjor UKK towwwnnes...' I fell down halfway through the first sentence having not taken a breath.

'Interesting,' said Marcia. 'It's OK, you can stop reading. By your lack of speed in drinking the water and eating the orange, I didn't think you would get that far. So you did better than I thought you would. Well done!'

I sat in my chair breathless and a little bemused by what was going on.

'I have a theory as to what's wrong,' said Marcia. 'Your brain is not telling your mouth when to breathe. You seem to run out of puff before you get anywhere.'

Marcia then pointed at the newspaper article again. 'Now I want you to try reading again. But this time I want you to take a deep breath before you start, then every time you encounter any punctuation: full stops, colons, commas, question marks etc. I want you to breathe in or breathe out. Do you understand?'

I nodded, then started to read the article again. 'There are railway stations in all of the major UK towns and cities. These include Birmingham, Brighton, Bristol, Cardiff, Derby, Edinburgh, Glasgow, Leeds, Leicester, Liverpool, London, Manchester, Nottingham, Newcastle, and Sheffield. Most cities now also have a tube or tram network which connects people to their shopping centres. Food halls and pedestrianised centres have improved the shopping experience, but now this is all under threat from the internet...' I was startled by the improvement. I could understand and hear what I was saying much more clearly, and more importantly, so could Marcia!

'Fabulous,' said Marcia.

'Thank you,' I replied, my new-found confidence and ability to talk made me cry. But my joy was short-lived when I got handed my homework. I was asked to read at least one newspaper article aloud every day for the next week until we saw each other again the following week.

On my way home, Marcia's words echoed around my head. 'Your brain is not telling your mouth when to breathe.' My first thought was 'Oh my God, Myrtle has been talking to it, and clearly she wants to kill me!' I looked at Myrtle on the way home and she didn't deny it. She even looked a little sheepish. What was that, how? Well, she pulled the sleeve of my jumper tightly around herself as if wearing a fleece, and then looked back at me, shrugging a French gesture as if to say, 'Who, moi?'

When I got home, I told Rachel of my experience with Marcia. 'I never stopped to question just what on earth she was asking me to do: eating oranges and drinking water. She was just so upbeat that I accepted everything she said, and I felt that I could completely trust her.'

'Oh, it's because she's a posh bird,' said Rachel. 'That's what it is.'

'They know who Myrtle is; I saw her name in my file.'

'Well, I suppose it's fairly small scale in the scheme of things, and you're not a danger to yourself or others by giving your arm a name.'

'Oh thanks.'

There was a lot of truth in what Rachel said: I have always had a thing about posh women in authority. Most of my TV crushes were newscasters; and yes, OK, she was probably right that naming my arm Myrtle was not hurting anyone. After I had finished telling Rachel about Marcia, I read aloud to Rachel for what seemed like ages, and we both cried and hugged each other. I was made to feel like I was a new television or radio reporter. She would switch me on by asking me to read aloud all sorts of things: newspapers, passages from books, even my own poems just for the sake of her hearing me speak more clearly. I tried to stop after my tenth recital: she'd asked me to read the instructions for our new iron, but I protested I was tired.

'No, you're not!' she countered. 'You have a lovely voice and I've missed it. I want to hear it, loud and proud!'

Chapter 43: Finding Neuro

'How did your neuropsychiatry appointment go today?' asked Rachel.

'It was OK,' I replied, 'when eventually I found it. Neuropsychiatry is on a similar level of conversational fame as mental health. It seems to be a phrase that no one has heard of at the Prince Regent Hospital.'

'How weird,' said Rachel, not realising the irony of her words.

'Saying the words "neurology" and "psychiatry" in isolation is fine. People even smile and say, "Oh yes it's over there," even pointing as they answer. But putting the two words together somehow places a blanket over them and makes them disappear. "Hello, could you tell me the way to Neuropsychiatry, please?" I asked several people, when all the corridors and had taken on a "sameness" which would confuse a maze designer. Then I was confronted with a confused blank look, as though I'd asked them to divide 977 by 15. Myrtle didn't help; she would wave like an attention-seeking, naked glove puppet. "It's OK," I tried to reassure them. "The appointment is for Myrtle. She's my left arm, that's why she's so interested".'

'Hmm, maybe not your best move.'

'Well, two people stroked Myrtle as if she was some sort of hairless Chihuahua. Maybe I shouldn't have sung the question, "Do you know the way to neuropsychiatry?" You know, like the Burt Bacharach song; still, it makes a change from San Jose.'

'Neuropsychiatry sounds like a doctor for a Roman emperor,' laughed Rachel.

'We've been together too long,' I laughed. 'You are definitely my wife.'

But as I was to discover, there were whole sections of the Prince Regent Hospital who had never heard of each other. My first meetings there were with the consultant neurological psychiatrist, Dr Madden. Rachel did not go to my neuropsychiatry appointments, as we had an agreement that I would attend alone. The first time I sat in Dr Madden's waiting room, a strange, small, unkempt man entered. Although it was a hot day, the man had his thick coat buttoned all the way up. He sat opposite me looking around constantly, like he was checking in case he was being followed.

We were separated by a pile of well-thumbed copies of *Hello*, *Chat*, *Bella* and something called *Coarse Fishing*. I thought the latter was a magazine for people who never caught anything whilst fishing so swore a lot. Occasionally the man stared at me, making me feel uneasy, so I looked the other way.

'Are you up before the beak?' the man asked.

'Sorry?' I replied.

'Madden,' he added curtly. He shifted uneasily in his chair, puffing a lot and folding and unfolding his arms. Myrtle didn't like him. She thought he was showing off.

Finally, he got up and said, 'Look I can't do this, it will have to be another time. Tell him I can't make it today. Tell him they're following me again.'

'I will tell him, but what's your name?'

'Oh, you'd like to know that, wouldn't you?' he returned indignantly. 'I suppose you want my address and a picture of my grandmother too. Well, tell him he'll never get me committed, because I'll admit to nothing. See!' Then he left.

I was left open-mouthed. I stammered an explanation of what had happened to the receptionist, but she didn't seem unduly worried. She just tutted, sniggered, shook her head, muttering the word 'Murray' under her breath over and again.

Dr Madden was a tall, blond, rather gaunt-looking individual who wore gold-rimmed spectacles. He had indeed got a large nose, or beak as Murray had observed. When I entered Madden's room, Myrtle went into overdrive. She was out to impress and played his desk like it was a grand piano and she was a slightly neurotic Liberace [ask your parents]. Madden watched Myrtle's actions with a degree of bemusement. He was one of those ridiculously calm people who would politely and rationally question everything, like Fred from *Scooby Doo* but with a medical degree. After watching Myrtle for a few seconds, Madden looked at me over his gold-rimmed spectacles and asked softly, 'Do you hear voices?'

'No, of course not,' I answered firmly. I was being defensive just in case it was a trick to get me committed.

'That's a pity, I do. I think there's somebody next door who has turned up late for an appointment. Excuse me for a minute,' and with that he left the room.

It turned out that Murray, the man from the waiting room, had returned. I sat there, not knowing quite what to think. I had built up the appointment in my head all day, worried sick in case Madden would take one look at me and decide to have me sectioned. Now he had buggered off, a minute into our meeting!

I looked around the room and then at Myrtle. She seemed disappointed that we were being left alone and seemed to think it was my fault. She slapped me across the face as if to say, 'Why did you send him away?' or 'What have you brought me here for if nobody wants to see me?'

'Oh, will you stop it!' I tried to remonstrate with her after the third left cheek slap. 'If this guy sees both of us arguing he'll have me sectioned as sure as night follows bloody day.' As I ended my sentence, Madden came back in. I sat back looking sheepish and down at the floor.

'Sorry about that,' he purred. 'Who were you talking to?'

'No one. I was just saying a prayer. I tend to do that when I'm nervous.'

'Do you ever see visions?'

'Sadly not,' I replied, keeping quiet about the Paul Bindon bullying episodes and the reappearances of my dead parents in my dreams.

'You have an interesting condition; I see from your file that you have seen and stumped a lot of my colleagues at some other hospitals. And that you call your left arm Myrtle.'

'Yes, I've met a lot of clever people but sadly I haven't got very far on what's wrong and how to put it right.' I didn't acknowledge his second point about Myrtle, which she stropped at, banging on the desk with her knuckles.

'Hmm. Well, I think we can help.'

'Well, that's a welcome change.'

'What is?' enquired Madden.

'You seem very confident and positive. My sessions with Marcia Makepiece have helped my voice no end. I still speak incredibly slowly when I meet new people, otherwise things ecomdumbled [become jumbled] because I get very nervous.

'Well, no need to be nervous around me,' smiled Madden.

I wanted to say, 'And no need to be patronising around me. When you tell someone not to do something such as "Don't be scared, nervous or whatever", that's generally what they become,' but I didn't, just in case my sudden ire made up Madden's mind about my mental health. So, although the visit was productive, I was still considering what I should reveal about myself.

'Your nodding actually coincides with my speech patterns,' I said, 'so that's good. I can tell if somebody is understanding me by monitoring their nods and pauses.'

'How am I doing?' said Madden quizzically.

'You're doing well so far.'

'I take it others don't do so well.'

'No not really,' I replied, 'they tend to nod along without really taking in my speech and do it in the wrong places. I'm a musician and people's conversational "nods" to me are musical beats. My speech is the lyric. It's a test I use to see if we can play together.'

'And can I play with you? Let me rephrase that. Do you think I can help?'

'Yes. You corrected yourself, so you're prepared to try, and you look at me when you speak. That wins you extra Brownie points. Some people at work can't even be bothered to look at me when I speak to them. They think they will somehow offend me by looking at me or catching my eye.'

'And this annoys you?'

'Yes. It makes me feel ugly or unclean if people can't bring themselves to look at me. Besides, it takes me a lot of time and effort to get my words out and I don't like to see them wasted. Some people give up without really trying; they fear I'm too much like hard work or too complicated, so they tend not to go overboard in their communications with me, especially when we first meet.'

'Do you think your appearance or condition is off putting to them?'

'Yes. I think I'm scary and embarrassing to quite a few people. Oh, I'm not exactly Hannibal Lector or Frankenstein's monster. But mental illness is much harder to understand or accept for some people than, say, broken bones. It's not immediately visible what's wrong, for a start. No bandages, spots, rashes, splints, cuts or bruises to heal. You are outside the normal, you're different. There is an ugliness about it in most people's eyes, mine too, which is tremendously off putting. I realise I'm passing my own standards on to other people here, but I have no other frame of reference. When you have mental health problems, it's almost as if you have not passed the 'how to be a human being' test. You are defective. People don't seem to realise that if you look past the shaky arm and facial gurns, I'm just like them. I'm just trying to muddle through like everyone else. It's just that my path is more stony and slippery than other people's. My emotions are always out on display; I'm a terrible card player, I can't do bluffing or contain my feelings. The more stressed I get the more Myrtle intervenes with her terrible tremors. I just wish people understood that a bit more.'

'Yes well, as I said, I think we can help I would like you to try something called Cognitive Behavioural Therapy (CBT) across the road at Owsley Hospital. And I would really like to write a paper about you sometime.'

'If you cure me, you can write a whole blessed book.'

CBT was also part of the treatment programme Professor Khan had recommended, so hearing it recommended by another source carried a bit of added cachet.

It was at Owsley Hospital that I met another superhero to rank alongside Marcia Makepiece – a man who shall simply be known as Len. Yes, I know, Len is not exactly a great name for a superhero. Len is not much of a name at all on some levels. If it was a bedcover, it would hardly cover a person's eyebrow let alone his personality. But he had a huge influence on my life. He looked a bit like one of those Open University lecturers from the 1970s. He had lots of different-sized teeth waiting like a small bus queue across his gums. He wore a beard, jeans and a cheesecloth shirt. I think they all came in the same dressing-up box. Len lived in the bowels of Owsley Hospital, just across the road from the Prince Regent.

Rachel did come along to my first CBT session. We went through the whole story: my accident, the operations, my perception of work, work's perception of me, the whole shebang. There was laughter, tears and sneezes (the previous occupant of the room wore too much perfume). We sat in a sort of group of chairs, and I tried to open up. It was not difficult because Myrtle was the perfect exemplar of first-night nerves; she shook solidly throughout the first half of the performance, which helped me get over the conversational barriers.

'Your arm has finally stopped moving,' noticed Len after thirty minutes.

'Yes, she's probably exhausted,' said Rachel. 'Even Myrtle gets tired.'

'You-are-good-but-you-are not dat good,' I added.

'Let's see if I can improve,' said Len. 'Adam and I will meet here once a week for the next few weeks. Your brain has rewired itself. We must change it back to where it was, re-educate it. We must challenge your current perceptions and break you out of them. We must work out how you got to this point and then retrace your footsteps; give your brain a reboot to the last known place it worked properly.'

'How long will it take?' I asked.

'It will take time. Everybody is different. There isn't a magic wand I can wave. I wish there was. The other things you're doing in tandem, like speech therapy and exercise, will complement the work we do here. They will boost your confidence.'

And that was basically how the next six months of my life shaped up.

Chapter 44: Just to Be Able to Talk Again

In my second meeting with Len, I was very nervous. I was alone in a room with a man I barely knew who asked me to find some common ground and talk about myself. 'Tell me about your family,' asked Len gently, trying to ease me into things.

'There's not much to tell. My parents are both dead. My mother died when I was 24, my dad died about 7 years ago. I have a brother and sister, neither of whom I talk to easily or that often.'

'Why do you think that is?' asked Len.

'What do you know about Dystonia?' I asked tersely. *'Get the madam!'* I even chastised myself at my own remark. Not even two appointments in, and I was already asking the therapist to present his credentials. 'How rude I was!' I mused. 'I never had to prove to him I was ill. Shouldn't it work the other way around?' the reasonable side of me asked. 'No, of course not, I'm scared!' my unreasonable side retorted. 'Besides which, he knows how this therapy stuff works and I don't! And if he's having me committed, I'm not going down without a fight.'

I surprised myself by twisting things around in my head and using my anger to appear more confident. But then at that time I could turn the most irrational bollocks into some form of justification for my actions. That said, my bollocks *were* becoming irrational too. I tended to need the toilet far more than I used to; perhaps Myrtle had been speaking to them too, whilst I was asleep. Anyway, back to the story.

'I'm sorry,' I asked, 'but why are we talking about my family?'

'We have to get back to who you were before the accident. To do that we have to know how you got to here,' replied Len calmly.

'OK, I'll play,' I mumbled, feeling slightly ashamed for questioning him.

'To answer your other question,' continued Len, 'Dystonia manifests itself in a variety of ways. Mostly in the arms and legs and the face. Some people become really handicapped by it. Yours is actually milder than some cases I've seen.'

'Milder? Don't bet on that!'

'Bet Milder? Sounds like some sort of conservative lounge singer. Yes, I know that's probably not much comfort to you. But Dystonia is not as rare as you think.'

'What is the treatment for it?

'There isn't one.'

'What do you mean, there isn't one? Thirty seconds ago, you said lots of other people have had it or still have it. Surely there must be a cure if it's been around for ages?'

'Well, lots of people have various forms of cancer, but there's not yet a cure for some of them either.' Len was one of those people who could answer everything you threw at him with a positive comeback or devastating remark. It was quite an impressive, or annoying, feat, depending how you wanted to think about it.

'What do we do then?' I asked. Myrtle then jumped up, perching herself on the chair arm as if to say, 'He knows nothing. Talk to me instead!'

'Yes, thank you, Myrtle. We'll work our way through it. We get that you accept who you are now, we understand what that means, and we'll try to get you a good quality of life.'

Speech therapy ran alongside my Cognitive Behavioural Therapy (CBT). Whereas CBT was calm, soft and gradual; speech therapy was always noisy and more positive.

Marcia Makepiece said, 'Your voice is probably the most common way people judge you, after your appearance.'

Her words resonated with me. At first, I thought whenever I met someone new, I should use my reinstalled speech to explain Myrtle's tremors and shakes.

'Oh no,' said Marcia, 'you don't have to do that with everybody. Just the ones who matter. Otherwise, you'll be explaining yourself forever, and drive yourself mad.'

Rediscovering my voice again was such an amazing thing. Previously at work I would try to go as long as possible without speaking, and it's surprising how far you can get with just a nod. But then the phone would ring, and I would have to answer it and all my problems would be out on display. My voice, more than anything, severely affected my standing at work and made people decide that I could not cut it anymore. To my mind almost anyone can wear nice clothes, but not everyone can speak well. I used to be a wonderfully lucid speaker: funny, erudite. I had people glued to their seats when I presented. Then suddenly I was stuck in the land of Dystonia, and I was a braying donkey on a good day, and a stuttering stammering shire horse on a bad one. It sounds like some dreary politician's mantra, but the best treatment for mental health can be self-help. As I made 'reading aloud' part of my regular day, my voice began to improve, and I became more confident. Each week I went back and got a little better and people started to notice: mainly Marcia and Rachel at first, but then so did Jerome over the phone and their positive feedback made me feel good.

At the end of the first month of speech therapy, Marcia had two assistants with her. They were called Nadia and Natalie. They were training to be speech therapists and the Prince Regent Hospital was their first work placement. They took me on as a side project. The assistants were both young and pretty. I stared at Nadia as we mouthed vocal exercises together. As I later told Rachel, 'It's the weirdest thing having a pretty young woman sit in front of you mouthing OOOH noises. I quickly became transfixed and found it disconcerting. I completely lost my thread while watching as she puffed in and out with her cheeks. I tried to do the same, but it didn't feel like my mouth was working properly or that my face muscles were moving correctly. In my mind I could not seem to copy her facial movements at all.'

What happened? Glad you asked. Well, she stopped and looked kind of annoyed. I think she thought I was not taking the exercise seriously or going to make a smutty remark. I apologised and said, 'Look, I'm not trying to gawk at you. It's just that I don't seem to be doing what you're doing. My face muscles don't feel like they're doing the same thing as yours.'

But Nadia said, 'No, you were doing it.' She held up a mirror as I did the exercise again so I could see. I was relieved, to say the least.

In the coming weeks, Natalie, Nadia and I did vocal exercises together, reading some of my poetry along with newspaper articles and tongue twisters. It may not sound much, but it was a very big thing for me; people were now taking my written and spoken word seriously, and it felt like a long time since that had happened.

'I'm really pleased with the improvement in my speech. It makes me feel much more confident,' I said to Marcia at the end of the fourth session.

'Wow,' said Marcia. 'You have equated self-confidence with speech so early, usually it takes people a lot longer. Adam, you're a remarkable and interesting man.'

'I think you're being fast and loose with the word interesting,' I responded. Nadia and Natalie both laughed. 'But thanks for the thought,' I continued. 'I haven't missed being able to speak, but I have missed being understood and taken seriously.'

Chapter 45: It's Beginning to Look a Lot Like Me, Again

That announcement said our train's being diverted, so we might have to rethink our journey. I remember I had a lot to adjust to after the accident. After about six weeks of treatment, Rachel and I met with Dr Sharma at the Medical Centre to discuss my progress. It became apparent that for the first time in my lengthy case, medical opinions were starting to come together. Dr Sharma nodded when he read a letter from Professor Khan, and then smiled when he looked at the letter from Dr Madden.

'I can see what they're saying here, and I must agree.'

'What are they saying?' asked Rachel.

'They're saying that Adam's arm cannot move itself, and that at some level the command must come from his brain,' said Sharma directly to Rachel.

I suddenly felt scared, thinking I was being blamed for the arm movement, as though I was putting it on like some errant child, benefit cheat or just a liar. I reacted badly, my voice immediately faltering. 'Mmnot cheattin!' [I'm not cheating].

'Adam is suggesting we think he's doing this on purpose,' translated Rachel.

'Yes, I rather got that from his body language. No, of course not,' said Sharma, trying to calm the troubled waters that his conversational pebble had stirred. 'But your arm cannot control itself. At some level your brain must be sending messages to make your arm move. The brain can rewire itself after a traumatic incident.'

'That would make sense,' agreed Rachel. 'I know that look. No, Adam, we're not turning against you.'

'Feels sat way,' I mumbled indignantly.

'He said it feels that way,' said Rachel.

'Yes, I got that one as well. And no, not at all,' said Sharma looking at me.

'I don't think you understand what we're driving at,' added Rachel.

'Your brain controls your body,' said Sharma. 'If your brain rewires itself, then it makes adjustments that you don't recognise. Before you know it, you get behaviour which is completely out of the ordinary, or just plain odd. And so your arm may appear to be possessed by somebody else, or seem to have its own personality.'

'Exactly,' added Rachel. 'That explains the appearance of Myrtle.'

'Okay, I ged it,' I nodded.

'Your speech is much improved,' said Sharma. 'I'm going to reintroduce some physiotherapy to help support the other work you're doing. It will make you stronger.' Then he added, 'You should try to capitalise on your efforts.'

'What do you mean?' I asked, pensively.

'What about trying to return to work?' asked Rachel. 'I could speak with Jerome; we could ask them to make reasonable adjustments for you.'

'I agree. I'd recommend a phased return to work,' said Sharma. 'The quicker you get back into some form routine, the sooner things will return to normal.'

'You always knew you would have to go back,' said Rachel, looking at my ashen complexion. I had rather got used to being at home.

After a few moments, I said, 'OK, I'm willing to try.'

'Good man,' said Rachel.

Sharma wrote a note showing my fitness to return to work and added, 'You will need this.'

And so, the next phase of my journey began. The physiotherapy started first, and it was nice to see Nurse Ruth again. She did a double-take when she saw me. 'Wow, Adam, it's like looking at a different person,' she said, giving me a hug. 'You look fitter and your speech, wow. I thought Anthony Hopkins had turned up.'

Whilst this was nice to hear, it did make me want to get her a hearing test.

Chapter 46: Breaking Out of the Cocoon

Being at home recovering from a serious injury had 'cocooned' me from the rest of the world. I didn't really have to make any decisions, because everything was decided for me by doctors, nurses and Rachel. It was almost like a second childhood, and I was not entirely convinced that I was ready to become an adult again. The road back to the world looked dank, dark and difficult and other firms of dodgy accountants.

Return to work? Christ, what have I agreed to? I found the thought of going back terrifying. So, I sought a second, third and fourth medical opinion from the other professionals in my life. Surely *somebody* could see this was a bad idea? Unfortunately, everybody else seemed keen on me going back.

'Good for you,' said Nurse Ruth, the physiotherapist. 'You have a lot to offer the world and you can't hide away forever.'

'Marvellous news,' said Speech Therapist Marcia Makepiece. 'Having to see more people each day will do wonders for your self-confidence and speech.'

What about my Cognitive Behavioural Therapy Counsellor, Len? He's a rational man. He could see this was not a good idea. It was too soon for me to go back surely. Well actually no, he sided with the others as well. The rotten sod even added, 'Well done, that's the best thing for you. It will build on everybody else's good work.' He even gave me homework to prepare for it. 'When you go home, get yourself out doing shopping or posting letters, anything where you see other people. It will help soften the blow of being around them when you go back to work.'

Rachel quickly figured out I was scared, and after I had told her of my assignment from Len, she took me out to events so that I could get used to being around other people again. We went shopping too, well I did. Rachel would deliberately forget things and send me out to buy them. She tried to ensure that there was an event every other day to get me back into a routine of waking up, eating breakfast, then going somewhere. The thought of returning to a world where I would be around the very people who had sent me away had a bizarre effect on me. As soon as I pictured the faces of my work colleagues, my world telescoped, I would get dizzy and then gently fall over. The most prominent occasion when this happened was at a concert in Regent's Park. It was freezing cold and pouring with rain. As Rachel and I stood watching the Ukulele Orchestra of Great Britain, my legs became terribly cold and I elegantly sank to the floor like a giraffe having a drink. Rachel and another woman quickly managed to get me to a chair and give me some water.

'What happened?' asked Rachel.

'I don't know. My legs just went numb, then they went cold and gave out.'

'How do you feel now?'

'Yam ok.'

Myrtle sat up as I spoke and stroked my face, seeming concerned.

'I suppose you know nothing about this?' glared Rachel at Myrtle.

Myrtle shook her own hand from side to side as if to say no.

We went to see Dr Sharma about the falling over, and after testing my reflexes and heart he suggested it might have been a panic attack. Once again, we were told just to keep an eye on it. The implication was that once I had returned to work and the ordeal was overcome, the situation might remedy itself. However, there was still one other person to agree the return to work with, and that was Jerome.

I rang him on speaker phone and Rachel sat quietly by my side.

'Hi Jerome, it's Adam', I ventured tentatively.

'Hello, Adam. Wow, your voice is sounding good. The treatment programme you mentioned in your email must be having a positive effect.'

'Thank you,' I replied. Rachel gave me a thumbs up from her chair. 'I'm very glad you noticed. I'm feeling OK now and I'd like to try to return to work.'

'That's great news,' Jerome replied.

'Well, not just try to come back, I want to succeed.'

'What did you say that for?' mouthed Rachel, looking at the ceiling in dismay.

Sadly, I was overcompensating in a bid to convince Jerome I was fine. This made me sound super-confident, superhuman and, on reflection, supercilious. But it got worse 'I'm very determined. This time it's Persil!' I added trying to lighten the mood.

'OK,' replied Jerome, clearly baffled. 'Well, in terms of the actual return, Human Resources (HR) are saying that you must be assessed by Occupational Health in Harley Street before you can come back. It's nothing to worry about. It's just HR wanting an independent analysis to fall back on in case something goes wrong. Not that it will, I'm sure! I mean it's for your own protection. I'm sure you understand.'

'He's worse than you!' Rachel mouthed again, quietly.

'Once their assessment is complete, what I was thinking is that you could do one short day per week for the first month or so. We can then look to increase that to two days as you get back into the swing of things. You could carry on with your physiotherapy and CBT as normal, in between. How does that sound?'

'It sounds good. I'm there. It's fine,' I answered.

'Great, I'll set up the Occupational Health appointment and we'll take it from there.' And with that he rang off.

'Well done,' said Rachel. 'I know that was hard.'

'I was an idiot.'

'Yes, but you are my idiot.'

We didn't mention the falling down episode to Jerome, thinking he would be completely over the top about it, "by trying to do the best possible thing for me - according to HR."

I had only seen pictures of Harley Street in films. It was supposedly where some of the greatest medical minds in England were located. Unfortunately, the Ministry of Paperclips version of 'Occupational Health' was in a cupboard in the middle of Harley Street. To cap it all, it was on the top floor of the middle building. They still made a big thing about Harley Street on their letter heading, so obviously there was some cachet in being located there. But the Occupational Health office in Harley Street was singularly one of the most unimpressive places I've ever been to. There was a 'lift' which took you to their floor: more like a bird cage where you pulled the bars across in front of you. Myrtle thought we were in prison and wished she had brought a harmonica with her. She was flapping around because I was apprehensive. The lift took ages to get anywhere and creaked terribly when it did. 'Maybe it has Dystonia too,' I mused to Myrtle, trying to calm her down.

When eventually we arrived, I introduced myself to the receptionist and went into the waiting room. It was expensive looking: the magazines on the shiny antique tables were *Tatler* and *Country Life*. The doctor was very nice: a very posh, Scottish woman who asked lots of questions, but she did eventually confirm Sharma's diagnosis that I was ready to return to work. 'Why don't ye take in some biscuits to work with ye? That always wins people over.'

'Good idea,' I replied. That was not exactly rocket science, trying to win over office workers with food, but all the same I smiled and added, 'Thank you.' I was just grateful to overcome the Human Resources hurdle.

Chapter 47: The condition my condition should be in

Well, that's good; the train seems to have righted itself and we're back on our original route now that the town of Doncaster is out of the way.

My workmates tried to 'right themselves' too when I returned for the second time. They were taking no chances and tried desperately hard to show they cared. I was met at reception by Jerome and escorted up to the office. By now they had acknowledged that my accident, which was a life-transforming condition, had happened during work time. Whether or not the threat of a possible lawsuit concentrated people's minds, I didn't know, but I wasn't going to complain as it meant that they would do their best for me.

The discussion about me being back at work began innocuously.

'How are you feeling, being back here?' Jerome asked.

'Apprehensive and a little scared,' I replied.

'Well, in just a few days it will feel like you've never been away. I want you to know that, before we get into the mechanics of your return, I really want this to work. I'm glad Occupational Health gave you the OK to return. We want you back and we'll do our level best to show it.'

'Thank you,' I replied, a little taken aback by his enthusiasm. 'I will do my best to repay your faith in me.'

'Do be open with me. I'm your friend. You can bring in the Trade Union representative at any time you want. I welcome the opinions of others to help get things right. I'll give you lots of room and time to undergo your medical treatment. I know you have lots of Cognitive Behavioural Therapy, Speech Therapy and Physiotherapy to do. We can fit these appointments into the work time. I know it might be hard to get into a routine, but we can try. Do you have any preferences about which day you want to be in the office for the first month?'

'I think Mondays would be good to start with. I have to attend therapy sessions on Tuesday, Wednesday and Thursday at the moment. Although some of these will become fortnightly soon, with the exception of CBT.'

'You must be making good progress if they are spacing things out.'

'Well, most of physiotherapy exercises I can do alone, because I know them off by heart now. I can also do telephone assessments on the speech therapy side too. I have balance issues and can't really stand for more than half an hour, so coming in on the later, less crowded, trains would be helpful. It would also work better for going home if I could leave before rush hour. I would still work the core hours, 10 a.m. to 3 p.m.'

'Agreed. Peter Moores has said he doesn't want you travelling on busy trains because he's worried about you falling over or getting jostled about. He wants to see you next week to say hello, and he's really looking forward to catching up.'

'That's nice of him.'

'The Mayor of London is bringing in the 'Please offer me a seat' initiative on trains and the tube. You should apply to join it when it comes in.'

'Thanks, I will.'

'Following the Occupational Health assessment, Human Resources (HR) have made some suggestions about your office equipment – your chair and phone. One of their representatives will come and see you later today to talk these through.'

'Thanks, that's really good news.'

I was especially pleased and relieved at the promise of equipment and HR being involved, as I had previously felt as though I could not ask for any changes to my desk area without being labelled difficult. The episodes on the phone when I could not write things down and hold the receiver to my ear at the same time suddenly flashed through my mind and I shuddered in dread.

'You can be as open with me as you want,' continued Jerome. 'Are there things you don't want to talk about? I'm aware from the last time that you found other people speaking and speculating about your condition disconcerting.'

'Yes, that was hard. I felt on trial last time, and people's comments made it worse, mainly because they were usually wrong and rather negative.'

'I'm not sure I can stop all of them talking. Then again, how much do you want me to tell other people about what's going on? How specific should I be?'

'Well, I don't want to be the talk of the office. But on the other hand, I don't want special privileges either. We should tell people only what might affect them.'

'How do you mean?'

'Well, I should probably have a Personal Evacuation Plan (PEP) in place in case there's a fire or whatever. This should list what help I need in case you're not around. Whatever is listed in there is all they need to know.'

'That makes sense. When you've settled back in, you could have a look at your calendar and see if there any particular days off you want as leave.'

'OK, but at the moment I can't think of any that aren't to do with hospital appointments.'

'Well, we can come back to that. What practical changes can we make to help you, such as access to the tea point, toilets or emergency exits? One of your colleagues told me of your difficulties in working the soap dispenser.'

'I don't know yet, let's see how it goes.'

'We'll keep it under review and talk together at least once a week.'

The meeting went well. I was glad that Jerome was overseeing this. It felt like the fastidious side of Jerome's nature was being put to good use. This time around it certainly seemed as though there was a lot more consideration as to how things might work. My "managed return to work" would only really work because I had a manager in Jerome who wanted to meet me halfway and try to help.

On the first afternoon I was back at my old desk I had a visit from a strange bloke from Human Resources called "Cockney John". He was there to carry out a workstation assessment. Cockney John was a man of many words and few teeth. He smelt of rolled up cigarettes, strong aftershave and sweat. He was rather dishevelled, unshaven and wrapped in 1970s style knitwear.

'Hello, I'm Cockney John, and I'm a bit mad,' were the first words he said to me.

'Not exactly politically correct,' I mused under my breath to Myrtle. 'But maybe he's trying to show himself to be one of us.'

'Just to clarify things, there's another bloke called "Irish John", but he works in furnishings, so you probably won't meet him,' he continued.

Cockney John worked to his own timetable and appeared in front of various people unannounced. He spoke, as his name suggested, in a clipped Cockney conversational dialect. 'HR sent me. We need to measure fings [things] so they're right.' Every other sentence of Cockney John's contained the phrase 'I'm a bit mad.' This was his Cockney, cheeky chappie persona. He studied me "sideways on" at my desk for nearly a minute, then asked, 'Would anedset help you?'

'Sorry? Anedset?' I replied, quite confused.

'Anedset.' Cockney John covered his ears with his palms.

'Oh, a headset!' I nodded as the words finally registered. 'I thought there was something wrong with you. Yes, really good idea. I can't write and hold the telephone at the same time, so a headset would improve things, yes,' I smiled.

'How about a one-handed keyboard? Something small so you can reach around it better. You could be like Rick Wakeman.'

'He uses two hands, doesn't he?'

'Yes, but sometimes he plays two keyboards at once, with one hand on each.'

'That sounds really useful,' I replied, thinking that having a one-handed keyboard would mean Myrtle didn't have to join in work at all if she didn't want to.

Cockney John had worked at the Ministry for Paperclips for many years. He was one of those people who try to prove themselves to be a good person by telling you who their friends are. 'Do you know Andy Gorman?'

'No,' I replied, worried in case a 'yes' reply would meet with disapproval. I had learned in hospital to appease my care providers.

'Neither do I,' said John smiling and then adding, as he saw my face lapse into a smile, 'Told you I was mad. You should get one of those specially adapted chairs which supports your whole body. The chairs themselves are just a frame, like a skellingtonne,' said John, opening a brochure and pointing at page 27. 'Just look at her! She may look like one of them supermodels, but she's *so* comfortable it's like sitting on a big, bearded fat bloke called Trevor!'

'OK,' I replied, feeling rather dumbstruck by John's description.

'Unfortunately, they take weeks to deliver.'

'Can't it come any quicker?'

'Sadly not but I can measure you today.'

John was a man of his word and the very next day I was issued with a "nedset" for my telephone.

Chapter 48: How Was It For You?

I attended my next Cognitive Behavioural Therapy (CBT) appointment the day after I'd met with Jerome and Cockney John. It was at the rather foreboding Owsley Hospital. I sat in reception studying the hospital sign which contained the phrase 'works closely with the Institute of Psychiatry' and it was now dawning on me as to where I was and that I was there alone.

'Yes,' I mused to a shaking Myrtle, 'I am in no doubt as to where we are.' As I waited, I started worrying that I might not be released if things went badly. When Len arrived, we went to a different room from last time. It had a very heavy metal, cream-coloured door – a bit like entering a secure prison wing. I gulped noticeably when the door electronically clanked itself shut behind us.

'This is a more secure room than last time,' I said.

'It's just what was available,' replied Len. 'Nothing more to it than that.'

We sat on opposite sides of a heavy pine coffee table. The furniture was fastened to the floor. The decorators had clearly gone for claustrophobic over cosy.

'How are you getting on?' asked Len.

'Yam fine,' I replied, noticing a big red alarm button on the wall.

'It's just a room,' said Len after a cavernous pause. 'Four walls and a ceiling. Try not to make any more of it than that. How did you get on at work yesterday?'

'I think it was OK.'

'Only OK? You did a huge thing yesterday. Returning to work is hard. It's like visiting a former life. These are important steps.'

'My boss asked good questions. They seem to want to put things right.'

'Was it how you expected it to be?'

'No, I felt it was much easier. I didn't sleep well the night before, but I never do when it's something important. A strange bloke called Cockney John came to see me from Human Resources about how my desk was set up. He kept telling me he was mad.'

'Well, that's different.'

'I think he's like that with everyone. Probably he was trying to be funny and show he was "one of us". Maybe he thought seeming mad would somehow make it easier for me to talk to him – trying to show empathy and all that. He's ordering some equipment for me: a nedset (headset), a one-handed keyboard and a chair.'

'He sounds well-meaning at least, and the equipment sounds great. But more than that, remember you did a good thing by going back to work. That's a huge step; now the recovery work can begin in earnest. What were you like before the accident?'

'I was confident, I even had a career path and a retirement plan.'

'And now?'

'I'm no longer in the same place. I feel as though somebody has lifted me off the "well lit" side of the mountain and placed me in a ravine.'

'That's all very dramatic, but I see what you're saying. The walls look dark, slippery and treacherous. You can't see anything more than shadows in front. It looks daunting and different. Uncertainty was probably the first tangible thing you got hold of after the accident, just before uncertainty's best friend "fear" arrived. You are probably terrified that the world has moved on and that you won't matter anymore. You feel different, uglier, more burdensome, and that nobody will ever like you again. You have no confidence because everything in your world has changed. You can't find any familiarity. Is that anything like you?'

'Close enough for jazz. I play guitar,' I replied, sensing that he was preparing me for what was going to be a long walk back to normality.

'Good, it's important to have something besides work to identify yourself with.'

After another pause, I added, 'By the way, I couldn't even contemplate not turning up for work. There were too many people who had done amazing things just for my benefit. Speech Therapy, this Cognitive Behavioural Therapy and plain old physiotherapy, not to mention Rachel, her family, my family and some people at work. It makes me dizzy just to think about it. I feel I would be personally letting each of these people down if I didn't give it my best shot. The stigma of that would kill me. I **know** that. And that's not just because I have been imbued by marriage with Rachel's Roman Catholic guilt. No, if I don't do this properly, I will have to live in a hole in the ground or roam the earth like some sub-standard creature that only comes out at night to vote Tory and/or score some heroin.'

'Well, it's nice that you put me in the list of people who have helped. But you're putting a lot of pressure on yourself,' said Len. 'What will happen will happen anyway. You may have to face up to the fact that you may not crack it this time either.'

'Well, you're cheery. I'm demoralised now. I was quite chirpy when I came in.'

'I'm not trying upset you. I'm just trying to get you to be more realistic and more forgiving of yourself if things don't immediately go to plan. What did you learn from the last time you returned to work?'

'Last time? I wanted it too much! I had this idealised shape of what "doing it well" should look like. I exercised hard and I lost some weight. I had a lot of motivation to succeed and prove the doubters wrong. If I didn't, I would die trying.'

'OK, well this time maybe not trying so hard is a good thing.'

'I don't really know how to be any other way. It's in my nature to have a go. My wife Rachel says I'm an all or nothing kind of guy. I don't do moderation. She says that's why our house is full of DVDs, CDs and guitars.'

'But you don't give yourself any space or wiggle room.'

'Well, I'm scared of losing my job. I can't really do anything else.'

'That's not true, is it? You can adapt.'

'How do you mean?'

'Could you envisage yourself living with only one fully functioning arm?'

I shook my head.

'But you do, and you do it well.'

'But I have a terrible fear of failure. It gives me headaches just to think about it. So many people have helped me. It makes me cry. I feel I don't deserve it.'

'You don't get to choose how much people invest in you. They do it because they want to, because you're a nice bloke. It's not an equation, and there isn't a right answer. And if you do fail, the people who already like you will still like you.'

'You sound like my wife Rachel.'

I found this hard to accept: not the advice, but having two versions of Rachel in my life. Two lots of positivity in two strands of life that don't normally meet was going to be difficult to manage. 'Oh my God, two people being right in my life. When do I get to do it?' I mused on the way home. 'This mental health stuff is really tiring.'

Part 5

Chapter 49: And Then the Wind Changed

Eventually there was a proper welcome back to work for me from my old team. Jerome escorted me round the office in an event powered almost entirely by small talk. There was lots of smiling, nodding and empathetic head bobbing going on, with everybody on their best behaviour. But as I got to see people up close, their conversations seemed rehearsed and a little odd.

'You'll never guess what?' the Zombie Twins (Roderick and Sam) asked me in unison in some strange tantalising, infantilising, pantomime speak.

'I-I don't know,' I replied, rather embarrassed by their enthusiasm.

'We have a new photocopier,' they both said again in unison, stepping aside to reveal it. 'TAAADAAAR – it's fabulous.'

'It prints in colour,' said Roderick.

'And it staples too,' added Sam.

'That's good,' I replied. 'The old one was worn out.'

As I walked away, I heard Sam say to Roderick, 'Told you speaking together was daft. But you wouldn't listen.'

I learned later that Jerome had asked people to make "Adam feel included" so that I would feel part of the team again. This was easier said than done. We all struggled for things to talk about, including me. Mary Swanson (Peter Moores' PA) even asked me what medication I was on to fill the silence. So, I reeled off the list of my heart medications: Ramipril, Simvastatin, Aspirin, Bisoprolol, Amitriptyline and Isosorbide Mononitrate, as if it were a version of the Lord's Prayer.

And the attempted empathy? Well, that was 'Oh, my dad takes those.'

'Really,' I mused to Myrtle. 'I bet he doesn't take Amitriptyline. Not unless he's going mad.' But I saw Rachel shaking her head in my mind's eye. I just smiled to myself. 'I know they're trying their best, and so must I.'

'How do you think it went?' asked Jerome in the canteen later.

'I feel a bit disconnected,' I replied. 'Next time I should take off my gas mask!'

Jerome looked startled and his jaw dropped. 'You're wearing a gas mask?'

'No, of course not! I thought it was fine and thank you for arranging it. I must buy you a sense of humour for Christmas. Honestly, I thought it was good. The team's changed a bit. Darren Jones and Diane weren't there.'

'They've moved on to different offices,' said Jerome tactfully, as if hiding something.

As promised, later that day Jerome took me to Peter Moores' office to say hello. There was a hug between the two of us and a few laughs. I found conversation with Peter much easier, maybe because our relationship was simpler: I still saw Peter Moores as the team leader.

'Do you remember this?' asked Peter showing me a photograph.

'I do. It was the office Christmas party 2008.That's Jerome, Harry and Jenny Talbot, you and me. We all look to be having a good time.'

'It was an amazing team and it's even more amazing that there's only you, me and Jerome left from that time. That's why I wanted to see you. I wanted to tell you in person that I'm moving on. I didn't want you to hear it from anyone else. They've said they want me to manage a new team in the Olympic branch – the Games are only a year away now.'

'Good for you,' I replied, wondering what on earth a paper company would have to do with the Olympic Games before adding, 'The world really is changing.'

We shook hands and hugged again. 'Stay in touch,' said Peter.

'I'll do my best.' It was one occasion when I meant what I said.

The phased return to work helped me a lot. It gave me an umbrella under which to shelter. I kept to a strict 10 a.m - 3 p.m. routine, so that like before, by the time I got overly 'worked up' about being at work, it was time to go home again. Certainly, that made things easier to cope with. Arriving late and leaving early may not seem much, but when you throw in how much I was having to adapt to, such as having Myrtle travel with me, it was certainly enough for the time being.

I'd had initial thoughts about coming back to work and proving all the doubters wrong. I'd thought about buying a great coat to look like Napoleon, which I would wear whilst planning my "return revenge strategy".

'You do know Napoleon lost, don't you?' said Rachel when she caught me looking at overcoats on the Internet.

'My plan is to ease my way back in slowly and carefully,' I replied, like a camp Bond villain. 'I'll use the negativity of last time to fuel my positivity. Then when they least expect it, I'll go for promotion. After all, I have a point to prove.'

'Excuse me, Mr Blofeld, but could we wait a bit before you have your revenge on the world?' asked Rachel. 'Maybe two years or so to build up your strength.'

'The first time I went for promotion I had a heart attack,' I replied, stroking the kettle. 'The second time I broke my shoulder. I'm not sure I have enough body parts left to work at the next grade up, but I'm determined to try.'

But then something happened which pulled the rug out from underneath everything – Jerome told me he was moving on too! He went out of his way to bring the bad news to me in the gentlest way he possibly could. He took me out to lunch.

'I suppose you're wondering why I've brought you here,' he said after sipping some water.

'Before we start, I'm old enough to be your dad and I'm happily married.'

'What do you mean? My partner runs a health spa.' Then the joke dawned upon him. 'Heh, heh, no, that's not it, I haven't brought you here on a date. I've had a job offer and it's too good to turn down.'

'Then you must go for it.'

'How will you feel about me going? Will you be OK? Will you cope? I realise it's a shock and probably a bolt from the blue,' he said, thankfully pausing. I was just about to speak, but Jerome resumed. 'Only we've got quite close over the past two years. I know so much more about you now, and I'm kind of used to having you around. I sense you feel the same.'

'What will your new job be?' I asked.

'Running a secretariat. It's a promotion, of course.'

'Look, please don't think of me as an obstacle. I would be mortified if you did. Please take it. Don't give me a second thought.'

'I suppose you're adaptable and flexible,' he said.

'Absolutely, I'm also collapsible too. My mother got me from Ikea. I came free with some flat-pack furniture.'

Then Myrtle raised herself up in a slow but deliberate wave.

'I will miss you too, Myrtle,' said Jerome and with that he reached and shook Myrtle's middle finger. We sat in the strange silence that working friendships sometimes afford. It was a parting of the ways; a minor footnote in my return-to-work evolution, but a worthy one, nonetheless.

Leaving aside the rather ham-fisted farewell, I did have to admit that I would miss Jerome. I spoke about it that night in bed with Rachel.

'I got some news today: Jerome's leaving, and so is Peter Moores.' Then I flicked off the lights. 'Ah well, good night.'

'Just a minute, mister,' said Rachel, turning the lights back on. 'What was that? Jerome is leaving and Peter as well. Why do you always raise "stuff" when we've just turned off the lights and are going to sleep?' asked Rachel curiously.

'I don't know, maybe it's because it feels like we're the only two people on earth when we're in bed. I enjoy the confessional side of it. It's the only time I can properly open up.'

'Well, I applaud the sentiment but not the timing. When did you find out?'

'Jerome took me out for a farewell meal today. Yes, I know. I've done nothing but complain about this man. I said he was interfering, overbearing, high maintenance, and kind of annoying.'

'But there were some nice things about Jerome. He was straightforward, trustworthy and most importantly you had grown used to him. You only know what you've got when it's gone.'

'He told me over lunch. That was typical of the man,' I reflected before correcting myself. 'Now I've gone the other way, haven't I?'

'You have rather, yes. Jerome moving on is like a death. No doubt he'll be given a sainthood and forgiven all his transgressions – offices are weird like that.'

'The world is changing,' I said, turning over and yawning.

'How do you feel about that?' asked Rachel, sitting up in bed.

'Well, I'm very philosophical; as you know, I don't really do emotions.'

'Oh, you're *such a hard man.* You idiot! You're the softest person I know. You cried when Bambi's mother died, and you've been an emotional wreck ever since.'

'No, I'm not,' I whined, semi-indignantly.

'Yes, you are. Well, Jerome wasn't family. But he and Peter were both nice.'

'I still think that as a manager Jerome was an overbearing busybody who often talked down to me. But there were advantages to him being around.'

'They do say better the devil you know,' said Rachel. 'I always felt that Jerome had more than a touch of the Mary Poppins about him. I could easily imagine him saying "I'll be here only until the wind changes".'

'Yes, that's true, he did once give me a spoonful of sugar and say "spit spot" when he wanted some urgent papers doing. But he knew me, and I hope he respected me. I wish he could have said he was leaving a bit earlier, then I would have been able to prepare better for when he goes. I'm not sure how I'll take to someone new.'

'Peter could be the harder loss,' said Rachel. 'I always felt he was the one who made sure things happened properly and in the right order.'

I would soon find out what Rachel meant by this, but for now I slept, as getting back into the pace of my old job after a long time out was tiring.

Chapter 50: All Change, Please

Over the next few weeks, I found that the merry-go-round of life which had previously revolved around home had now spun off to an entirely new vantage point at work. With the imminent departures of Jerome King and Peter Moores, I now had an entirely different set of people to get used to. There were three new "careerists" in the immediate management team closest to me: Wendy Plant (the new Jerome), Nigel Foster-Kramer (he was short, power-dressed in expensive dark suits and organised performance meetings) and Mary Black (a woman who seemed to be fifty-feet tall and was in charge of finance).

Of course, you have no say in who takes over, and soon I was ushered into a meeting room to meet my new boss. Wendy was a cold rather pallid-faced woman. If Jerome had no sense of humour, it was hard to tell whether Wendy even had a pulse! She sat at the table in a dark-blue polyester business suit like an emotionless Gothic armchair.

Jerome attended the meeting as part of the handover and did his best to talk me up. 'This is Adam, he's very good, very motivated. He knows lots about the job, including where all the bodies are buried. Yes, he's been here for years. He needs virtually no managing, he does it all by himself.'

I reached out my right hand toward Wendy and said, 'Nice to meet you.'

Wendy shook my hand and muttered 'Likewise,' but she didn't look at me or make eye contact.

In her own way Myrtle tried to impress Wendy too, by pirouetting back and forth across the desk, using her fingernails as ballet shoes. Wendy just looked on impassively from within her crash helmet of coal black hair.

'Well, what did you think?' asked Jerome after the meeting had finished.

'It was hard to get much of an angle on Wendy at all,' I replied. 'She's quite circular and not the most open sort of person.'

'Nobody opens up straight away,' reassured Jerome. 'It will be fine, I'm sure.'

My end of the day conversation with Rachel about Wendy had a similar shape.

'She seemed cold,' I blurted out to Rachel. 'Jerome, for all his fussiness, at least seemed to care. His obsessiveness was at least well meant. I suppose it also helped that Jerome had seen me before the accident. He had some sort of affinity with me. We had a history. He could at least testify that I was a good bloke, reliable, dependable and other types of sheepdog.'

'Well,' said Rachel, 'with Wendy you'll both be starting afresh with a blank canvas. How long did it take for you to build a rapport and trust with Jerome?' I didn't answer because as usual I knew she was right. 'It was at least few months, maybe even a few years, and here you are judging this poor woman after a few hours. Give her a chance.'

The new management team had no sympathy, understanding or most importantly empathy with me. The link with the past was gone, and with it any semblance of anyone who knew about my capabilities from before the accident. Hovering above all this was Peter Moores' replacement: the foppish and ineffectual Gareth Cadogan. His 'anything for a quiet life' demeanour quickly earned him the nickname of Gareth Cardigan. The Wendy, Mary and Nigel trio quickly became a three-headed hydra, or triumvirate of evil, as I watched how they spoke in the open office about their new and "supposed" boss.

'Mary, are you wearing the Cardigan again this morning?' asked Nigel.

'Yes, it'll be the same as last week,' replied Mary. '"How do you raise a purchase order? Can you help me brief the board on the latest finance figures? Can you stand in for me at the directors' meeting, please?"'

'So thick!' said Wendy. 'He never remembers anything, but worse, he can't make decisions unless you hold his hand all the way through a subject.'

'Over promoted,' said Nigel.

'Absolutely,' agreed Mary.

'Over cautious,' said Nigel.

'Totally,' added Wendy.

'And over here,' they all chimed together.

After watching their behaviour, I suddenly felt very lonely, exposed and vulnerable. 'What has happened to respect?' I mused to Myrtle. 'If they do that to the supposed head of unit, then I'll be mincemeat in no time.'

In terms of "assistance for Adam", the new management team got together and talked about how to "handle it". I even saw it on a meeting agenda. The main thing wrong with this was that they didn't invite me to the meeting or tell me about it. The meeting happened one Tuesday, and as far as I could deduce, it went as follows.

'Now how we do handle the Adam situation?' asked Gareth. 'Ideas, anyone?'

'Oh, I'm sure we'll manage it,' said Wendy dismissively.

'We don't need to draw attention to it,' added Mary.

'I'm sure Adam would be embarrassed if he thought he was being treated any differently from the others,' said Nigel.

'But do we need to do anything extra?' asked Gareth earnestly.

'No, of course not. The situation will be closely monitored,' answered Wendy. 'We just need to follow the HR guidelines, that's all.'

'But is that enough? asked Gareth, looking at the three of them. 'What happens if the Adam situation worsens, or he relapses?'

'Then it will become a situation vacant,' whispered Wendy to a smirking Nigel.

'Don't worry, Gareth,' said Mary. 'The three of us will help you through it.'

And that was pretty much how most of the meetings about "assistance for Adam" went. Whenever Gareth got concerned, the other three would effectively 'pat him on the head' and close down the conversation and dismiss it as unimportant.

Back in the office at that time I knew none of this. I did eventually come to realise how important the word *respect* was in my working life. But for the moment I felt I might have a bit more freedom workwise away from Jerome's prying gaze and that felt good. I thought I could breathe more easily and loosen my tie without it being reported to all and sundry because they thought I was about to have a heart attack. But there's giving people breathing space and then there's ignoring them until they hyperventilate. Although I did not know it, I was heading for the latter.

Chapter 51: Am I Intelligible?

Well, I didn't quite catch that that announcement: something about the buffet car now being available in coach C.

Speaking of being understood, I was now approaching the end of my first month of speech therapy, so Marcia Makepiece decided it was time for me to take an intelligibility test. This was a bit of a surprise, and I was totally unprepared for it.

'Oh, you'll be fine,' said Marcia, noticing I had changed colour. 'It's just reading aloud, and you've been doing that every day, haven't you?'

'But I need time to prepare.'

'No, you don't. I will choose a block of writing and you'll read it into this microphone. It's connected to a tape recorder away in another room. I will be listening in, and I'll mark off how many of the words I recognise from what you say. It's important that you haven't seen the words before. Otherwise, it will skew the test result.'

'OK,' I said, 'I understand.'

I was always nervous when reading aloud. It took time trying to match my breathing to the punctuation. To me it was like reading a musical stave and following a rhythm. Somebody recording/listening into my performance was like being in front of an audience, and Marcia being a speech therapist made it like performing before a music critic. The text I read was another newspaper article about shopping. I got through it, but was covered in sweat as Myrtle tilted her imaginary sword at windmills.

'Well done,' said Marcia on her return. 'I know that was hard. There's no pass mark as such, but we expect over 80% for normal understandable everyday speech. This time you got 43%.'

'Forty-three per cent! That's awful.' The figure seemed very low, and I was shocked by it.

'Well, everybody's got to start somewhere. Remember what you were like when you first arrived. I think you were trying too hard in this test. Your speech was quite stilted, and you put emphasis on letters in words which have silent letters in them like *knew* and *butcher*.' I looked blank. 'You said *K new* and *Butt cher*.'

'All the same, forty-three per cent is disappointing; no wonder everyone at work thinks I'm stupid.' With my disappointment, out came some of my own disability prejudices.

'You're certainly not stupid!' countered Marcia sounding quite annoyed. 'Besides, I'd like to see some of your work colleagues come back from where you've been. It takes a lot of bravery and character. But it would probably help you improve if you did some exercises before you came into the room. It would help relax you and you could properly compose yourself before you took the test.'

I retook the test the following week, scoring 63%, and I was amazed at the difference. As I later confided to Rachel, 'I speak much more clearly when I'm relaxed, and my diaphragm is properly open. It's hard when you have the rest of your body trying to close you down.'

Myrtle realised she was being talked about and hid beneath the dining table.

'I did swimming exercises – breaststroke in the toilet before I went in,' I added.

'That's a good idea,' replied Rachel.

'Sometimes, if I feel brave enough, I exercise on trains, but mostly it's something I do in public toilets. When people see you doing the breaststroke, they're a little surprised. One bloke asked, "Are you expecting a flood?" Another comedian said, "Don't you need water to do that?" At first, I felt the need to explain myself, but then I thought what the hell. It doesn't matter, and what's it got to do with anybody else anyway? It's my life not theirs.'

'Good for you,' said Rachel, hugging me. 'I'm so proud of you.'

Chapter 52: We Aren't History

"We should look after our mental health", says the Minister. Hmm, that's all very well as a newspaper headline, but some people have the misconception that those of us who have mental health issues are not fit to work. They don't understand the value or benefit of human interaction, or even that people with mental health problems need to pay the bills just like anybody else. I rapidly came to think that Wendy could be one of those people. At the time I was buoyed by Marcia's comment about whether my work colleagues could come back from where I'd been. Rachel, of course, with her ridiculous sense of fair play, suggested that I should at least try to get to know Wendy before completely dismissing her out of hand. So, I agreed I would chat to Wendy to bring her up to speed. By trying to establish some common ground and share some experiences, I hoped we would develop a bond as Jerome and I had done previously. On paper, this seemed a practical idea: I would be taking control and helping to shape the terms of our relationship during our first chat. Sadly, the reality was markedly different.

'I yam quite prepared to learn how we can get through things together,' I began to explain to Wendy as we sat together either side of a meeting room table. I paused and looked for some reaction in Wendy's expressionless face. Realising this she suddenly woke up and filled the silence with a monosyllabic, 'Yes.'

Perhaps Wendy is shy, I thought, and so I continued enthusiastically, but on reflection rather stupidly, with 'I call my left arm Myrtle.'

'You call your left arm Myrtle? That's unusual.'

'Well, it's easier to battle with a person rather than a condition. Sometimes she wakes me at night with pain and this affects my whole day and it's hard.'

I should really have known my audience better and noticed that Wendy was starting to shift uneasily in her chair. But no! I blundered on like a condemned man giving more and more rope to his executioner. After all, I knew nothing about this woman and now I was treating her like my confessional priest.

'Of course, there's more to it than pain: it's about who owns the power...'

'Why are you telling me this?' interjected Wendy.

'Why am I telling you this?' I spluttered indignantly. 'Well, I think it's important that you know some of the things I go through each day. Sometimes I feel as if I've done a day's toil before I even get here. Sometimes I remonstrate with Myrtle just to get dressed.'

'I can certainly bear that in mind when it comes to performance review time, but I must judge you the same as everyone else.' Then Wendy promptly left the room.

I was left in the meeting room alone, slightly stunned. 'She's gone!' I mused to Myrtle. 'I had so much more to tell her, and she's buggered off.'

I didn't get the chance to tell Wendy that before each working day I neatly pile my clothes on the spare room bed in the order I need to put them on: T-shirt, underwear and socks. I stopped adding my shirts and trousers to the pile, as Myrtle kept throwing them to the floor which creased everything and got it dirty. I couldn't tell Wendy how Myrtle and I sit on the spare bed like an old married couple bickering about putting on my socks.

'Are you going to help me?' I ask Myrtle. When there's no reply, I try to taunt or goad her into action. 'My right arm is helping me. It's setting an example. Look, that's how things should be.' But then Myrtle gets frustrated and flings my sock or vest across the floor as if to say, 'Your right hand is a SWOT! And it lives in a village called Crawley Bumlick. I will never kowtow before the likes of you.' Myrtle is my body's equivalent of Cornwall: she desperately wants her independence but cannot reconcile herself to the fact that she is inextricably linked to the rest of me.

Once my socks are on and that strange "ribbed bit for your displeasure," is settled around my toes, I step carefully into my underwear. This is not because my underwear is enormous. No, it's easier that way. Once I have got each foot into position, I will then pull my underwear up over my knees. I do this slowly because Myrtle once gave my penis concussion when she pinged the elastic waistband of my underpants against it. Myrtle offers no help at all; bending is literally beneath her.

We used to do the putting on my shirt 'waltz' together each morning, although this did rather depend on what was on the radio. If it was Motorhead, or something fast and loud, I ended up chasing Myrtle round the room, like dancing a frantic Charleston with the Invisible Man. One morning Rachel caught us both 'tango-ing for control' of my shirt and she stared at me in disbelief.

'What *are* you doing?' she asked, laughing at my poor dancing pose.

'Getting dressed. Only Myrtle is being a bitch.'

'Are you having a spot of bother?'

'I've got this covered. I know what I'm doing. No, I don't need your help or advice. I've been doing this quite successfully for a while now.'

'Why don't you put Myrtle through your shirt sleeve first?'

'OK, I maybe do need your advice, because I hadn't thought of that,' I said, admitting that this approach hadn't occurred to me, but it would do from then on.

Once the shirt is on I must button it up, and this is more difficult. I usually end up bargaining my way around this part. Yes, some people may be able to fasten a button with one hand whilst smoking a cigarette or conducting the Royal Philharmonic with the other, but I have sadly never been one of them. On bad days there is usually bribery and corruption involved, and I attempt to reason with her. 'Myrtle, if you agree to help me fasten my shirt, I will get you a manicure.' No reaction. 'It will be professionally done! You will look so much nicer than my right hand. Honestly, all you must do is to cooperate.' Then Myrtle will move in front of me, from side to side, which means she is thinking. Then, and only then, she will reluctantly grab hold of a button and start the process of doing up the shirt.

It's odd but these things work. I reason and argue with Myrtle all the time. Sometimes I barter. I once swapped one week's worth of getting dressed for the application of some fancy hand lotion. Myrtle chose it when we were out in a supermarket. It was either that one or using salad cream – she grabbed a bottle of that last week in Sainsbury's and put it in my shopping basket. Kleptomania anyone? Another time I persuaded Myrtle to help me put on a tie by offering to buy her a new pair of satin gloves and a pearl bracelet. 'Clearly Myrtle has an Audrey Hepburn fixation,' observed Rachel.

But sadly, none of this information about my trials and tribulations was imparted to Wendy because she had chosen to leave the room.

Chapter 53: Pictures of Mental Health

Wendy did not mention her conversation with me to anyone else. When she had her management review with Gareth Cadogan (he was still her boss, after all), I understand their conversation went roughly as follows.

'How are you finding working with Adam?'

'Oh, fine,' said Wendy.

'Have you worked with many disabled people before?' Gareth asked prying a bit further.

'No, but I'm sure I can handle it. Mental illness is something a lot of people exaggerate to get special treatment. They always seem to want so many adjustments and then use the lack of them as an excuse for why they can't do their job.'

'Really? In Adam's case I'm quite worried that we might break him.'

'Don't worry, I can cope. I'm quite worried about how his being here affects the younger team members. I mean it's not good for morale having someone like *that* around. Heaven knows what visitors will think if he's the first person they meet.'

Gareth winced at Wendy's last comment but did not challenge her over it.

What this meant in practice was that Wendy gave me jobs that she felt were simple and out of the way, such as photocopying or getting rid of mountains of filing and shredding. Gone were the days when I would engage with people, because these were jobs that kept me out of the public gaze in the basement photocopier room where the shredder was located. I now received work in bundles in an in-tray with a set of instructions from the other members written on a top sheet such as 'Please shred this' or 'Make X number of copies of this'. I was now Wendy's 'quasi admin assistant', condemned to wander the bell tower of the Ministry of Paperclips forever.

'How are you getting on with Wendy?' asked Gareth one day when he met me in the lift on the way to lunch.

'The photocopier made me deaf, and the shredder made me dry, but she gave me water,' I replied, my face twisting up and head bobbing to and fro. Whenever I met with those in charge, my Dystonia became more pronounced and the confidence I'd got from my improved speech momentarily went away. I always felt 'less than' whoever I was talking to, and vulnerable and powerless. During those times I used comedy to deflect people's attention away from my condition, but it didn't always work.

'OK,' said Gareth, staring at me and not really understanding the 'quasi admin assistant' reference to my being like Quasimodo from the *Hunchback of Notre Dame.*

I very nearly said, 'I think Wendy and the others are ashamed of me. They have no idea about my disability. In their eyes I've gone from competent to incompetent and they give me work three pay grades below what I used to do!' But the thing that kept me in check was my own belief that the office was doing me a favour by keeping me on.

I did try another charm offensive on Wendy. It was a disaster. I still cringe about it now. It happened one Wednesday afternoon in the Ministry of Paperclips canteen. Following Rachel's instructions, I tried to be more pleasant and welcoming whenever I saw her. I was having lunch and Wendy saw me and came over. After a few seconds of my stupid grin, Wendy said, 'You look pleased to see me.'

I followed the line of her gaze and looked at my trouser pocket and then hurriedly said, 'Oh no, it's just my glasses case.'

Wendy quickly made her excuses and left. Neither of us ever spoke of the incident again, thankfully. As I mused later to Rachel, 'Perhaps Wendy doesn't know how to talk to me. She never asks how I'm feeling. She just sort of reacts and seems to want to close down whatever I'm saying as quickly as possible.'

'You need to stand up for yourself more,' said Rachel. 'I keep saying this.'

'That's much easier to say than do. I wasn't good at confrontation when I was healthy, let alone after the fall.'

'Then talk to your Trade Union or find a sympathetic ear in the team.'

'Well, trying to find a sympathetic ear that's not attached to a young ambitious head in this current office is hard. There's no Jerome or Peter around now to protect me. And Sam and Roderick are in another team now. There's a taint or a mark of Cain about me at work, which I can see in other people's faces. My brain disorder doesn't conform to what some people think of as a nice disability. I'm not one of the more media-friendly autism cases. There's no novelty value. I've got no special skills. I can't do huge mathematical calculations or memorise the phone book. I'm not a Rain Man; in fact I'm a bit of drip.'

I base the evidence of my disability being unpalatable on personal experience. One afternoon I was at my desk when Ralph Durrant came over with a new member of staff called Robin. They stood looking me for a moment.

Ralph asked, 'Who did the song, 'Is Vic There?'

'Department S,' I replied without hesitation.

'Told you,' said Ralph to Robin. 'You should ask him about old films.'

'OK. What connects *Goldfinger* with *Chitty Chitty Bang Bang*?' asked Robin.

I looked at the floor, then stuttered, 'Ian Fleming wrote both. Gert Frobe was in the films as Goldfinger and Baron Bomburst. So was Desmond Llewelyn, he played Q in the Bond movies and the scrap-dealer Coggins in *Chitty Chitty Bang Bang*.'

'Wow', said Robin, suitably impressed. 'Do you watch a lot of old films?'

'Not really,' I replied forlornly. 'I'm just old and I remember useless rubbish.'

As they walked away, I half heard what Ralph said next. It went something like, 'We could clean up at pub quizzes, but he won't do that. He doesn't like being on display because he shakes in front people. What a cop out!'

After that conversation, I felt used and slightly soiled. It was like someone wanted me as their own novelty memory act. But I took solace in that I had not fallen for their Svengali act and gone into show business.

'I'm not being somebody's performing monkey,' I said to Rachel. 'My memory is impressive, but I had that before Myrtle came along! Ralph didn't know me then. It's not a new skill that came free with the Dystonia.'

'Yes, Dystonia doesn't come with superpowers.'

'And sadly, that means in the eyes of some of my esteemed work colleagues that my disability has gone against the two cardinal rules: it's ugly and it's dull. It's always there, too. It never really changes that much. Once you got used to the waving, shaking and the funny voice, it's like 'Adam, change the record please. We get that you have problems. But why can't you know lists of things, reams of information or calculate big sums? At least that would be interesting, or funny and chic.'

Chapter 54: To Affinity but Behind

One night, as I was putting my mobile phone on charge for the next day, I noticed it had a new email from Wendy. It was ten-thirty in the evening. Thinking it might be important, I cautiously opened it. It was simply a list of the documents she wanted printing for Thursday's board meeting. Given it was only Monday, I was a little surprised to receive it so early.

'Are you OK?' said Rachel, walking past.

'I've just had an email from Wendy.'

'Is she OK?'

'She's fine. It's just a printing request for Thursday. It's not important. I get them at all hours of the day from her. I never print anything until just before the meeting, because the document orders and final versions always change at the last minute.'

'Maybe this is her way of showing how committed she is,' said Rachel. 'Or how committed she expects you to be.'

'My job ends when I leave work. I know Wendy's out of hours emails, pointing out how much she does, upset Nigel and Mary. They feel it makes them look bad.'

'Wendy seems to be one of those people who lives through work and identifies herself by her job. She probably defines how good a person she is by how high up in the organisation she's reached. People look for validation in all sorts of ways. Maybe it's because she doesn't have any friends, or that her family life is bad.'

'Well, she's definitely weird. She collects those ornaments they sell in the Sunday newspaper magazines: teddy bears, porcelain dolls etc. - so there's clearly no end to her depravity. I saw her showing one to Roderick the other day. He doesn't like her; he's joined another team and so has Sam Maxwell.'

'Or worse still,' said Rachel, 'maybe she's competitive. Competitive people are horrible. They don't care who they trample on to get to the top. Watch your back.'

'Well, the other two are competitive as well. It's a strange alliance they have. They're united when they have a common enemy. But when they don't, they split up and turn on each other at a moment's notice. I did hear that a deputy head post is being created, and maybe that's what Wendy is vying for.'

'That would be interesting. The other two *will* feel threatened by her.'

'Yes, I overheard Mary say through gritted teeth to Nigel that "Someone needs to have a word with Wendy about her late-night emails." Nigel agreed with her, saying, "I don't know what she's trying to prove, or who to." It was quite brutal.'

'But if they can turn on each other that easily, you need to be careful. You're easy prey on the office Serengeti, my little wildebeest.'

Rachel's words chimed with me, and over the next few days I watched the interactions between Wendy, Nigel and Mary in a slightly different light. I was reminded of hyenas that come out of the womb squabbling and fighting with their siblings. It was weird how the Wendy, Nigel and Mary triumvirate would disband at the drop of a hat and sometimes reform into a duo to criticise the remaining one. Sometimes this was Wendy and Nigel against Mary, other times it could be Wendy and Mary against Nigel. They may have collectively thought little of their boss Gareth Cadogan, but if one of them started to make the other two look bad or court praise, then whoever was listening was quick to bring them back down to earth as the next example shows.

'I thought Wendy did well with her briefing for me yesterday,' said Gareth.

'Oh, I wrote that,' replied Mary dismissively. 'She's not that great on the page.'

As for the outsiders, people like me, well, we quickly learned to keep quiet.

Wendy had no truck with mental illness, not even a go-cart. I didn't realise how much my time away at hospital appointments irked her until we had another one of her less than illuminating management meetings. We sat in silence for a few minutes. By now I had decided that I didn't like her and wouldn't therefore make her job any easier. So I waited until she spoke first. However, I wished I hadn't when eventually she did.

'Do you know why you never get any interesting work?' Wendy asked.

'No,' I replied. Even Myrtle slowly shook her fist from side to side, not sure where this was heading.

'It's because you have so many hospital appointments,' added Wendy.

'Well, I can't help that,' I replied, rather bemused.

'I'm not saying you can,' said Wendy, 'but it's about perceptions, and you not being here won't help that. Perhaps that's why you don't get volunteered for anything. If you aren't here, then people will see you as unreliable.'

This was one in a series of little jibes which over time chipped away at my self-confidence until it was full of more hairline fractures than a piece of nineteenth-century bone China. I wanted to say, 'Are you saying I shouldn't go to any of these appointments because it would make me look better at work?' But of course, I didn't. I was quiet and took it on the chin, because like so many people in my situation I thought *this* was the only way forward.

More was to come at the end of the next quarter. I sat in another meeting with Wendy about my new performance agreement. Without warning or context, she suddenly asked, 'Can't you see him at the beginning or end of the day?'

This comment was oblique, but I quickly recognised that it was another reference to Len, my Cognitive Behavioural Therapist. It was a weird thing to say. She made it sound as if by doing CBT I was cheating on work with another man.

'Well no,' I answered, slightly shocked. 'CBT appointments start at 10 a.m. and finish at 4 p.m. so I'm doing the best I can.'

'We're trying to rehabilitate you back into the work environment and that's not easy when you have so many medical appointments and aren't here.'

'As I've said before, I can't help that.' I was left wondering how being dumped in the photocopier room rehabilitated me at all. But she wasn't finished. It affects your profile, and other people in the team are starting to realise you're never here and always at the hospital.'

'Wendy, these people who think I'm never here,' I replied, getting annoyed. 'Is this actually coming from just you? Because I haven't heard it from anyone else.'

Wendy said nothing and our meeting gradually fizzled out.

Chapter 55: Exclusion

A notice went up on the wall of the office about the arrival of a new team administrator. The new appointee was the aptly named Dave Small, and he was due to start at the end of the month. He was someone I'd never heard of. But more importantly, his post sounded remarkably like my own job, or rather the job I had been hired to do when I first joined the team.

'I wonder whether people are trying to tell me something by appointing this new guy?' I confided to Rachel. 'I'm feeling left behind: I keep hearing of meetings after they've taken place. A curtain seems to have gone up in front of me. My name is being left off meeting lists and invites for things. I asked Wendy about it. She said, "Perhaps that's because people think you're never here, so they don't bother to invite you".'

'That's horrible,' replied Rachel. 'You need to get out of there.'

'Yes, I do. I'm being excluded. It feels cold, a sort of draught exclusion.'

'Hmm, you're still trying to be funny, at least. It's your go-to place,' mused Rachel. 'They know nothing about your previous reputation for good work, do they?'

'I don't think it would matter if they did. They push old stagers like me to one side in their desperate quest to get on and do well.'

My first proper experience of how much things had changed came in the way I was ousted from being Secretary for the Paper Board (a senior meeting) without even being consulted. I was told in an email that Nigel was taking over.

'What's Nigel like?' asked Rachel. 'You should offer to do a handover.'

'I already have, but he's not interested. He's one of the most ambitious, short people I've ever met. The first thing he said was, "Yes, I'm brief, but I'm also brilliant".'

'Oh God. And is he brilliant?'

'Not really. He looks as if he should come free with something. He tries to make up for his lack of size by making pronouncements on things he doesn't really understand, which gives him the bonus of being quite annoying.'

'How do you mean?' asked Rachel.

'Well, he once said, "Anyone who's not on the fast-track management scheme is stupid, and I would question their loyalties." A visiting Jerome said, "I'm not on a fast-track programme, but I have a master's degree, so does that include me?"'

'What did Nigel say to that?'

'He muttered something about exceptions to rules and then went to lunch. Jerome said, "He seems to regard himself as a patrician and somehow above everyone else." The rest of us are probably just plebs or commoners. When he first arrived, he said that he was "born to be in paper" and that he "rustled" with delight when he got his job here. Yes, it was pretty hideous.'

Gareth Cadogan sensed that Nigel's taking over the meeting was not handled well. He tried to smooth this over with me. 'It's nothing personal, and we should try to broaden your palette of skills. You've been in that job for quite a while.'

This chimed in my head as polite speak for 'You've had it, mate!'

When I pressed Gareth as to why the change was happening, I was met with another cowardly platitude. 'The DG thinks this should be done by a higher grade, so it's out of my hands, I'm afraid.'

However, the first meeting wasn't completely straightforward for Nigel as I was brought back in just before the start as an emergency minute-taker. Someone was off sick, and they were desperate. When I arrived in the meeting room, I watched Nigel floundering around, trying to impress people.

'You know it's such a pain that we have to have this meeting; I would love to sit and listen to you speak,' he toadied to Sir Rodney Bike from Legal.

'You're confused, son,' said Sir Rodney. 'I'm from Yorkshire I don't do flattery.'

I saw the pain of rejection on Nigel's face. I wanted to laugh, but thankfully I managed to stifle it. After that Nigel did not want me anywhere near the meetings in future, in case the attendees looked to me for advice instead of him. It was noticeable to Nigel how many of attendees come over and said 'Hello' to me before the meeting started. Nigel looked on furiously when the area manager (an altogether rotund bloke), James Doyle, smiled and said, 'Are you back now?'

'No,' I replied, 'this is only a flying visit.'

'Pity. You're missed. This man's a twerp. He's got the papers wrong. These are the minutes for July; we needed the August minutes as it's bloody September now.'

I said nothing, but the look in Nigel's eyes towards me was one of total hatred.

Chapter 56: Nigel's Revenge

A few days later, Nigel had his revenge for my daring to "help out" during the Paper Meeting. The occasion happened during the team hot desking period, when Nigel sat at the next desk to me in the basement. By now I had my new "nedset," a one-handed keyboard for when Myrtle was at her most uncooperative and a designated desk. This was in the days before I had my replacement chair and I was still sitting in one of the old bucket seats, which meant Myrtle was unsupported. If Myrtle could talk, she would have said something along the lines of *'Un-supported, darling, I was downright ignored, I tell you! It was arm neglect!'*

Every half an hour I used to get phenomenal backache because I was holding Myrtle at a ridiculous angle. During these periods, I stood up because it eased the pain. Then after the pain subsided, I resumed my seat again.

As I stood up, I heard Nigel muttering something under his breath.

'Sorry?' I replied. 'Did you want something?'

Nigel looked at me standing beside his desk and ordered me to 'Sit down!'

'But my back hurts,' I winced.

'I've been watching *The Apprentice* and I'm trying to improve my assertiveness skills.'

'I'm sorry,' I replied, not really believing what was happening.

'Sit Down! SIT DOWN! You weirdo!'

I noted the blazing glare in Nigel's eyes and registered the lack of please or thank you in his voice. I sat down crestfallen, thinking he was going to attack me.

'Nobody has ever ordered me to sit down before,' I mumbled in shock.

'Oh, get over it,' Nigel sneered.

I didn't sleep that night. I couldn't tell Rachel what had happened at first, but she repeatedly pulled on the 'Oh, what is it?' conversational cord until I did. Of course, she applied reason and logic to what had happened. 'Perhaps you were standing too near Nigel's desk, which scared him,' she said. 'After all, you're a big man and from what you've told me he isn't.'

'I can't help that.'

'Well, whatever the reason for his anger, I feel he could've handled it better.'

'It was horrible. It made me feel like a freak.'

'You could make a complaint.'

'And let him know that he'd made a one-armed man cry. No, I think in some way he would regard it as a victory. Besides, the others will only think me a troublemaker. I don't really have any friends in the team any more to back me up.'

To be fair, I don't think Nigel felt good about the situation either, because the next day he sat in another part of the office, well away from me.

I thought that was it and over for Nigel and me. However, during the next month I was given the job of organising the team away day and once more I found myself nervously sitting opposite Nigel in a meeting room.

'Gareth wants the theme of the away day to be the staff survey,' said Nigel, as if Gareth was his best mate. 'Any ideas on how to take it forward?'

'We could try to address the bullying side,' I answered nervously.

'Sounds like a good idea. Let's do it.'

'There's quite a lot of bullying within the team. It was mentioned in the staff survey. So maybe we should have a workshop about that? Eight instances of bullying have been recorded in the first half of this year alone.'

'I don't want to say anything about them in case any of them involve me.'

I could not believe what I was hearing! Nigel seemed to know, or at least recognise, that he was horrible. It seemed preposterous that anyone would or could bully him! He was like a homicidal baby tortoise, with his narrow eyes and long neck protruding out of his pin-stripe shell. The most laughable thing of all was that Nigel Foster Kramer eventually became our Diversity Officer. It was like putting King Herod in charge of a children's home, but I'm sure it looked good on his CV.

Amongst the other lowlights of the staff survey there were complaints of sexism, misogyny and lack of women in key roles. Needless to say, senior management's outlook on the results did verge on the strange.

'We have women here; look, there's one,' said Gareth Cadogan, pointing at Wendy during one of the larger team meetings.

'Yes, Gareth, we have fire extinguishers too,' snarled Wendy. 'But because they're there doesn't mean anybody listens to them either.' It was one of the few times Wendy and I were in total agreement.

Chapter 57: A Well of a Time

I didn't notice until he'd gone, but Jerome had turned me into a project. He had assembled all the records about me, including my hospital letters and emails from Human Resources, in a huge ring binder called 'Adam'. He kept it in his cupboard, which was now where Wendy kept her things.

Jerome never told me he was doing this, and I discovered the folder one afternoon when Wendy asked me to pass her something from the cupboard.

As I saw the bulging file, I immediately did a double-take because my name was written in huge letters down the side. Fortunately, Wendy was so wrapped up in herself that she didn't notice. I waited until the others had gone to lunch, as for some reason I felt guilty about looking through a file about myself. As I turned over the pages, I looked at how my accident had worsened and become more serious. I noticed too how I went from 'poor Adam' to 'Mr Wright' when legal services got involved. The tone of the emails got much more formal, and there was a commentary too. People were quick to suggest what should have happened to me, and how a tribunal might reflect upon this if it didn't or hadn't.

I reflected later to Rachel, 'I suppose I should be glad that somebody was doing something, but it wasn't very nice to see in black and white that their motives were driven by their legal defence, rather than by altruism.'

'Well, they're a business,' said Rachel. 'So you can't really blame them.'

When I saw Jerome later, I asked him why the book was still there. He answered meekly, 'It helped me keep track of everything.'

'Really?' I asked. 'How would you like to have your intimate records available for anyone to read? It's not very nice, is it?'

He apologised and agreed the book should be destroyed.

For a time, I did wonder what else I was not being told. Within the overall office, there was a strange atmosphere: a smiling two-facedness. People would pretend they were OK with my disability, but behind my back I sensed they might be behaving differently and having a good old backstabbing party. However, this was offset when occasionally nice things happened to me, which even the new team members could not control.

There was a visit from Sir Brian Willis, a board member who'd been behind my ill-fated training course trip when I had my fall. Nathan Brock, the visitor I mentioned earlier, worked for him. Nathan had obviously mentioned my accident to Sir Brian, because although Sir Brian was here to meet Gareth Cadogan, he walked straight past him and hugged me instead.

Gareth seemed taken aback by Sir Brian's action, because when Sir Brian had gone, he came over to me and said, 'You're remarkably well connected.'

'Yes, you're a fantastic networker,' echoed Nigel.

'Thanks, I just try to be nice to people, and sometimes it pays off.'

Wendy even conceded in one of my reports that I was very popular, even if it did probably nearly choke her to admit it.

And the actual away day itself? There's not much to tell. I decided to focus the event around 'what makes a good manager' and encouraged everyone to chip in thoughts about people who'd inspired them during their career. Nigel took it upon himself to confuse everybody with a presentation about what diversity actually meant. To Nigel it was some kind of Welsh underwater village.

The head of unit, Gareth Cadogan, joined in the good manager section and told the team with a tear in his eye about someone who'd inspired him in his youth. As he said it with conviction, for once, he did not look vastly over-promoted and out of his depth. Neither Nigel, Mary nor Wendy contributed much to that part of the debate. I recall seeing them sitting together during the break sessions oozing vitriol like gossiping snakes in a launderette.

'What are we doing here?' said Wendy.

'I have no idea, its ghastly' replied Nigel.

'Indeed. The whole thing is pointless!' added Mary.

I wanted to say to the three of them, 'WHY DON'T YOU GET IT? THAT THIS DAY IS ACTUALLY ABOUT YOU! The rest of the team are all saying what terrible managers you all are!' Of course, this would have gone completely over their heads.

Chapter 58: A Light in the Black

God, that ticking train door is annoying. It's like being stuck in a bad Star Trek episode where the doors keep constantly clicking instead of swishing open. It seems to have stopped now, thankfully.

Back to the story. There were moments of kindness and understanding amongst the bleak landscape of my return to work. Speech therapy was one. As time went on, my test scores improved and my sessions with Marcia's team reached the end of what they could usefully achieve. This culminated with a final sign-off test.

After my pre-vocal exercise, I was shown into the tape recorder room where I dutifully read into the microphone for my last intelligibility test. With an ominous feeling and a dry throat, I read from a newspaper article about travel. It was over with in a moment, even though when I looked at the clock, I'd been reading for at least five minutes. When Marcia came in with my score, she looked different somehow.

She sat opposite me, frowning, and then asked, 'What is a buzz?'

'A buzz?' I replied, 'It's a big red vehicle with wheels and passengers.'

'Oh, you mean a bus!' [She said 'bass' like the fish, which most posh people do.] 'Oh, I thought you'd relapsed, but you're just a northerner! I'm afraid I can't cure that.' And with a rather wicked grin she added, 'You got 98%.'

Despite losing two points because of where I was born, I felt on top of the world.

'The speech therapy sessions have improved my confidence no end,' I sobbed in a rather emotional goodbye to Marcia.

'Well, you did it. We just helped a bit,' Marcia replied.

'You made my returning to work so much easier, and you helped me talk to people. I think you're amazing. Without you I'd have given up.'

'Thank you. From our side you helped us diversify. You brought down our average patient age by a lot. We normally work with far older people: stroke victims, dementia patients and so on. The results are dramatic, but they take longer.'

As I said to Rachel later in bed, 'Marcia had such a positive effect on my life. It was as though she understood where I was and guided me back to the real world.'

'I agree. She's improved your quality of life no end. Being able to communicate makes such a difference. Now, if we could just get you to stand up for yourself more...'

I pretended to be asleep, by snoring aloud.

'I know you're still awake,' she said.

Chapter 59: The Lack of Christian Chair-rity

People often remarked about how tired and spaced-out I looked in my work pass photograph. I joked that I only managed to blink because somebody poked a hotdog through the curtains. Most supermodels say the best weapon in your make-up bag is a good night's sleep; Myrtle constantly waking me up during the night was probably why my supermodel career never really took off.

The photograph on my pass, of course, was from before I got my new work chair. By now we were four months into my second return to work, and the new chair (the one I had spoken with Cockney John about weeks ago) had still not arrived. Each day was an ordeal. I had chronic back pain from holding myself in one position during the day, and this would impact on how I slept at night. It was not a quite a vicious circle, but definitely an unfriendly one. At Rachel's behest, I kept asking Wendy whether she had heard anything about when the chair might be delivered. She would look across at me through her crash helmet fringe and say rather patronisingly, 'No, it's still not here, I'll chase it up again.'

So, out of frustration and being fed up with the pain, I took matters into my own hands and went to see a wonderful smile of a lady called Helen, who worked in the Administration Support Team. She was one of those cheerful, helpful types of people with short red hair almost as upright as she was. Much more importantly, she was also one of those people who secretly run the world without any fuss or favour, yet never get any of the credit for it. However, I didn't realise the cross-ripple effect that this would have, mainly because Helen, unlike Wendy, actually *did* something.

One day Wendy called me into a meeting and said, 'I've been speaking with Human Resources (HR) and they say you should not be here until the new chair is delivered, in case the chairs we use cause you any permanent damage. You will be placed upon gardening leave until your chair arrives.'

I found out later that HR had contacted Wendy in reaction to Helen's enquiry. It was five months too late to worry about whether the other office chairs were hurting me. But I didn't say this to Wendy. To be truthful, I was glad to be away from her and the job. Rachel thought that I should have been more upset than I was. After all, I was being sent home again with no idea when I would return, because work was being incompetent in not getting me a basic piece of equipment.

I think Wendy sent me away to be 'out of sight and out of mind', but she severely underestimated Helen. Helen was one of those sorts of people who would not stop until a task was completed. I was sent home Thursday lunchtime and by Friday night two chairs had arrived. A third was delivered on Monday, and they had to be kept separately in case they had babies and I came back to a fleet of footstools.

Incidentally, the cause of the non-delivery of the chair in the first place turned out to be Wendy. She had been sitting on an email for two months which required her approval. Of course, Wendy never admitted anything was her fault, but it was helpful for me to know where I came on the list of her priorities. But this was not the end of it. When the chair did arrive, and the extra ones were returned, it sat in its box because nobody would help me assemble it. Three dreadful scenes unfolded as follows:

One: 'I am not trained to do this,' said Wendy at 10.30 a.m. 'I might make things even worse and cause you permanent damage. I've got to go to a meeting now.'

Two: 'Don't they send a fitter?' asked Nigel at 11 a.m., his patrician upbringing and the need for servants showing through. 'They should at least send a fitter. It's the SMG meeting now, so see you later.' I now thought the SMG stood for Selfish Moronic Gits rather than the Senior Management Group.

Three: 'I'm off to a meeting; it's a big box, though, isn't it? It is rather in the way! Could you move it, please?' said a wet Mary at 11.30 a.m. It's raining outside.'

I sat staring at the box like the fox and the grapes fable. Except I knew that the grapes inside were good, but I couldn't get into the box by myself. I had all but given up hope, when smartly walking around the corner came Helen.

'Oh, it's here, how exciting!'

'Yes and no,' I mourned. 'It's here but nobody will help me unwrap it or put it together. They're all worried they'll do it wrong and hurt me.'

'The rotten lot!' said Helen, and within two minutes she had all the packaging off; after five minutes more the chair was assembled, and I was sitting in it. I hugged Helen. I didn't know what else to do except to say 'Thank you' over and over.

After Helen had gone, I sat crying in the chair. The incident had opened an emotional gateway and seemed to mirror my life now in microcosm: obstacles all round me, but a better life over the next hill. The chair had quickly become a chink of light in the darkness of work, and I needed little victories every now and again. It gave me hope.

As I later told Rachel, 'I had to wait an awfully long time for the chair, but now it's here it makes such a difference. In the most bizarre of people there is always wisdom. Cockney John was right, the chair did not look much, but it provided support for my entire body. It may have looked like the supermodel Kate Moss, but it was more like sitting on the *Carry On* film star Hattie Jacques.'

I even named the chair Hattie. I was so relieved not to be sat in one of those old bucket chairs. But the best thing was that I didn't have to hold my body in such a way that it gave me acute backache. But then an ugly backache would have been even worse.

Chapter 60: Over Empathy, I Feel Your Pain

I tried to explain to Len, in yet another CBT meeting, that Myrtle always gets very excited whenever she sees other visibly disabled people.

'OK, how do you know?' returned Len quizzically.

'She waves at them and dances about. I think it's to show solidarity, that she's "one of us" or at least "one of them". In Myrtle's mind, she's their kindred spirit and has membership of their club. Myrtle feels that she's club president and in charge.'

'Why are you telling me this?'

'Well, there are other symptoms beyond Myrtle's club membership. When I see people who are palsied, I fall into similar mannerisms. My head begins swaying, twisting from side to side, and my face starts gurning. For anybody who sees me do it, I'm certainly not taking the micky or mimicking other people's problems on purpose. I just seem to absorb their condition and I can't help it.'

'I don't think you're taking the micky. I think this is your brain trying to process what's happened to you. You seem to think your version of Dystonia should identify with other conditions, so people can better understand it. It's a defence mechanism.'

But as time went on, another far more horrible thing started to happen to me. The first time it properly occurred was when I was watching television curled up like a cocooned bug under a blanket. Rachel would wrap me up because my heart medication reduced my blood circulation, body temperature and I would get cold legs. On the television screen somebody was hit by a car, and they rolled over and over. Suddenly, I felt as if the exact same thing was happening to me. I screamed repeatedly in pain and agony. Rachel was upstairs, but she soon came running in when she heard my screams.

'Oh my God! Are you OK? What is it?'

I was rolling about and writhing in my chair, curled into a ball.

'The television,' I moaned repeatedly. 'THE TELEVISION! THE TELEVISION!'

Rachel looked at the person lying down on the screen. 'What about it?'

'I can feel it! Turn it off. TURN IT OFF!' I rolled around in frenzied anguish.

'Feel what? You're scaring me!' said Rachel, turning off the TV.

'His pain! I can feel his pain in my legs.'

'What? You're having sympathy pains. Are you pregnant?'

I glared back at her holding my legs.

'Too soon?' she said, putting her hand on my forehead. 'You know, I felt it was. I was joking that you had Couvades Syndrome, but without the relationship and the being pregnant part.' As she hugged me, the ache went out of my limbs. We sat in each other's arms for what seemed a long time but on reflection it was probably only a few moments. I was crying and Rachel held me saying, 'It's gone now, you're OK!'

After a few more minutes Rachel said, 'So what just happened? Somebody got run over on TV and you experienced their pain?'

'Yes. Except it wasn't sympathy, or empathy pain, I was engulfed by it. Whilst I was sitting here in this chair, my legs began to throb. I felt like my whole body had been hit with a hammer, like it was on fire.'

This episode was the beginning of a whole plethora of me experiencing all manner of horrible things that happened to people in TV dramas, plays, movies, even cartoons. To this day I still have to leave the room when such things appear.

Chapter 61: Performance

One day Rachel and her mother were sitting in the kitchen having breakfast.

'How's Adam doing?' asked Maxine.

'He's doing OK, I think,' said Rachel.

'You don't sound sure,' said Maxine.

'Work are trying to help. They've given him a headset and a one-handed keyboard. And finally, they've got him a chair.'

Just then I came into the room, wrapped in my big blue dressing gown.

'Morning, Rachel. Morning, Maxine,' I said breezily.

'How are you doing? Rachel tells me you have a new chair.'

'Yes, it's called Hattie.'

'You call your chair Hattie.'

'Yes, he does,' said Rachel. 'I've decided to find it charming.'

'The equipment is fine,' I said. 'But the managers are horrible. I'm embarrassing to them, so I now live in the basement with the photocopier and the shredder so I never see anybody.'

'Your voice is sounding better,' said Maxine. 'Speech therapy really helped.'

'It's always easier around people he knows,' explained Rachel. 'He doesn't have as much to prove around people who know about his condition. Well, except for Wendy. She's probably setting his therapy back months by keeping him locked away.'

'She tells me she doesn't want to send me to the more "complicated" meetings in case I feel out of my depth. Besides, they'll want someone "more experienced" to attend. "After all, these will be quite senior meetings".'

'She sounds gruesome,' said Maxine.

'Yes, she is,' I said. 'I want to say that "Of my course, my shaky arm and speech difficulties have nothing to do with your decision, do they?" But I never quite seem to have the courage'.

'Oh God, that's so terribly British,' said Maxine.

'There are occasional rays of light,' I continued. 'One of my managers from three years ago, Ben Shackleton, wrote to me the other day and said, "It's nice to see you back at work, taking part in a meeting and arguing your case." Today is performance review day. So, lots to look forward to. Not.'

Like everything you don't want to happen, the time of the review came around all too quickly. There I was sat with Wendy in a cupboard-sized room which smelt of paint. She had a comfort blanket of papers with her.

'Oh, it's not the biggest room, is it?' said Wendy, failing to break the ice.

I nodded my agreement, and then there was a pregnant pause worthy of triplets while we both struggled for something to say. Most performance reviews in the Ministry of Paperclips were like that. Somebody (having been on a week's course, now crammed into a day and half) who had neither the experience nor the capability was suddenly given the power of evaluating somebody's career and their future.

'How do you rate your performance in relation to the other team members of the same grade?' asked Wendy.

I should have said nothing, or 'I don't know, why don't you tell me?' But instead of this, I wanted to protect my colleagues because I still thought they were my friends. So, I said, 'Oh, they're all much better than me.'

Wendy took me at my word. It was like I'd given her permission to do so. 'I agree,' was her rather glib reply, and worse was to come. 'In other areas I'd like you to stick to the line management parameters more. You must not speak to Human Resources again without going through me!'

'Do you the mean the chair episode?'

'Yes, I feel I was bypassed.'

'Well, I didn't speak to HR to make you look bad. I needed the chair because I was in pain'.

'I understand that.'

'It was a recommendation which Occupational Health made months ago.' I was becoming annoyed, so I added, 'I also hear that the programme booklet which I designed for the team away day was no good either. Some people criticised it.'

'Some members of the team felt under-represented in the format you used.'

'Well, I agreed with Gareth that the meeting should try to be as inclusive as possible. I was asked to get the lower grades and some of the wallflowers to speak.'

'That's highly commendable, but the seniors, meaning Nigel, Mary and me, felt left out. After all, we do contribute a lot to the running of the team.'

'But that was kind of the point,' I replied. 'The other team members don't have a voice, and there are fifteen of them and only three of you. And you guys speak regularly at weekly senior management meetings. So, with the greatest respect, this was not about you, it was about the others. Besides which, if you three felt left out, then nobody had bothered to talk to me about it. Gareth said he liked it.'

'It might be something to bear in mind for next time.'

'OK, will do and point taken. But whilst we're talking about being left out, I don't feel that anybody in the team really notices me or cares. I just do routine stuff, like booking meeting rooms, shredding and photocopying. It was not what I signed on for. I don't even go to meetings any more since Nigel took them over.'

'Well, us three seniors – Nigel, Gareth and I – got together and discussed what would be best for you when you arrived back at work from hospital.'

'Really? Nobody told me about that or asked me what I wanted or might need. Incidentally, what medical qualifications do *any* of you have? How do any of you know anything about what is best for me?'

Wendy did not reply, and the meeting ended in awkward silence.

Chapter 62: Len-atomy Lesson Part 1

The CBT appointments were unlike anything I had ever done before. I was not sat in a wicker chair with a box of tissues whilst a new-age hippy repeated the phrase 'How did that make you feel?' over and over. No, the CBT at Owsley Hospital was far more challenging stuff. It was not just a talking shop either. There were practical exercises too. One of my biggest fears was crowds and people, and suddenly I was having to face up to both of these things.

'What is about crowds that scares you?' asked Len.

'I don't know, I suppose it's being trampled underfoot,' I replied.

'Do you think it's likely that will happen?'

'I don't know. I suppose I must do. Otherwise, I wouldn't get so scared. I fell over in the middle of a crowd. It's my recurring nightmare. I have flashbacks.'

'Do you dream about it a lot?'

'Yes. Falling over took so much away from me: my job prospects, reputation, autonomy, speech, even the ability to wash properly. I fear it might come back and take the rest of whatever I have left.'

'I was expecting you to say what you did, but the order of it was interesting. I would have thought you would place speech much higher. You're very articulate.'

'I don't know. I did not think about the importance of the list and or even whether it was full.

There are lots of other things in my world that are important to me: guitar playing, for example. Now I'm thinking a lot about my job, where I was and where I am now. It feels like I've lost the old me. That person is dead.'

As I spoke, Myrtle began throwing herself around in strange jerky movements, finally landing like a spider on Len's desk.

'I think Myrtle agrees with you,' said Len. But the "old you" is not dead. He's just different. We need to get you to accept him. The person you are now is a good man with a wealth of experience and understanding to offer other people.'

The following week Len once again picked me up from reception, but instead of going to the room, we walked down the road to a supermarket.

'I want to try something different today,' said Len.

'OK,' I nodded, nervous and rather flummoxed as to where we were going. Myrtle began a strange tremor wave, hitting my chin with her knuckles.

'One of the few good things about Dystonia from a therapist's point of view,' said Len, 'is that you can quickly tell how the patient is feeling. I know you're scared, but don't worry, you'll be fine.'

'OK,' I replied, 'you're the boss. Let's give it a try.'

'I can't recapture the accident,' said Len as we entered Sainsbury's. 'But we can provide crowds and simulate a similar situation. Now I want you to walk around the supermarket, up and down the aisles. I'm going to walk with you. When you see a group of people together, I want you to walk through the middle of them, even if there's a pathway round. Do you understand?'

I nodded and walked around the vegetable and fruit aisle. The store manager was talking with a customer and two employees. I followed Len's instructions to the letter, and walked through the middle of the group. They did look puzzled: after all, there was space at the side of them which I could have used, but they did move. With Myrtle flapping around, I must have looked quite a sight. When I passed through the cereal aisle, I did the same to two women who were talking to each other over their shopping trolleys and children. It felt weird, but I did it and continued to do it.

'Well done,' said Len as we walked through the door and back to the hospital. 'You took a big step today.' At first I thought he was just being patronizing, but when I saw the steel glare in Len's eyes, I realised he was deadly serious.

So, I returned with, 'Yes and thank you.'

Myrtle also waved. I think she knew that it was special moment for both of us.

After the supermarket episode, I got more homework. Each morning and evening I had to walk into work taking the 'most tourist populated' way, by the Houses of Parliament. I had to walk through all the tourists who gathered there and through their seemingly endless lines. I had to admit that I got a small amount of pleasure knowing how many photographs of Big Ben I would ruin.

Chapter 63: Len-atomy Lesson Part 2, God Gets Bored

They just announced that there's no heating in Coach D. Maybe this train is what they call 'old rolling stock'. No wonder it's cold.

Thinking back, some of the CBT discussions I had at Owsley Hospital didn't have much warmth in them either. At the third session of CBT, the subject of the discussions got a lot harder. Whilst I was not surprised by this, it still did not make it any better or easier to cope with.

'What do you think when people see you?' asked Len pointedly.

'I - I don't know,' I stammered.

'Think about it for a moment.'

There was a pause while neither of us spoke. I looked outside at the sunshine, trees and grass, wishing I was there. The contrast was stark when I looked back around the room: bare cream walls, a box of tissues on a cold smooth knee-high coffee-coloured wooden table, two stiff-upper-lip bucket chairs and a big green nipple-shaped alarm button behind Len. Seeing no other alternative, I broke the silence with, 'They see a horrible old half man made more repulsive by his body.'

'Why do you think you're horrible?'

'I feel horrible around everybody else.'

'And why half a man?'

'I can't hold my wife properly or protect her. I can't do everyday things or stand up for long. I feel our roles have changed and she protects and looks after me.'

'Well, maybe she does. But she does it because she wants to, and she loves you. You're very lucky. And you're not ugly or horrible.'

'Really? I don't see anybody else whose face twists and contorts on its own. I don't see anybody else who has lost control of their body like I have. The rest of my body hates me! It attacks me. Myrtle slaps me all the time.'

'I want you to talk about the accident. I think part of the problem is that you've not accepted what's happened to you and your mind is going around in circles because of it. I notice that whenever you talk about the injury, you wince and recoil in horror. So, I'm going to show you some pictures of broken bones to get you accustomed to looking at them. Then let's hope you can face up to your own injury.'

'That sounds horrible,' I protested. 'I really don't want to do this. Is there no other way? Can't we talk about me as a new born baby or something?'

'Do you remember that far back?'

'No, of course not.'

'Then we can't do it.'

I wanted to leave there and then! But I knew damn well that Rachel would turn me round and send me back. So, I replied with, 'OK, maybe you're right. I'm not saying yes or no, but maybe. What if I do have difficulty in accepting this alien piece of plastic that is now inside me? What then? There's no alternative path that I can see. I don't see my bone growing back. There's no other option except amputation.'

'Well, we can hope to stop your body and mind from rejecting the new joint; then you'll get past this to reach some inner peace.'

'OK.'

'OK, what?'

'OK, I'll do it.'

Things started off fairly innocuously by looking at pictures of people in slings and bandages. But it rapidly descended into a kick-boxing match where one of the fighters broke his leg after kicking his opponent.

'Oh, my god that's horrible! TURN IT OFF!' I screamed as we watched a YouTube video of a poor man's shin swinging loose from his knee.

I got out of my chair and faced the wall, cradling Myrtle between my right arm and my body. I was crying. 'I feel sick! This is repulsive it hurts so much!'

'But it's only a guy with a broken leg,' countered Len. 'They fixed him up and he was back fighting again in six months.'

'No, you don't understand. It's as though I can feel their pain. I get this horrible cold steel jab in my left arm when I watch or look at things like that. It's unbearable. It's horrible! It's right where the shoulder joint is. I have to look away or think about something else until it passes. The pain is overwhelming, it engulfs me.'

'I know, but we need to get past this,' said Len, calling time on the session.

The following week Len started showing me actual X-rays of injuries. It was truly revolting, and clearly my appeal for mercy had not worked. So I tried anger. 'What are you, some sort of sicko or broken bone fetish merchant? This is truly vile! WHAT THE HELL IS WRONG WITH YOU!' Len and I had hit an impasse.

The way forward came when real life chose to intervene. Rachel and I went to a football match: Brazil versus Ghana at Craven Cottage. It was a weird evening. I was in a huge crowd of people looking around for Rachel after collecting our tickets for the match. I was screaming

Rachel's name in vain and trying to locate her. But all around me were strangers, thousands of them. I was scared and started to have a panic attack. I was being jostled and pushed, carried along in a wave of happy people. It seemed to go on for ages, but looking back it was probably no more than a few minutes. Then I realised I had survived. I had been jostled and had fallen to the ground, but my arm had survived. 'Len is right: I'm much more durable than I thought,' I said to myself. 'I'm still alive!' I declared to a rather bemused Ghanaian. 'I am alive!'

'Yes, well go and be alive somewhere else. You are sitting on me rucksack. You better not have broken me rum, man.'

I was amazed that I'd survived being jostled at that football match, and it proved to me beyond reasonable doubt that my arm was OK. As I said to Len at the next CBT session, 'You were right: my arm is just as strong as before. I'm sorry for being an idiot. I don't really recommend walking through twenty thousand people to find out my arm joint is still OK, but it worked for me.'

Chapter 64: Trying to Find the Door Marked Exit

That bloke's got snow on him; perhaps he's from Coach D. Speaking of frosty atmospheres, I finally realised I was wasting my time in the team I was in. I also felt I was talking to a brick wall when I tried to speak up for myself with the senior management team. I needed to get out but was not sure how. I began to research possible next moves but was left bewildered by what was on offer and how to get to it. I had not applied for a job for *literally* years.

'I'm not sure how to discuss Myrtle's arrival and long-term stay in job applications,' I said to Rachel. 'I keep sounding like an old hippy: I was spending more and more time with my body, man! My arm in particular. We had to get re-acquainted after she went to live in another place. It just sounds daft.'

'It's not daft; you came back from a serious accident. Not many folks could have done that, especially that unfeeling cow Wendy! It's an achievement. I'm very proud of you mister, and don't you forget it'. And with that she hugged me.

Rachel's encouraging words aside, I soon found out what I was up against in the new cut-throat world. I opened the new Ministry of Paperclips recruitment website and got quite a shock. A strange new set of buzzwords leapt out at me. I was used to adverts which asked for people who were 'honest', 'trustworthy', 'self-starters'. Now phrases like 'dynamic innovator', 'not afraid to punch a puppy or poke the bear' and 'ocean boilers not required' were the first things I saw. I had no idea what it all meant. 'What exactly is a "first class communicator"?' I mused to Rachel. 'Does this person only talk to posh people on trains? And who "persuades people to get on or off the bus"?'

'It's just like learning a new language,' said Rachel. 'You couldn't do this when you left college, but you learned how. You just have to do it again.'

'OK,' I replied, 'but look at this police recruitment advert. What is "organised crime"? Does somebody wander in halfway through a bank robbery and start advising people or telling them where to stand? Now, Roland, hold your gun up, dear! Yes, that's it! And remember when we're in a robbery, we announce our demands, we AN-NUN-CI-ATE, dear! Annunciate, drag those syllables out! Make them work for you! Remember dear, voice commands!'

Joking aside, the new buzzwords seemed a horrible, unreal set of platitudes. The person had disappeared completely and been replaced by a set of ideals called competencies. Rachel was right, it was like learning a new language and people would constantly and rather earnestly ask, 'But what did you actually do in your last job or task? What was your role? What did you contribute?'

Whilst I was working my way through the recruitment maze, I was told that my current post was coming to an end. I was being placed in the redeployment pool.

'This is horrible,' I said to Rachel. 'Chucked on the scrap heap. Wendy even smiled when she told me. I suppose in her mind she's getting rid of me.'

'No, it's good,' said Rachel. 'It solves the problem of how you leave your current team. Being on redeployment means that you'll get to see vacancies before they're advertised to the world at large. I'll help you compile a CV, and then we'll just have to wait for people to be interested enough to offer you an interview or chat.'

'Having to make myself interesting is hard enough in person, but on the page it's ten times worse. How will I explain my working career over the past two years?'

Rachel went automatically for the positive: 'It's a fight back which you should be proud of! Not everyone could come back from where you've been.'

'Well, they probably could if they had a Satnav,' I countered.

I must have done something right because I did get interviews and I rehearsed ahead of them. With the added stress, my speech again became blurred and sometimes words elongated themselves into each other. 'Hello, I'm Adam' became 'Nellow armedem.' To improve my intelligibility, I reviewed the work I'd done in speech therapy and practised reading aloud. I also did swimming exercises (breaststroke arms mainly) and breathing exercises to reduce tension. I requested a chair with arms for my interview, so that Myrtle was properly supported.

The first interview really set the tone for all the others. I sat in my best suit opposite three senior types, shaking like a leaf. I dare not eat anything beforehand in case Myrtle chose to throw it all over me and render my appearance of looking neat and tidy null and void. I was hungry on my journey in, and periodically my stomach would make weird jazz noises like 1970s progressive rock music.

'Is that the band Yes on your iPod?' asked a balding hippy on the train.

I did not have the heart to say, 'Sorry, that's my stomach.' I just nodded. 'Yes. It's from their Tales from the Lack of Weetabix album.'

'Oh, I don't know that one, it must be a reissue.'

During my interview phase, when I told people I had Dystonia, they started speaking to me very slowly, in very quiet whispered voices, as if they were doing a bad Sir David Attenborough impression. They moved with military precision from general ignorance to majorly patronising. During the first interview there was a heavy pine table separating me from the panel, but it may as well have been an ocean. I sat there feeling that there were a million spotlights on me. There were two nodding, smiley middle-aged women placed like elegant gargoyles either side of a gaunt man in a pin-stripe suit. At the start, Pin Stripe said, 'This morning we're going to ask you some questions about your experience in relation to each of the competencies. We'll be taking notes for our records so that we can make our assessment. Does that sound OK?'

I nodded, wondering slightly what would happen if I said no.

'Oh, and please don't worry,' Pin Stripe added, 'we're all friends here.'

Myrtle, perched on the arm of the chair, nodded, which was noticed by the panel. As the questioning went on, Myrtle regarded it as a duel and pretended to thrust and parry their questions to coincide with my answers.

'How do you keep abreast of the latest news?' asked the right-hand lady.

'I have to confess it's only newspapers and TV for me,' I replied. I spoke deliberately slowly so as not to exacerbate my Dystonia.

'Do you use the newer technologies?' asked the left-hand lady.

'I'm quite old-fashioned, I don't do Twatter,' I declared, not even noticing what I had said, but Myrtle had noticed and looked startled by turning her palm towards me and shaking her wrist in mock disbelief.

'You don't twat then?' said right-hand lady. I could see her top teeth pressing down on her bottom lip to suppress her laughter.

Suddenly noticing what I had said, I blushed. 'Sorry, I didn't mean anything by that. It was an accident.'

'It's OK,' said Pin Stripe, 'we rather guessed that.'

The lady let out her suppressed laughter and I mused that at least I'd made someone smile. Humour was always my go-to place in difficult situations.

I didn't get the post, and was left feeling my disability created complications.

'Well, it looked a really busy post and fairly thankless,' said a sanguine Rachel.

After being rejected from similar further posts, I sat with Rachel reviewing a failed application for a Filing Clerk job.

'The feedback's good, but you need to realise that the Dystonia gives you the upper hand in interviews because people will be sympathetic,' said Rachel. 'You're a great catch and you could also truthfully say that apart from the fall you've had no other days off except for medical appointments; also, you've had to adapt to a totally new way of living. Plus, you tick all their diversity boxes.'

'I agree,' I replied. 'Now if I could just find the right opportunity.'

After a few days, I noticed a job advert looking for people to work in the design team for the Ministry of Paperclips' contribution to the Olympic Games. This had a great deal of appeal. It was one of those nice moments when work and history coincide. It was a monumental event, one to tell the grandchildren about.

'All right,' I said to Rachel, 'we don't actually have any children, so it's probably something that we could tell someone else's grandchildren about, but either way it's special. It will also be an opportunity for me to prove that I can still do it, take part and make a difference at the highest level.' I read the advert over again, musing, 'It has me written all over it. I can see quite a few A, D and Ms.'

I quickly assembled another tailored CV with an elegant collar and nice lapels. I arranged a meeting with the team leader, the amazingly cheery Jackie Hill. The first time I laid eyes on Jackie, she was giving a presentation about her work in the Olympic Games team and asking for volunteers. She seemed nice and friendly, but more importantly she had no side to her, so yes, she was a funny shape.

'You come highly recommended,' Jackie began as we sat down together.

'Thanks, well I do know quite a few tall people,' I replied. Thankfully Jackie laughed. It also turned out she knew Jerome and he had spoken up for me.

'Do you know Roger Mogg? That's who you'll be working with, he's the other poster manager. Is Canary Wharf OK for you to get to?'

'Sadly not,' I replied.

'And there it was, my dream job torpedoed in the water by a simple tube journey,' I mourned to Rachel over the breakfast table.

'Well, the journey is actually quite long: it involves four train changes to get there from our house,' she replied. 'And there's also the fact that you can't currently stand up for more than about twenty minutes without falling over.'

'Yes, it's so disappointing, I want to cry, die and all manner of other three-letter words. *Tit.* Yes, I'm probably one of those too, Myrtle.'

'Well, hug is another three-letter word, so come and have one,' said Rachel.

'This is torture,' I cried. I'm on the brink of getting a new job but can't quite seem to manage it. I want to show people that I'm still good at what I do. I want to join another team, to prove the doubters wrong; I just need the means to do it.'

One day I was sat on my own in the works canteen, considering to how to make myself more interesting to potential recruiters in the job world. I had written down a few ideas. 'Change my name to David' was the first. I'd reasoned I needed an image makeover, and David Beckham and David Attenborough were very popular. Become a Labrador puppy was the next idea; clearly the thought process had not gone too far.

Suddenly, I saw Jackie walking towards me. She stopped at my table and said, 'If we based the post here and took out the commute part, would you come across? You could join in on the meetings by teleconference.'

'That would be brilliant!' I blurted out enthusiastically. My eyes welled up with tears.

'Then welcome aboard,' smiled Jackie, shaking my hand.

'Thank you,' I beamed, and this time I was crying for the right reasons.

Part 6

Chapter 65: Freedom

'My new job is brilliant,' I beamed to Rachel as I got through our front door. 'There was a triumph today, or at least an old Vauxhall Viva. I gave a presentation at work to a big group of people, and they liked it!'

'Oh, that's wonderful, I'm so glad,' said Rachel, hugging me in recognition that her efforts in bringing me back from the abyss had been worth it.

'These days small victories seem like big things. I'm sure my old boss Wendy wouldn't like it, because it proved her wrong, but there you go.'

'Who cares? Wendy was so bad for you and badly dented your confidence.'

'People came up to me after I spoke and said it was like listening to the old me. There's a compliment in there somewhere. You just have to know where to look.'

'Sounds like the change of line management is paying dividends.'

'You would think that, working for the same company, we would all have common ground. But I couldn't have found two more different people if I had tried. There's Wendy: controlling, clumsy, awkward during social interaction. Then there's Jackie: calm and understanding, able to inspire and put people at their ease with just a look. I'm suddenly being given autonomy and put in charge of things. It takes some getting used to after where I've been. My new team is much nicer too. When they ask me to do things, I look behind me in case they don't mean me. "Yes, we're talking to you," says Jackie. "Honestly!"'

'She sounds lovely.'

At first when I joined my new team, I would ask permission to do just about everything. This raised surprise and laughter amongst everyone when I said, 'I'm going to lunch and will be back in twenty minutes.'

'You don't need our permission,' said Jackie.

It was wonderful. I suddenly felt that I was relevant again, as if I'd stepped out from behind a curtain. And I remember the first review went well too.

'How are you doing?' asked Jackie.

'To be completely honest,' I said, 'I love it here.'

'Great,' said Jackie. 'I'm really pleased. We love having you here too.'

The *esprit de corps* in my new team permeated across all grades during the Games. One evening I was on the phone to the print shop whilst several people gathered around a television watching the Olympic Games ladies' boxing quarter finals.

'So, have the programmes and posters all been delivered now?' I asked.

'Yes, they got them at 3 p.m. today,' replied the Storeman called Norman. Norman Foreman was his name, so his parents obviously loved him a great deal.

Suddenly the words 'KNOCK HER ON HER ARSE!' were screamed at the television by one of the female directors.

'Sounds like you're watching the same thing we are,' laughed Norman.

'Yes,' I replied, 'I think we all are.'

Chapter 66: Are You Sure You Want to Do That?

Do you hear that woman shout *'I'm on the train,'* just now? Then she followed it up with *'Now Monica don't sign anything until I arrive'.* Not sure we all needed to know that.

As my return to work improved, I grew in confidence and went to more events – concerts and football games. Rachel always secretly arranged it so that somebody went with me. However, when I arrived at one concert hall to see Iron Maiden, I was on my own. There were thousands of people standing in line at the venue, but my next-door neighbour Tommy, my chaperone for the night, was not one of them. He was running late.

'I'm dead excited,' said the large gentleman in front of me, who wore a baseball cap to disguise his receding hairline.

'I'm just dead, I ate too much,' his only slightly slimmer partner burped.

The hold-up as always at the event was security: people in dark T-shirts checking tickets and taking the tops off bottles of water. After this there was a pat down search, which I felt made some people's evening. Certainly, it reminded me of my sister Agnes's disappointment at the 'No thank you' she got from the handsome young security guard when she asked him if he wanted to search her when the metal detector went off during a recent Tower of London trip.

But this was another day, and as I got closer to the head of the concert queue, Myrtle took it upon herself to shake and tremor so violently that I nearly fell over. My head and neck swayed too; yes, this was Myrtle in full takeover bid. I was wobbling like a ship's mast in a force ten gale. Of course, Myrtle's antics had sounded alarm bells ahead of me. A security guard called Rick gave me a strange pat down search in a "Sorry, but this is my job" sort of way. Thankfully he only smiled as Myrtle kept giving him an accidental raised palm borderline Nazi salute-cum-wave. Security Guard Rick looked at my ticket and his brow furrowed as though he was trying to spell chrysanthemum or do his 97 times table. Then he called a colleague over.

'What's wrong?' I asked, rather confused.

'This seat is very high up, sir,' said Rick very slowly to me as his colleague arrived. Note that the phrase 'This seat is very high up, sir' contained no words which asked me about anything, an automatic assumption that I could not get up high because I was disabled. I was amazed that somebody could suddenly decide that I couldn't even cope with sitting down!

'I'm worried about you getting hurt,' said Rick.

'Dank you, but my friend will be here soon, and he will look after me,' I ventured, my voice started to crack as I felt I was having to justify myself to someone who was questioning me.

'No, you'll have to change seats,' said Supervisor Mick. He then stared straight at me and said quite loudly and slowly, 'TOO HIGH FOR YOU!' for my benefit.

'Die will be all right,' I reasoned. 'My friend is coming to meet me. He's not as big as your friend, but he will look after me.'

'I can't let you have these seats on your own,' said Rick. 'We will get you a different seat. The views not as good but it's definitely safer for you.'

Thankfully, at that moment my friend Tommy arrived. He too had come straight from work in his pin-stripe suit and sensible beard.

'Hi Adam, are you OK?' Tommy ventured.

'My friend is here now,' I said. Then we went through the situation again.

'These seats are too high for him,' said Rick.

'Don't worry, I'll look after him,' replied Tommy.

'You don't understand: the floor on Row T is very steep,' added Mick.

'Have you asked him how he feels about it?' asked Tommy.

'Well no, but it's too high,' said Rick.

'Do you want to move to the new seat, Adam?' asked Tommy.

'I want to sit with you,' I replied, my head bowed in embarrassment.

'Then you shall!' said Tommy.

'You don't understand, sir,' said Rick.

'NO, YOU DON'T UNDERSTAND! I WILL LOOK AFTER HIM! I'm a lawyer. If you don't leave him alone, I will take legal action against you and this venue. He has a valid ticket, and he has paid to use that seat. I will look after him!'

With that, the security guards both backed down. Rick realised his well-meaning approach was almost like bullying in this context. This was one of the few times when somebody was able to do my confronting for me. I just wished Tommy could have been there all the time, but of course lawyers are expensive.

Chapter 67: Hold the Phone

I told Rachel about the concert incident, and she was quite alarmed. She thought about it and what might have happened if I had been at the concert alone.

'We should get you a new phone,' said Rachel one morning over breakfast. 'It won't really help with what happened at the concert last night, but it will make me feel better about it. I don't mind arguing with security on your behalf.'

'OK,' I replied, not really looking away from breakfast TV news.

'I'm being honest now; your brain condition and heart attack make me worry.'

'OK.'

'We can get a really snazzy phone that does weather and train times.'

'OK.'

'And gives you the internet so you can look for concerts.'

'OK.'

'I know you and technology don't really get on. What do you think?'

'OK.'

'You seem stuck in some monosyllabic universe.'

'OK.'

'Do you want a slap?'

'OK. I mean no, of course not. I'm just agreeing with you.'

And there the subject was quietly left, for the time being. I didn't know it at the time, but the phone was Rachel's way of electronically tagging me to ensure she knew where I was. She was determined that I would at least have the means to tell her where I was and whether or not I was dying, even if she could do nothing about it. This covered not just finding my way to and from work, but also coming home after concerts and the other events I went to.

I didn't give much more thought to the phone until one evening when we were having dinner. After dutifully sawing up my steak and kidney pie until it looked like a blown-up council estate, Rachel sat down to her own dinner.

'I just wondered if you had given any more thought to your new mobile phone?' she asked after her first forkful.

'I don't know,' I replied, wanting to change the subject, but not knowing how. She then tried to entice me.

'We could get you one of them smartphone fancy things like David Gilmour used to record that French railway noise on for his last album, *Rattle That Lock*.'

It was an unwritten law between us that Rachel oversaw our information technology. She has researched, bought and assembled all the computers we've ever had. My sole contribution was to name each one of them Clarence. We are now on Clarence V now. As I once said to a technician who was advising me about an iTunes problem, 'Clarence's middle name is not Virgil, the V means Clarence 5.'

'It's not a good combination, is it?' I replied, remembering the iTunes incident as I ate my dinner.

'Technology and a 50-year-old man. It's never going to end well.' Then Myrtle hit me on the chest.

'What's the matter with her?'

'I think it's her way of saying it will have to be a really smart phone to improve someone as dumb as me. Thank you, Myrtle.'

'You've learned how to redo most things in your life one-handed, so I'm sure you can learn how to use a phone.'

Just to show she was serious, Rachel took me to the Fancy Mobile Phone Shop and spoke with a man called Gary. I stood holding different sized phones up to my ear and saying 'Hello' into them, followed by 'Nicole, I told you not to call me at work.'

'We're outside!' said Rachel. 'People will think you're weird.'

'Sorry', I said, catching the salesman's eye. 'That pesky Miss Kidman, she won't stop bothering me. I'm disabled and I need a mobile phone,' adding as my arm began to wave, 'This is Myrtle.'

'Well, you've come to the right place, sir,' said Gary, looking at my shaking arm, quickly changing the subject and laying out five different mobile phone models. 'We have lots to choose from.'

I picked up a phone and tried to send a one-handed text on it. Whenever I looked blank or phased by the buttons, Rachel kept repeating the mantra, 'You can do this, you're not stupid!' Occasionally this would be peppered with an additional but more encouraging, 'Which button do you think it is?'

I tried countering by saying, 'Yabooey who ha.' This was my regression into infancy; it was something I used to do pre-accident, when the world got too much. Sadly, it was met with, 'Stop it, you're not a child! You can do this.'

Rachel did all the talking, asking intelligent questions. But Gary the salesman didn't seem to understand that women can know things about IT too. He directed all his answers to me, deciding that either I knew lots about phones or that I needed to know lots about phones. But then I suppose he could have been talking to Myrtle, but either way Gary didn't pick up the tell-tale signs that I knew nothing.

'This one has more memory,' smiled Gary.

'Remembering everything is not necessarily a good thing,' I replied, 'Not being able to let go could lead to problems later on. Some people bear grudges and cannot let them go. It's why we had the Cold War.'

Gary laughed nervously; to change the subject, Rachel held up what looked like a metal bar of chocolate and asked, 'What's the battery life on this one?'

Gary turned to me and said, 'A very wise choice. That's one of our best sellers, would you like to give her a try, sir?'

'What's the resolution of the camera?' asked Rachel.

'Well, that is high-definition, sir.'

'How much is the contract on this one?' Rachel continued. 'I assume the rental maintenance agreement is with the parent company for repairs if it breaks down.'

But Gary once more turned to me and said, 'Yes, sir, all repairs and maintenance are covered for two years.'

Finally, I had to say, 'Look, mate, I really don't have a clue what you're talking about. I don't know what biggergytes are, and if you don't answer my wife's questions about how much alimony we'll have to pay the phone's parent company if it breaks down, then we're going to register a complaint.'

'I'm so sorry, madam, how can I help?'

Eventually we came away with a phone. And so began my battle with smartphone technology. I named it Narnia – a world totally unfamiliar to me.

When I returned home from work, Rachel asked me, 'What did you think of it?'

'It's quite a lot to get used to.'

'OK, let's see if we can simplify things. Pass it over then.'

Rachel looked at the phone, adding, 'You found the camera, that's good.'

'Did I?' I asked, somewhat bewildered.

'You've taken some pictures.' She opened the gallery. 'Who is this bloke?

'No idea, I think it's the person who sat opposite me on the train home.'

'Why did you take his picture?'

'I didn't know I had. Perhaps it was Myrtle.'

'Did he not notice when you took his picture?'

'I don't think so, but I don't remember. I was too busy trying answer your call.'

Maybe Myrtle had a camera fetish, because over the next weeks she took lots of pictures of people on trains and train toilets, but thankfully not the two together. Perhaps it was her comment upon society. In those days my mad phone escapades on trains were sad and numerous. The problem was that I could not get the hang of answering the call whenever my phone rang.

'Right, when the green light is on and flashing, you have a call,' Rachel said as she rang me. 'So, we put our finger on the button and slide it across to answer it.'

I followed the instructions and then held the phone to my ear. 'Hello,' I said, but nothing happened, and the phone was still ringing.

'My finger slider doesn't work,' I said forlornly.

'You're doing it wrong; here, let me show you.'

Rachel and I would practise finger sliding until I got it right under the controlled conditions of our front room. But no matter how many times we did this, it never quite translated across to those times when I was on the train alone and somebody would ring. In those days (before I started keeping the phone in my inside jacket pocket) there would be a blind panic blur as I could feel the vibration of the phone but couldn't locate it. 'Why does my coat have so many pockets? Why does my bag have so many compartments?' I would ask people nearby. Myrtle joined in shaking up a storm, like a drunk bidding at an auction.

When I did eventually get to the phone, the person had rung off, or it had gone to answer phone. Of course I didn't register this, so out of frustration or blind panic I started to flick and scratch the screen, and this rather confused the phone. It opened the camera page and I either took a photo of my foot or the person opposite, so I ended up with a load of phone messages, usually from Rachel, and a gallery of photos of people I didn't even know.

At the beginning and for some time after, there was also a problem when I tried to end telephone calls. I was left in some curious limbo with whoever called. Then everyone nearby on the train could hear Rachel's little Borrower voice asking, 'Hello, can you hear me?' Or worse still, the bellowing of 'Hello, it's Agnes, are you still there?'

I also kept opening all these phone pages and didn't know how to close them. My phone told me that I couldn't open any more internet pages. Rachel explained, 'It's just your phone saying you have too many internet pages open and have reached your internet capacity.'

'I think that happened a while ago,' I replied.

At the end of each week Rachel closed everything.

'At the concert last night, I nearly blinded myself.

'How?' asked Rachel.

'Because in my mind the phone camera is like one those old Kodak instamatics which had a viewfinder or lens which you looked through. When I try this with the phone, I end up seeing pink and yellow dots and have a big close-up of my head.' Clearly the digital age was not something for everyone.

Chapter 68: Myrtle's Big Break

If the accident had done one thing, it was to show me the lack of knowledge about disability in the wider world. More specifically, there was a considerable lack of understanding about my own condition, Dystonia. I had been told I was 'interesting' by several eminent people at some of the finest hospitals. I didn't realise what being 'interesting' meant in medical terms until one day when the phone rang.

'Hello, could I speak to Adam Wright, please?' said the male voice on the line.

'You are doing!' I replied. I was abrupt, thinking it might be Telesales.

'Adam, this is Dr Madden from Owsley Hospital. Do you remember me?'

'Yes of course,' I replied, slightly stammering. 'How can I help?'

'I'm attending a conference on Dystonia, and I wondered if you would let me film you and use the footage for a workshop discussion.'

'I don't know how I feel about that.'

Rachel, who was watching TV, had noticed my reaction and quickly switched the TV off. The doctor's voice was quite loud, so Rachel caught his words quite clearly.

'I understand it's a difficult thing to ask for, and I would totally understand if you said no, but the footage would help enormously to promote recognition of the condition. So it would be used for a good reason.'

'OK, I'll say yes to you filming me and showing it as part of your medical conference.' I spelt out the subject of the telephone discussion so Rachel would hear and understand it.

'Thank you, that's excellent. Can you pop in on Tuesday? At 4 p.m and we'll record something?'

'Yes, that would be fine.'

'I'm so proud of you,' said Rachel as I hung up. She hugged and kissed me.

'I'm not keen, in fact I'm quite scared, but if it helps others, that's good enough, isn't it?'

'Yes, it's more than enough.'

Myrtle absolutely loved the idea of being on film; she even picked out a book on Method Acting when I was shopping in Foyle's bookshop.

When I sat in Madden's office being filmed, Myrtle was in orbit. She had tremored the whole time. It was horrible. It affected my speech: the stammer and facial grimace returning with a vengeance. Madden asked one his colleagues, a Dr Cushing, to be the cameraman. Myrtle was horrified that she had no dressing room or trailer, and with how low-budget and low-tech the whole thing was. Cushing used his mobile phone to capture the whole thing. Although I tried to focus on my face, Myrtle decided to intervene by periodically dancing her way into the shot. The whole thing lasted about ten minutes, but felt like about ten hours. Myrtle tremored her way to exhaustion whilst walking across Madden's desk. Towards the end she became like Little Orphan Annie, trudging her way across through a snow blizzard.

'Would you like to see what we recorded?' asked Madden softly.

'Absolutely not,' I said. 'I never want to see that as long as I live! I found me repulsive even before the accident. I can't bear to look at me now. I'm happy to sign any rider you want to give you permission to use the footage. But I don't want it ending up on YouTube, is that clear?'

'No worries,' said Madden, nodding. My tone must have hit home because Madden hurriedly designed a written agreement giving him full control of the footage, which he and I signed, and Cushing witnessed. Myrtle refused to speak with me for several days because I didn't want to watch her cinematic debut. But I have never wanted to see the footage since that day and probably never will.

Chapter 69: Getting My Life Back

Last year I was going up north to visit my sister Agnes. The purpose of the visit was twofold: firstly, it would stop Agnes's relentless *'Can I come and see you again'* pangs over the telephone; and secondly, Rachel said it would be good for me to travel somewhere alone for the first time. Rachel packed my bag – one of those suitcases on wheels that we nicknamed the "mother-trucker". Quite a lot of thought and coordination went into my journey. Rachel would take me to the station and my niece Paula would be waiting at the other end to pick me up.

On the big day, Rachel seemed tearful at sending me off on my adventure, as if it was my first day at school. 'Now I've packed your meds in the very front of the bag. There are some guitar magazines in there too. Oh, and a pen and paper in case you feel inspired to write some poems or songs.'

'Thank you, you're an amazing wife,' I said.

'Do you have any tissues? I packed you an extra jumper.'

'Yes, I'm fine, and I've done my number twos.'

'Course you have, you brave boy.' Rachel then hugged and kissed me and escorted me to my seat on board the train. After a combined platform waving ceremony which made *Brief Encounter* seem like a comedy, I realised I was alone, and all the bravado stopped. Myrtle suddenly was in full tremor performing mode. My face too was growling and gurning – the type of grimace normally reserved for old men from the West Country or creatures in horror movies. I was perspiring heavily too, and the other passengers noticed.

'Mummy, what's wrong with that man?' asked a posh-sounding little boy as he noticed me from his seat opposite. There was no reply, so the boy asked again, this time much louder.

'MUMMY! What's wrong with that man?'

'Rufus, darling, we don't point.'

The child began to wave his arm up and down, twisting up his face like mine.

'And don't copy him, it's not polite,' continued his mother.

'Why?'

'And don't talk about him, he might hear.'

'Is he working class?'

'No, Rufus. Look, there're some nice cows like the ones on Grandpa's estate.'

For a few seconds I toyed with the idea of explaining myself and telling Rufus what Dystonia was, but I let it lie. Mother seemed a hysterical type. But the fact remained that the child wanted to understand, and the grown-up thought it all too embarrassing. It seemed somehow like my real life in microcosm.

Just then I heard the words 'Tickets, please' gradually becoming louder as the inspector moved along the carriage. He stopped at me, and with Myrtle still shaking, I presented my ticket. 'Where are you go-wing to?' he asked slowly.

'To Congleton, to see my sister,' I replied, almost mimicking the inspector's patronising tone. I noticed that he didn't take my ticket or look me in the eye. Myrtle shook the ticket toward him, like she was trying to emphasise the seriousness of the situation.

'It's OK, mate, you have enough to contend with,' and the inspector continued on his way. He was polite, but I found his assumption a little disconcerting, about me having enough to contend with and thereby treating me differently and not even looking at my ticket.

'Perhaps he thinks my disability is catching,' I mused. Myrtle nodded. He spoke very slowly too, as if disability equates to stupidity. I kept expecting him to say 'How!' as if addressing a Native American in an old cowboy film.

'Mummy, that man is talking to his hand,' said Rufus, still watching me.

'Rufus, stop it. Here's your colouring book. Paint me a picture,' said the mother. Then she turned to me and said, 'I'm so, so sorry.'

'That's OK,' I said softly. 'People always stare if you're different. Your little boy is curious because he doesn't know what's wrong with me.' Turning to Rufus, I said, 'I fell over and hurt my head a few years ago. Now my arm shakes and I can't stop it.'

'Does it hurt?' asked Rufus.

'Sometimes', I said, 'but it hurts a lot more when people treat you differently. I'm glad you asked about it. I like it when people ask rather than thinking they know.'

'It must be difficult to eat when your arm does that. D'you want a toffee?' asked Rufus, pushing his bag of sweets over.

'Thank you,' I said.

'You do very well,' said the mother.

'I have a lot of help. The lady who helped me on the train is my wife. She helps me a lot. I'm very lucky.'

'I'd be scared to go out if I were you,' said the mother.

Sometimes I am scared. People make up their minds all too quickly when they see something is wrong or out of place. Anything that's too hard or too personal to ask about – they don't. Instead, they talk down to you. But most mean well.'

Chapter 70: It All Comes Round Again if you Let it.

Within the second month at work, I met my new incoming head of unit, Elspeth Dropper. She was a set of jolly hockey sticks morphed into a gangly posh lady. She was, and I hope still is, one those inspiring figures that the world needs to involve every now and again to get things done. She was always well dressed, with a flouncy, full-bodied curtain of black silken hair which she would casually throw about in gay abandon like Miss Piggy on steroids.

'Adam, how are you?' she enquired in her deep and breathless way whenever we met.

'Die am OK,' I replied cautiously. Elspeth always made me nervous, and when I was nervous, I stammered.

'So good to see you.' She was very tactile, which was OK, but then she'd playfully hit me right on the tip of Myrtle's elbow. It was more like a palm slap than a hit. This was the sort of thing children do: touch each other to express affection or to size each other up. But whatever it was, she had quite the jab on her. It made my eyes water and the plastic joint inside my left arm complained bitterly and chimed out my pain like the muffled clapper inside an old church bell. I would recoil inside, but for some reason I could never let my pain show outwardly.

'She's a director,' I mused, 'she would be upset if she knew she had hurt me.' But to the more observant person, my anguish was obvious as my eyes would water and I would wince. Elspeth was a rather self-unaware lady who would continue her slaps all the way through our conversation. I tried to take evasive action and quietly move away or around so that my good right arm and shoulder were facing her. But she would move around with me, and we would revolve together in circles in some strange non-touch waltz.

'It's surprising what people do in work to seem normal,' I said later to Rachel.

'Why don't you tell her she hurts you?' said Rachel. 'I'm sure she'd stop.'

'I don't want to make any fuss or to rock the boat.'

'No, you're just happy to let the poor woman unintentionally maim you. I'm sure she would be mortified if she knew.'

'OK, I'll say something.'

Rachel, not too surprisingly, was right. It was her most infernal of habits. But Elspeth was fine about it. She initially made a breathless apology for hurting me, which made Marlene Dietrich seem like the high-voiced comedian Joe Pasquale. But from then on, she was careful around me. And I wondered why everyone else couldn't be as accepting like that.

During my early days in the new team, I often thought about my time with Wendy and became angry at the injustice of it all. I could not change what had happened to me, but it still grated. It must have showed sometimes at work, because several people asked me whether I was OK when they caught me looking off into space. Totally by accident, I talked to the bright young thing, Peter Graydon, about it. I didn't know him, and thought he was another one of those 'knife your granny' types with a floppy haircut and very tight trousers, who happened to be in the toilets at the same time.

'How are you getting on with your new team?' he asked.

'I'm enjoying being here so much,' I replied. I have a new sense of purpose. This morning I was talking to the Games organisers, those who are involved in a press release. It's so good. I feel like I matter.'

'That's great. I hear lots of good things about you too,' he said.

I suddenly went quiet, my eyes welled up with tears.

'What?' Peter asked.

'People value my opinion here, they listen to me, and they trust me. Over in my old team, I was nothing, I was made to feel small. If this was Eurovision, I would have been in Switzerland *nul points* category.'

'Well, we like having you here,' he beamed, 'so enjoy it.'

During my Olympic Games post, I was part of the Team of the Year.

'It just shows what having the right supporting mechanisms around you can do,' said Rachel as we looked at my certificate.

'Well, they insisted it's just not just a sympathy vote.'

Chapter 71: You Can Do It!

My new-found confidence brought with it new responsibilities. At team gatherings or events, whenever there was a request for a volunteer, in my head I'd hear the voices of Marcia Makepeace and Rachel shouting at me, 'Come on then! Off you go!' And I would try to argue back with, 'This subject is not really my strength or forte.' This of course would be to little or no avail.

'What's that got to do with anything?' asks Marcia.

'I agree, on your feet, matey,' joins in Rachel. Two "gobby women" constantly giving me grief in my head could make life completely awful. But I must admit they have made me do things which got me noticed. And if the voices in my head were not bad enough, Myrtle still raises herself up, like putting your hand up at school, and volunteers me anyway, just to be spiteful.

'She likes to push me into things where she feels I could fail,' I confided to Rachel in one of our end of day chats. 'It's a no-win situation for me. I always end up being pushed forward or forced to take part against my better judgement.'

'How does it make you feel afterwards?' asked Rachel in her finest hippy guru voice.

'All right, OK, I feel great when it's over and people say that I was good. But it's still hard work. Tomorrow I'm taking part in an event to talk about and demystify disability. Myrtle is deliriously happy about the whole thing of course. She regards it like attending a film premiere. But I keep on asking myself, 'What on earth could people possibly want to know about some broken down, tired old twerp like me?'

'They want you because you're interesting and funny,' said Rachel.

Myrtle joined in the argument too, rising up as if to say, 'Speak for yourself. I think you'll find it's me they want.'

On the day of the presentation, I was there with three others: a blind person, a lady in a wheelchair and someone with multiple sclerosis. We sat behind a table in front of a hundred strangers taking it in turns to talk about ourselves and how we coped. My speech was as follows.

My brother turned 50 last year and I said to him, 'Brian, I love you, how would you like to celebrate?'

He replied with, 'Drive the Stelvio Pass.'

'Where's that?' I asked.

'Italy,' he said adding, 'I want to recreate the opening of *The Italian Job*.'

'OK,' I nervously replied. My idea of "living on the edge" is to eat some out-of-date boiled ham.

What was the big deal? you might ask. Turning to the audience, I explained.

'Well, I'm disabled; I have a condition called Dystonia. My brain re-wired itself after a fall in 2009. What this means is that sometimes I lose control of my left arm, known fondly as Myrtle. She tremors and shakes. My sense of achievement can vary anywhere between buttering toast and playing the guitar. But I had agreed to go on the trip, and before we knew it, we were in Italy.'

At Milan Airport, we were met by the smiling stylish Pietro. In his dark T-shirt, he looked like a recently ironed tom cat. He brought with him Gina, a thoroughbred open top black BMW Cabriolet. Rachel, my wife, came along too as navigator, carer and best friend. The roads were amazing and scary, as if an Italian giant had been throwing spaghetti against a wall to test if it was cooked. Imagine all those fairground waltzers from when you were a child, turned into hours of twirling tarmac. That was our 136-mile drive.

Within the first afternoon of being in this gorgeous open-top BMW car, 'our Gina', the sun beating down turned my head into a tomato, while my eye sockets behind my sunglasses turned into panda eyes. I looked like a very irate Noel Coward! All very *Italian Job*. We drove through huge, long tunnels that made the car engine sound like James Earl Jones humming *Nessum Dorma*. The Italian people were wonderful. We stayed in the village of Colico on the side of Lake Como, it was magical. We drove to the town of Bormio at the base of the Stelvio Pass. I had my photo taken at the top of the pass: in my dark suit and guitar tie, I looked all very Mafioso, provided he was called Norman. My brother was busy with the Stelvio bends so we forgot to play the Matt Monro soundtrack but hey, nobody's perfect.

I rounded off my presentation by explaining that 'I made this journey because I refuse to be beaten by a medical condition. I can't let it dictate my life terms to me. All the aches and pains of going through airports and sitting in a car for hours are my way of proving I'm still alive!'

People liked what I had to say. Somebody came over to me and said, 'You have no need to apologise for your voice, it's fine. You are perfectly understandable.'

Wow. It was like being freed or absolved of something. And my feelings afterwards were a mixture of relief and confusion, which meant I was just plain glad.

Chapter 72: How It Shall Be

And now we're getting toward the present day. Things are still sometimes ten steps forward and eleven back, that's life. And Myrtle? Well, she can still make her presence felt. I was at a concert, David Gilmour from Pink Floyd in Brighton with Rachel, and I wanted to buy a T-shirt.

Rachel said, 'OK, but you can do the asking and buying.'

I nodded an OK, feeling quite scared at the prospect of having to speak and pay quickly. It was very busy, with lots of people milling around. As we waited in the queue by the merchandise stand, we both tutted at the couple ahead of us who were still choosing when they got to the counter. I'm very precise in my T-shirt buying and was determined not to hold anybody up, even though I had a speech problem. I rehearsed in my head what I was going to say when we got to the counter. Then I started muttering the mantra repeatedly under my breath: *'Hello, I'd like the guitar T-shirt in XXL because I'm big. Hello, I'd like the guitar T-shirt in XXL because I'm big. Hello, I'd like the guitar T-shirt in XXL because I'm big, etc.'*

We reached the counter for our turn and the doe-eyed, gorgeous sales lady looked at me and said, 'Hello sir, how can I help you?'

Myrtle leapt up and started her waving routine which totally threw me and my first words to her were, 'Hello, I'm enormous.' Thankfully the lady thought this was hysterically funny. It probably helped that Rachel was right by my side. I turn red now even thinking about it.

I don't know what all this, the accident the recovery and so on, has taught me. It isn't a *carpe diem*, 'Seize the day,' thing. If it was, then Myrtle would probably have got hold of it first and thrown it at somebody.

I don't have any advice that I can give to others who find themselves in the same predicament. But maybe I have come to realise that the thing which I thought defined me, my job, didn't really matter or define me at all. What mattered more was relationships and feeling that you are recovering with or for somebody. Having people around you who care makes a huge difference. I think people need to remember that disability is 24/7. It isn't necessarily going to stop, so brace yourself! But it's surprising what you can get used to and turn into something good.

And here we are now, pulling into Edinburgh station. It was nice talking to you, and I hope you enjoy the rest of your journey.

My phone is ringing. 'It's my wife, excuse me. Hello, we're about to pull into the station. The journey? No, it's been fine, I found a new friend to talk to...'

Epilogue: The Present Day

This book is based upon my own life story. The events depicted are mostly true, but the people are fictitious and not based on anyone I know. I still have one of the many varieties of Dystonia and that will probably never change. If you want to find out more about Dystonia, do contact the Dystonia Society, https://www.dystonia.org.uk/.

I still have good days and bad days, but thanks to my wife, more of the former than the latter. 'Are you having a good day?' was something that I heard that last week in Sainsbury's. It was lunchtime and I was in the sandwich queue. Myrtle decided, because I was outside and there were people around to notice, to flap around and tremor. The place was quite warm, and the rapid shaking movement made me start to sweat. So, I was stood in a sandwich queue, holding my work rucksack and a tuna sandwich, with my left arm shaking with all the ferocity of a force ten hurricane. People stopped what they were doing and stared at me. When I caught one of them looking, they quickly turned away again like a 'found out' voyeur. Myrtle always makes sure that *she* is the first thing they all see. This appeals to Myrtle's sense of performance, and the more they stare, the worse she becomes, so it's self-fulfilling.

When I got to the counter, the shop assistant looked at my shaking arm and started talking to me very slowly.

'How are you doing? Are you having a good day?'

'Yes, I yam OK,' I replied and smiled, even though her focused attention embarrassed me somewhat as it made me feel very conspicuous.

'What are you doing this afternoon? Are you doing something nice?' she added patronisingly – my embarrassed head droop gave her permission to continue.

'I am going back to work,' I replied. I know the lady behind the counter was trying to be nice, but she didn't ask anybody else in the sandwich queue that question. Part of me wanted to say. 'This afternoon I'm organising and attending a meeting of paper suppliers to discuss the performance figures and sales of a massive company,' but of course I didn't. I simply said, 'Thank you.'

As I walked away, I heard her say to the next customer, 'I like to talk to them a bit. After all, they have a terrible time.'

So now I'm not one of us, I'm "one of them." I suppose it's flattering because you sound like you belong to a special club. That might be where the term 'special needs' comes from. Some people see the *differences* between me and them first. They never choose to look for the similarities. I have just the same amount of daily awkwardness as them, only mine is out on display. But I don't mind people like the shop assistant: she asked questions and tried to understand, and in her own way was kind and polite. When you encounter someone with Dystonia, that's all I can ask you to do too.

Printed in Great Britain
by Amazon

37786340R00188